"I HOPE THE DAYS OF YOU DECKING ME ARE OVER."

And so it became childhood laughter that closed the breach between them. Jim Roice gathered Sarah at once into his arms, held her tight against broadness she recognized, lowered his mouth to hers.

Before she knew what she was doing, she had committed herself to his kiss, a kiss that was at once a commemoration and a burgeoning hope, a kiss as immediate as it was tender, so like him and so unlike anyone else in the world. Not until it was over did she realize what it meant.

The remembrance should have frightened her, reminded her that while she released herself now to discover these old, good things, he could not. Since she'd left the valley so many years ago, she'd unconsciously compared every kiss, every man, to this kiss and this man, and had found them lacking.

CELEBRATE
101 Days of Romance with
HarperMonogram

FREE BOOK OFFER!

See back of book for details.

Dear Reader:

Just a moment of your time could earn you $1,000! We're working hard to bring you the best books, and to continue to do that we need your help. Simply turn to the back of this book, and let us know what you think by answering seven important questions.

Return the completed survey with your name and address filled in, and you will automatically be entered in a drawing to win $1,000, subject to the official rules.

Good luck!

Geoff Hannell
Publisher

CHICKADEE

Books by Deborah Bedford

A Child's Promise
Chickadee

Available from HarperPaperbacks

CHICKADEE

Deborah Bedford

HarperPaperbacks
*A Division of HarperCollins*Publishers*

HarperPaperbacks *A Division of* HarperCollins*Publishers*
10 East 53rd Street, New York, N.Y. 10022

Copyright © 1995 by Deborah Bedford
All rights reserved. No part of this book may be used or reproduced in any manner whatsoever without written permission of the publisher, except in the case of brief quotations embodied in critical articles and reviews. For information address HarperCollins*Publishers,*
10 East 53rd Street, New York, N.Y. 10022.

Cover illustration by Jim Griffin

First printing: July 1995

Printed in the United States of America

HarperPaperbacks, HarperMonogram, and colophon are trademarks of HarperCollins*Publishers*

❖ 10 9 8 7 6 5 4 3 2 1

To my dearest instructors, Elizabeth Cowan Neeld and Madeleine L'Engle. Thank you is all, and is everything.

To Jack, Jeff, and Avery Elizabeth. Yours is the joy and the magic. I love you, all three.

To Grandma Mollie. Who has taught me so well to love chickadees.

Breath of morning,
    icebound, sweet,
       impressions of once-tiny feet.
Where you walk
I dare not go.
I balance on the melting snow.

As water moves
    so flows a life . . .
       . . . tossed by aches . . .
    worn smooth by strife.
Should I contend or make a vow,
    it takes away from grace somehow.
       But if I wander fully free,
         the joy,
          the current,
           comes to me.

This path long empty,
    timeswept, closed,
       is better open, I suppose.
Once last, best glory I have seen
    comes haunting through the evergreens,
       your tiny hand within my own,
      I finally, fully,
       seek my home.

—dpb

1

The waterwheel beside Hayden's General Store stopped turning the same hour Will Hayden died. Some folks in the valley said it was even the same minute, but since Will took his last breath at the hospital in Jackson some thirty miles away, no one could be totally sure of that. Across the way, at the Caddisfly Inn, Dora Tygum was just banking up the wood stove, finishing up from the noon crowd when it happened. The eighty-year-old relic *screeled* to a halt with no advance warning, its reflection slowly stilling in the pond beside the ramshackle store, the fingerling trout surfacing to feed atop mirror waters that, for almost a century, had never been without ripples.

"Did you see that?" Dora's waitress, Kimmy Jo, asked. "Hayden's waterwheel just flat quit over there."

"Those damned muskrats," Dora muttered. "Will's been trying to trap 'em for years. Probably got up inside and gnawed on something."

"Yeh," Kimmy Jo said. "I've seen 'em swimming."

Dora totaled out the cash register. "Wonder if anybody's thought to call Sarah yet. She oughtta know her dad's not doin' well."

"Sweet Bejesus, don't you think somebody's called her by *now*?"

"You never know. People around here don't forgive easy. You remember how she told everybody in her senior class she was too good for Star Valley?"

"Even so"— Kimmy finished wiping the last oil-clothed table and stared out across at the waterwheel — "somebody should let her know."

"Don't figure she'll be too welcome."

"Lots of kids leave town bragging and come back realizin' what they've let go of."

"Yeah, but Sarah Hayden left worse than most. Left her dad to fend for himself."

Just down the highway, at Jenkins' Building Supply, Dawson Hayes was talking about the same thing. "Old Will got any family besides Sarah?"

"Don't think so," said Jake Haux, who'd just bought a whole pickup load of sheet rock. "Think she's the only one."

"Guess she ain't in town because she figures she's still better'n nine-tenths of the people here."

Jake plopped a neon orange hunting cap on his head. "Could be because nobody's called her. You figure anybody at that hospital thought to call Sarah Hayden about her dad?"

"Not if old Will didn't do it himself. And the chances of that are mighty slim."

Those at Peart's Barber Shop, a little way down Highway 89 from the Pronghorn Motel, were the first to hear that old Will Hayden had finally died. Jim Mill Roice sat in the ancient leather chair, watching the mirror, thinking of nothing, while George Peart pulled a pair of long shears from the jar of blue Bar-bi-cide and began taking off snippets of brown hair around the ears.

"So how's the wife and that boy of yours?" Peart moved from the left ear to the right.

"Fine. Just fine. Victoria's already working up in Jackson Hole, getting ready for the runs to open December second. I keep trying to keep Charlie interested in quiet sports, like fly tying. It's amazing what happens to kids by the time they're in fourth grade. They turn into daredevils. He's skiing almost better than I can. And he's decided he wants to play ice hockey this winter, too."

"Hope you survive a winter of his skatin' on Greybull Pond. Kids practice out there even if it's twenty below."

When the door came open, a squall of November air came first, followed by Margaret Cox and her satchel filled with the day's mail. "Got your order from Cabela's today, George."

"It's a good thing. Been waitin' on that Thermax underwear for almost three weeks now."

"Did you hear about Will Hayden? I just delivered down at Doc Bressler's office and the call came in while I was standing there. He died a while ago."

If George Peart hadn't been poised with scissors open to go after Jim Roice's nape, he wouldn't've noticed the fellow stiffen up the way he did. "Easy, Jimmy. I just about snipped off this mole back here. No need to act like a jackalope when you're in this chair."

But Jim didn't lean back or lighten up or anything. "Old Will died? When?"

"As far as I can tell," Margaret said, "about two-fifteen."

"Seems like the end of an era in Star Valley," George said. "Won't seem like we're in the right place without old Will behind the cash register selling pac boots and milk that's almost expired. What do you figure'll happen to the store and the waterwheel with him gone?"

"Waterwheel stopped this afternoon," Margaret said. "Just up and quit about thirty minutes ago. Everybody in town's talkin' about it."

"Sarah'll sell the store," Jim said. "She won't come back to the valley." And, in his heart of hearts, he hoped he was right about that.

"Folks are wondering why she's not back already," Margaret said. "Will's been sick for a month."

"You figure somebody called her, don't you?" George asked, plunking the shears back into the Bar-bi-cide and opting for the buzzing razor.

"Oh, somebody would have," Margaret said.

"Dunno." George skimmed the razor across the back of Jim's neck. "Folks around here don't take to Sarah much anymore. Could be nobody took the trouble to let her know. And now that Will's *gone* . . ."

"Yeah," Margaret Cox said. "Don't know what'll happen now that Will's gone."

Jim said it again, as if saying it again would make things more certain. "Sarah won't come back."

"Sarah won't come back! Sarah won't come back!" The children hollered it, their voices ringing, as they gamboled about the tree that lay decaying in the ice.

"You're right. I won't. Not if you throw snow at me."

"Sarah the chicken," Jimmy Roice bellowed, making wings askew with his elbows and flapping them at her while he squawked.

"Shut up, Jimmy," she hollered from beneath a Scottish-tweed fedora that had been all but obliterated by winging snowballs.

"Come on, Sarah," called another child. "You're the best at building snow forts. You're the only one that can make the roof and keep it from caving in."

"I'm not coming back unless you quit whalin' into me with snowballs."

"Nobody's doing it but Jimmy Roice. And he's just doing it because he likes you."

"Jimmy? You gonna leave me alone?"

"We'll just see about it."

"I mean it. I ain't coming back unless you leave me alone."

"You're just a stupid girl. Girls are just regular and dumb."

"I ain't regular. And I sure ain't dumb enough to come over there and get walloped by another snowball, Jimmy Roice."

"Okay. Okay. I'll quit it."

"Will you?"

"I will."

"Don't think I trust you."

"You just trust me. You just trust me and see what happens."

"Come on, Sarah. If you don't, we won't have this thing finished before dinner time."

"It's his fault, not mine. Blame it on Jimmy." Sarah pulled her hat low over her eyebrows, dusted off her ragg-wool mittens, and made to go toward the hole in the log that would mark the entrance to their fort.

"Ah!" Jimmy Roice bellowed as he leapt off the log, coming after her in a wide-legged run, spraying snow in diamond reflections of red, blue, green.

He caught up and grabbed her, the snow spilling over into her pac boots. Her hat flew off as she fell. "Damn it," she said. "Damn it to hell."

"You cussin' at me? No eleven-year-old girl oughtta know words as bad as those."

"Get off me." She kicked him brutally in the shin.

He grabbed a handful of snow and palmed it into her blonde hair, grating it into her scalp with stinging precision.

"Get off me."

"Won't get off you."

"You'd better or I'll get my dad."

"Run to daddy, little daddy's girl."

"I'll slug you one."

"You've got me so scared, I might just pee in my pants."

"I mean it, Jimmy. Get off me."

"Make me."

"I'll belt you."

"You ain't brave enough for that." He shoved another fistful of ice into her face.

She spit snow back out at him. "That's it," she hollered. "I'll show you how brave I am." She hauled off with her left fist and let fly a good punch, an uppercut that landed with a crack just below his right eye.

"Dad*burn* it," he shrieked, jumping off of her and holding his face. "Dad*burn* it, Sarah Hayden. You've gone and given me a black eye."

She lay in the impressed snow, snow which held record of all their flailing, and smiled sweetly up at him. "I reckon I have, Jimmy Roice. And that's fine by me."

Sarah Hayden's colleagues at the international sales firm of Sandlin and Bonham didn't know what to say when the telephone call from The Valley Mortuary came. She lay the receiver into its cradle and turned to three gentlemen who were examining a project in her office. "My father has died," she said simply.

"Sarah."

She sat down heavily on the top of her desk and stared at a schematic that only minutes ago had seemed vitally important.

"Sarah. I'm sorry."

"Was he sick?"

"Yes. That's what they said. Only I didn't know." She hadn't spoken to old Will, much less to anyone else in Star Valley, in an inordinately long time.

"So sorry . . ."

"Is there anything . . .?"

"Need time off. You'll need time to regroup . . ."

She didn't remember buttoning her coat, tugging on her gloves, catching a taxi home. She sat alone on the middle floor of the brownstone walk-up on East Seventy-seventh Street staring at the crumpled red bag of unwrapped Christmas gifts she'd procured early at Brooks Brothers' to mail to her father. Home for the Holidays, the sack blazoned, and in it lay three selections that hadn't satisfied her. Nothing she sent him from New York seemed personal enough anymore; she didn't know what he needed now that she lived so far away.

Sarah didn't think to eat, or to be tired, or to even lament a man's death. She only sat in solitude, thinking of what they'd lost together and of what they might have gained if only he'd been able to forgive her, or if only she'd been able to live life his way. "Everybody's phoning and asking about a service," said Etna Bressler when she called from The Valley Mortuary that evening.

"Yes. A service. Of course there'll be a service."

"Did your family ever purchase a plot in Aspen Grove Cemetery?" Vera asked. "If old Will had left us any sort of direction at all, we wouldn't have so many choices."

"We buried Momma on our own land. Down across from the waterwheel." But Sarah hardly heard her own answer. The word *choices* took her back. Took her back to a day in the autumn once when she'd been young with her father, walking along beside Caddisfly Creek, just after they'd lost her mother.

"People dying has a way of making you think back on your own choices," he'd said then as troutlings rose to feed in the backwash of the water.

"I know that," she'd said.

"Things that look easy'll end up hard. Things that look hard may pass by easy. You see somebody laying in the ground like that and you know the big things in life weren't really big at all. It was the little decisions, the ones your momma and I made without thinking. Those were the choices that changed us."

But she'd been impertinent, thirteen years old, too young to understand all he was saying. "Don't have any choices in this place at all," she'd answered instead. "As long as I'm stuck in Star Valley, don't figure I ever will."

"Does he have other family, Miss Hayden?" Etna asked. "Yours is the only name the hospital was able to give us."

Sarah hesitated only briefly. "No. No one else. I'm his only daughter. And my mother died a long time ago."

"You're not married? You have no children?"

This time, her hesitation lasted longer. "No. No children."

"Will you be here for the service?"

"I . . ."

"It'd be a shame if Will didn't have any relations here. He was one of the last of the homesteader families we still had around."

"I know that."

"He had a lot of friends, with all the years he ran the general store. I expect he'll have friends at the service."

"I expect he will." Etna waited, obviously wanting her to commit to coming or not to coming. And, at Etna Bressler's silence, came the strains of guilt for Sarah. It had been so long, so long since she'd been near her father, held him, told him to his watery green eyes how much she loved him. And now she'd frittered away every chance.

Sarah didn't stop to consider how painful she'd find it to make a trip home to the valley. Things like that didn't matter when somebody died. It was a shame, as she measured it now against what they'd lost together, that it ever had to matter at all. But it mattered to her. Oh, it mattered more than anyone could ever know. Only her father, her father who loved her, had known it.

"I'll make plane reservations this evening," she told

Etna Bressler, knowing full well she'd have to catch at least one connecting puddle jumper, maybe two, to get to his home place. Five years ago, she'd taken a turboprop, bouncing low over the Northern Rockies to Bozeman and West Yellowstone before Skywest had ever brought her back into Wyoming. "I'll phone you back as soon as I know more about my arrival. We'll schedule his service then."

Strange thing about a funeral. Seeing somebody dead and laid out on satin, somebody all decked out in a Sunday suit with a tie bar and not a hair out of place, sure makes everybody think twice about being mortal. And—for a while at least—a funeral of somebody well loved like Will Hayden makes everybody think of things kind.

Best thing about old Will's funeral was that nobody cried. They all walked by him and doffed their hats, pausing to give their last respects in a place that held the cool stone smell of the past century. Then, as each one started up the aisle toward the front foyer of the old log Episcopalian church, they started telling stories about Will, how he handed out ice pops to kids when their parents hurried them through the store too fast for them to have any fun, how he closed down the place for an hour each Tuesday so the Friends of the Elk Refuge could have a meeting, how he kept the pond full of native cutthroats so the young ones in overalls could try their hand at a fly rod and a barbless hook.

By the time the folks of Star Valley made it out to the front stoop of the church, they were all talking about the first snowfall and telling jokes about Hillary Clinton. And that's when they came upon Sarah standing on the stairs. "Gonna miss him so much, Miss Hayden."

"Won't even seem like the same town without Will Hayden."

"Your father meant a lot to us, Sarah."

"Thank you . . . thank you." It seemed as if she said it a thousand times. "Thank you . . . thank you."

Then, "Yes, I'll be going back to New York just as soon as possible."

And, "No, don't know if anybody'll fix the waterwheel. No, don't know if anybody'll keep the store open. Depends on who ends up running the place, you know."

But silence came again suddenly when she met Jim Roice coming down the steps. "Hello, Sarah," he said. And he didn't extend a hand.

"Hello, Jimmy." Instinctively, she raised her chin.

"Sorry about your dad."

"Thank you."

They just stared at each other, remembering.

He wouldn't touch her, not even to offer condolences, not even to brush callused fingers across the sleeve fabric of her black Donna Karan suit. Instead, he wrapped an arm around the attractive brunette towering at his side. "Victoria, you remember Sarah Hayden."

"Of course I do," Victoria said pleasantly. "You were in my graduating class at school."

"My wife," Jim Roice said.

"Thank you for being here," Sarah Hayden said.

Silence again. Words came hard at such a time. For many reasons.

"Didn't think you'd come back," Jim said at last.

"Dad's life needed to be finished up. I came because I intended to finish it up properly."

Neither of them said the rest of it, though both knew the truth: There wasn't much she could make up for, because finishing up wasn't nearly the same as being a whole part of something.

Instead, Jim asked, "He always wanted you to stay, didn't he?"

"Of course he wanted me to stay. Every father does."

Victoria lay one hand on Jim's arm. "Jim. We should

go." She turned to Sarah half in apology, half in dismissal. "We won't come out for the burial. Charlie will be home from school already. I've got to take him up to Jackson with me this afternoon so he can use his birthday money on hockey skates."

"Oh!" And Sarah didn't look back at Victoria Roice, only at Jim. "You have a son."

"Yes," he said, taking Victoria's hand. "We do."

"How nice." She didn't know why she'd never thought of it before. Of course they would have a family. And a little boy, at that. But her father had only written her with news of the wedding, she supposed to bedevil her with what-could-have-beens. Old Will had never once mentioned a baby. Never once.

He smiled mildly, with some satisfaction. "Yes. It is nice."

This wasn't the time to speak of the past between them, of childhood memories, of separate lives. For, with them, the recollections began with much innocence and ended with much pain.

Remember when I walloped you in the snow?

. . . and I gave you that black eye?

. . . and you snuck three half-gallons of tin-roof ice cream from the store and we ate it all?

Remember when we sat by the trout pond, peeling threads of grass, and you held my hand?

Once, you fell in the snow and I kissed you . . .

. . . then your grandmother played her old Victrola and we danced . . .

. . . and we made love and the stars circled in the sky above us, as primal and new as on the day of the first stars . . .

Remember when I thought you'd marry me? Remember when I begged you to stay? Remember?

No, no, Sarah thought. This wasn't the time for remembrances.

Instead, she said it again, knowing him well enough to understand he wanted to get away. "Thank you for being here."

"I'm so sorry," he said once more, too, paying homage to a man he'd known since he'd been young. "I'm so sorry that the season came for Will to be gone."

"Yes," she said. "I never let myself think it could come."

For Jim Roice, there was nothing left to do except take his wife's hand and lead her away, down the church steps. He did so now, never once looking back at the woman who stood alone, wearing black, belonging somewhere else, anywhere else, except in this country place she had forsaken.

2

Everybody within thirty miles of Star Valley knew how Jim Roice worshiped his son, Charlie. Come summer, you could see those two together out in the Mackenzie boat, drifting down Caddisfly Creek, the boy on his knees in the prow, the father playing graphite rod and fly line, expecting action as the nylon arched in glancing strands of light toward the water.

"You got one, Dad," Charlie would whisper, knowing from long, patient lessons that he shouldn't shout, knowing to watch the boat's side for the liquid-silver flash as his father netted the fish, then bent to release it, freeing the cutthroat before it ever left the water.

"We'll tell them about this spot, won't we?" Jim would declare good-naturedly, ruffling his son's wheat-blond hair. "When they're paying us to find a good fishin' hole, we'll bring 'em back to this spot."

"Yeah. We will."

"We'll catch that fish all over again, won't we?"

"Yeah. We will."

"Only he'll be *twice* as big by then, won't he be?"

"Yeah. He will."

Father and son always landed the boat on the same bleached strip of pebbles, called Crazy Woman's Bar, and the two of them sloshed through the shallows to water's edge, river stones clicking together as they tugged the drift boat toward the Dodge truck that read: Roice's Wyoming Troutfitters.

"Look, Dad," Charlie would say often, stopping in the middle of the job to examine some wet, perfect stone or a black, swirled larvae casing. And Jim Roice would always stop to see, releasing his side of the boat to stoop back down and take in a boy's wonders.

"You'll have to keep it for your collection."

"Won't be as shiny if it isn't wet."

"Mom'll let you keep it in a bowlful of water."

"She will. For a little while. Until it starts to smell."

"Get them in your pockets then, and let's load up. It'll be dark before we get that boat onto the truck."

Charlie poked his newfound cache into pockets of Sears jeans, just bought and already too short around the ankles, while Jim secured the Mackenzie in waning light. When finished, he hoisted Charlie up into the passenger's seat of the truck and, with door still open and dome light on, dug into the wrinkled brown sack Victoria had sent with them for their supper.

She knew them both so well, knew their enchantment with the boat and the water, knew they'd launch into Caddisfly Creek and that, from there, the evening would become timeless. She'd filled the sack with staples from their pantry: a Baggie of broken nacho chips, a half package of Oreos, tuna sandwiches on white bread that had mellowed, warmed during the course of evening. Charlie unwrapped his sandwich and bit into the triangled half.

"She'd better have put napkins in here."

"Don't need a napkin." To demonstrate, Charlie ran the length of his shirt sleeve along the length of his mouth. And, as Jim watched the young, much-loved face, he offered up a quick and formless prayer, thanking God for this life, for this one particular boy.

They drove home still eating, the radio tuned to KSGT in Jackson Hole, playing something old by Kathy Mattea, Jim humming along occasionally in off-key tenor when he knew the tune. And although these nights happened often enough each summer to be common, they never happened enough to be ordinary. Jim felt a certain sense of melancholy when every mid-October came, when chunks of ice began to form on Caddisfly Creek and the time came to cover the drift boat in tarpaulin and leave it battened down with cord.

Now, in November, father and son kept each other company tussling on the rug or putting socks on the dog's nose or inventing some new sort of insect in the flytying vice, something concocted from banty feathers or swatches of elk hair or filigreed dubbing.

"Jim," Vic admonished, coming from the shower and towel-drying her hair. "Don't keep him up all night tying flies again. It's long past his bedtime."

"I know that."

"He won't be able to get out of bed in the morning. And I'm the one who'll get stuck dealing with it."

For some reason, on this night, the very night after he'd seen Sarah Hayden and had looked upon old Will's face for the last time, Jim didn't want to part with his son, even just for bedtime. "Let him stay up longer. I know you're tired, Vic. But I'll be in charge of everything. I'd enjoy him a while more."

"He hasn't even started on his homework yet."

"I'll make sure he does his homework."

"He'll have to read a chapter of his library book out loud. You'll have to fill out his math quiz slips and then he'll want Gatorade. You might have to rub his back, too. Sometimes it's hard for him to keep still enough just to go to sleep."

"I'll do all those things."

She sighed, finished drying her hair, and sat back to stare into the fire. "I wish you'd get him to go now. I had to jam a whole day's hiring into a half day for the ski corps. I'd just like to know that everything's finished for once, so I can relax."

He stared at her for a moment, baffled by his own feelings, and by hers, then realized the truth. She hadn't any idea what it had been like for him today, seeing Sarah Hayden, bidding Will goodbye, talking about Charlie. "Guess I'll do it now then," he said, not wanting to be confrontational and realizing she was probably right when it came to bedtimes. Charlie needed to keep to his schedule.

The nine-year-old boy appeared from his room wearing his San Jose Sharks jersey, the one he'd chosen months ago to be his nightshirt. They hadn't bought him a hockey stick yet, but he came at his father with Vic's kitchen broom, spinning one of his Nike Air Jordans across the pine floor. "Yah, Dad! Hockey time!"

"Fine timing, fine shot!" Jim hollered as he grabbed the woodstove pokers and moved as if to guard a goal. "Every bit as good as Mario Lemieux."

"No," Victoria said from the couch. "Not hockey time. Reading time. Find your books from school, Charlie."

"Hockey time . . . Lemieux back . . ." Here Charlie hurdled over the back of the sectional couch right beside his mother. " . . . and he shoots . . ." *Thwack*.

Jim blocked the second shoe with pokers and set it airborne, winging past Victoria's head, past a lamp with big, brittle photos on the shade, photos of Bridger-Teton backcountry and an old trundletail dog that had once belonged to her grandfather.

"I'm a good sport," she said, unflappable, "but it *isn't* hockey time. It's *never* hockey time in the middle of the living room. Hear me, you two?"

Jim brandished the pokers and had the grace to look sheepish. "We were just on our way to go reading, weren't we, Charlie?"

"Yeah, Dad," he nodded energetically. "We really were." And Jim supposed he loved this part best, when they ended up being coconspirators like this, and they crawled into Charlie's bottom bunk grinning at each other.

That night in November it was too cold to snow, one of those still, deep-breath nights when the sky was so clear that the eye could follow the stars up and up. From somewhere past the pond came the low, upslurred whistle of a saw-whet owl. Sarah Hayden sat alone on the rickety porch of Hayden's General Store, her feet in the sheepskin slippers that Will had worn for years, her shoulders wrapped in an old down coat that she couldn't remember ever belonging to anybody.

Inside the store, the phone kept ringing. She supposed she should answer it. She rose from the bench, opened the sagging screen door, and went inside without hurrying. "Hello?"

"Sarah. Where have you been? I've been calling for hours."

"I didn't answer the phone." The brusqueness in his voice did nothing except mildly annoy her. She'd long since grown used to his impatience. "I've had a tough day. You can probably figure that much."

Only at her show of vulnerability did he back off and show her a bit of his own. "I should be with you."

"There's no need. You know what these things are like."

"But you're by yourself out there."

"You make it sound as if I'm by myself in hell."

"That's always the way you've made that place sound to me."

"No," she said quietly. "It isn't that. This is just a little town filled with people who have known me all my life."

"It's a little town filled with *little* people."

"Marshall."

"It's a place you hate."

"Marshall."

"Why should it be any different now?"

"Because I buried my father today. Because I need to put some distance to my grieving before I can be nonchalant about this again."

He remained silent.

"I knew it would be difficult, coming home. If I could have done it any other way—"

"When will you be back in New York?"

"As soon as I can be. I know I'll be back by Thanksgiving."

"That's only five days away."

"It's all the time I need. Dad's buried. I've got to talk to a real estate agent tomorrow morning. And if she doesn't want to sell the place complete with inventory, I've got a meeting with an auctioneer tomorrow afternoon."

"You can disperse the estate that quickly?"

"I can get that much started. This isn't New York City. People have time on their hands."

"*Little* people with time on their hands, time on their sides, time on their minds." He made up the tune as he went, singing it to her in the form of a lurid country song.

"Marshall," she said again.

"Couldn't resist."

"Day after tomorrow, I've got to go through Dad's files. He's got paperwork from the store as far back as 1965."

"What about the personal stuff? Photo albums? That ought to take a while."

"He doesn't have much." She forgot, for the moment, to speak of him in past tense. "I helped him go through a lot of it when Mother died. There's a suitcase or two of old photos and letters that belonged to my grandparents. That's about it."

"Good," he told her. "New York isn't the same without you."

She smiled at that, the first time she'd smiled in hours.

"Take good care," he said quietly, knowing those words were the most he could say, knowing not to frighten her, knowing he couldn't say, "I worry" or "I miss you" or "My life is lonely, too."

She stood still, holding the ancient black receiver an inch above its cradle, listening a long time for the connection to be broken before she set the thing to rest. And, in the buzzing of the long-distance line, she could almost hear her father saying again, *"Look around this place, Sarah girl. By my hand, this is the place that made us a living so we could raise you. This is the land your great-grandmother homesteaded, the home of your grandparents, the place I took my first breath in. Won't take to the idea of you leaving it. After I'm gone, can't figure who'll mind the store."*

Hadn't he realized that people didn't live on the land of their forefathers these days? They lived in condos or second-story walk-ups, in brick houses that stood side by side along cemented suburban streets. They followed the professions of their choosing, not of their birth.

As a child, she'd listened from the porch at night, hearing only the water as it dashed through the flume and onto her grandfather's hand-wrought overshot wheel. Tonight the flume stood dry, its weir tightly shut against the flow from Caddisfly Creek. And, in Sarah's heart, something felt the same way. Dry and barren.

Worn from time, from use, from passage. Where before she'd had her father to contest, she now had only herself.

She tugged the coat tighter around her shoulders, sat outside on the smoothed half-log bench where folks had been stopping to read their mail for the last half century, gathered her knees beneath her chin, and stared out into the empty night. She already knew she wouldn't sleep.

From the pond came the sound of a muskrat swimming, probably come out to feed on cottonwood roots or willows. Although she couldn't see the road through the darkness, she watched thoughtfully in the direction of the highway, the upland route that soon disappeared over a crest and then cut into the trees. The night hours emerged before her, stretched longer now for her conversation with Marshall Upser from the city. She could work tonight if she didn't mind climbing to the attic and going through Will's boxes without the sun sifting in through the soot smudged windows. She lowered her feet and stood.

When Sarah went inside this time, she fumbled about the shelves in the dry goods section until she found a kerosene lantern. She carried it upstairs with her and lit it, not caring much for the dusty overhead bulb that swung above her. In a place like this, home, and alone, she wanted warm light, gentle and living.

Along the length of the north log wall stood the bulk of her father's antiquated filing system, wooden orange boxes lined one after another with Smead folders, all meticulously labeled in Will's strong script and alphabetically arranged. She sat at his oak desk for hours, rummaging through bills and correspondence piece by piece, beginning with the folder marked "Acidophilus Milk," knowing she'd continue until she reached the last one, "Zucchini, Special Orders."

Occasionally, she'd come upon something personal mixed in with the rest, like "Dentures, Upkeep and Downplay, Blythe."

"What's that mean?" she'd asked Will when they'd gone

through files together after Blythe died. "Why did you write 'upkeep and downplay' about Mother's dentures?"

He'd chuckled a bit, the first time he'd been jovial since they'd put Blythe in the ground down by Caddisfly. "She hated those dentures worse than a cougar hates water, Sarah girl. Your momma kept herself pretty for me a long time, a lot longer than most Wyoming gals keep their features. Only problem was her teeth. Started falling out just after her thirty-fifth birthday, a couple of years after you were born."

"Never knew this story, Dad. Just falling out for no reason at all?"

"No reason at all. Found her in our room one night, looking in the mirror at those gaping holes in her mouth and crying to beat the band."

"Poor Mother."

"Dentist said for a price he could build her some new ones and she could put 'em on, just the way she'd put on a new dress from the JC Penney catalogue. When they came and she put 'em in, I thought she'd be so proud she'd want to stand in the middle of the store and let everybody who passed through take a look at 'em. I even wanted to put up a sign in the window. But she says, 'No, Will. I'm not standing in the middle of the store so everybody can gawk at me. I've got these newfangled teeth and now I'm gonna downplay them.' 'Downplay 'em?' I ask her. 'After all the money we spent? What good's that gonna do?' I can see her now, standing in the kitchen with that yellow apron and her hands on her hips. 'Plenty of good, Will Hayden,' she says. 'They make it so people look at me and don't see what I'm turning into.'"

Sarah stared into the lantern light, her face illuminated by the flat, blue-gilded flame. *There was so much we could have been, so much we could have turned into, if only you'd both been willing to let go.*

Her heart stood willing, testing the feelings, searching

for something inside herself that felt strong and clean, yet finding nothing. She turned to the files again, thumbing through quickly now, stopping only when she found a topic she thought might pertain to the sale of the property.

"Galvanometer, Payments Outstanding." No payments were outstanding. He'd paid the bill off in 1983, two years before he'd stopped using the waterwheel for electricity and decided to run the coolers in the store on a generator instead.

"Labor, Hourly Structure." Records showed that, with the exception of one stock boy who'd long since grown and gone, he hadn't paid anyone except family to work for him.

Just past "Okra Gumbo, Canned," an envelope of photos fell sideways and she caught it and opened it. Her father hadn't owned a camera. But these were photos of her, carefully clipped from the wrinkled page of school pictures that had come each year, beginning with the toothless, joyous Sarah in first grade and ending with her senior portrait. At the end she'd stood in cap and gown, staring off into the distance with the same serious ease and resolve that everyone had come to expect of her.

Occasionally, when tourists passed through Star Valley, they'd stop at the store and ask questions about the mountains, the elk on the refuge, or the holsteins they'd seen grazing along the road. And when old Will gave his time to answer them, taking them out onto the porch and pointing to the Continental Divide or the road that led to Jackson, they'd always thank him, pull out their cameras, and shoot a picture of the store. He'd collected many such photos over the years, some mailed with no address to "The Star Valley Store" or "The Store by the Pond," others taken by Polaroid and delivered on the spot.

She held such a photo in her hand now, a summer picture, one with herself and Jimmy Mill Roice sitting on the stoop, bottled Coca-Colas in their hands, dust on their toes and their knees. She looked at the photo hard and long, longer than she'd allowed herself to look at his face today. For one moment—one short moment—she touched his face, touched it with a finger so tentative, so cautious, she might have been touching a wound within herself.

"See, Jimmy?" she said out loud. "I was right, wasn't I? Just look what you've found, too. A beautiful wife. A fine boy you wouldn't have otherwise."

The hour was long past midnight. She pushed the envelope back into its place and lifted the wooden box, knowing she could set it aside and remember precisely where to start working in the morning. But as she hefted the thing across the attic, another folder caught her eye, one newer than the rest, and one she hadn't seen.

She set the box on the floor and stared at the file, not daring to reach for it. "Sarah's Baby," it said, the label scripted in old Will's heavy hand.

"Sweet heaven," she whispered to the attic, to the quarter moon outside the window, to the flowing kerosene light. For this was something she hadn't told him, something she'd thought would be too painful, too unbearable, for a father to know. She didn't read the folio now. She stood alone in the nighttime, reminding herself that she'd promised she wouldn't care, pushing them away because she already knew what the documents he'd found would say. And inside the very depths of her own soul, Sarah could feel the barrenness stirring.

Charlie hadn't been asleep long, maybe thirty minutes. Jim sat beside Victoria on the couch and she watched him for a moment, her dark hair almost dry now and reflecting tiger-eye gold from the lamp. While he'd been with Charlie, she'd gotten up and poured herself a glass of chardonnay, which she sipped languidly as she sat sideways to him, both knees tucked up beneath her chin and showing him a great deal of thigh. "Well," she said abruptly, as if she'd waited for hours to say this, "you survived it, didn't you?"

And so, she did know some of his feelings. "Will was an old friend. I'll miss him."

"You know I'm not talking about Will, Jim. I'm talking about Sarah."

He met her gaze head on. "Sarah?"

"Of course."

He wouldn't act stupid. And, in a way, her interest pleased him. He'd heard buddies joke about this thing, about life boding well when wives stayed abreast—pun intended—of previous girlfriends. "And thus the reason city folks hate living in small towns. History never dies. Especially when the history is between people."

"Yes," Vic said solemnly. "History between people."

He couldn't help laughing at her then, couldn't help loving her, as he climbed across the sofa and gathered her into his arms. "History. I hated that subject in school."

"Did you? Really?" She reached up to him, swept his brown hair away from his face.

He kissed her neck once, twice. "Of course I did. Old treaties. Dead presidents. People dying in ridiculous wars. What use is it?"

She began to unbutton his shirt. One button. Two. Three.

"Good use. When we learn history, we keep it from repeating itself."

He spread her robe apart at the thigh, his hand easing up, up, his fingers heating against her skin. "Right."

"Right, Jim."

The robe lay open as he lowered his eyes to her, revealing her body. Tonight that surprised him. But he figured he should have suspected as much. She'd come to him in the middle of the evening with Charlie still awake, knowing that she would have him. He stared at her legs, at the hair where they joined. "It's that time of the month again, isn't it?"

She nodded, stretched her arms, and opened her legs to him, all sensuality and softness, as if readiness of body could transmit to willingness of soul. And he hated himself for it, but he felt himself wanting to pull away. "Your temperature is up?"

"Yes. I ovulated."

She'd wanted a baby for years, ever since they'd been married. And Jim wanted to give her one. But he wouldn't be brokenhearted if they never had a child between them. For, you see, he had Charlie. And having Charlie meant everything. Everything.

She sat up on her knees, the robe closing again, as she moved toward him. "C'me on, Jimmy." She unbuttoned the fourth button on his shirt. The fifth.

"Vic." She was a hell of a sensuous woman. She stood on her knees, undressing him, naked beneath the velour robe. "Sometimes I wish—"

"What? What do you wish?"

"That we could make love because we need each other, not because we need a baby."

"We do that," she said. "We do that every time."

She had a skier's body, lithe and long. Her body overtook him. It had been almost a week since they'd done this, since they'd found the time to be together and alone. For one second, one second only, he wondered if Vic had planned it that way. He held her neck in his hands, splayed his fingers out across her shoulders, eased the velour down her forearms until it lay below her breasts. She backed away from him then, waiting for him, letting him look at her.

"You're beautiful."

She smiled.

He lowered an open mouth to her right breast, taking it in and licking it, feeling it pucker beneath the grain of his tongue. Ten fingers dug into his dark hair, separating it into runnels. He moved to the other breast, stringing saliva as he went. He knew she loved it when his mouth made her wet, when he moved on to other parts of her and left moist skin to cool against the air.

She untied the belt at her waist and the robe fell open in heavy folds. "Yes," she whispered, drawing her muscles tighter, concaving her stomach as she held his face against her. "That's it, Jimmy. Yes."

She hadn't finished unfastening his shirt buttons. Jim stopped to take care of them himself, almost popping one off in the process. Next came his belt, which jingled as he ripped it out of the loops on his jeans.

She raised her arms above her head and stretched like a cat knowing he could see her. "Now," she told him. "Please. I can't wait much longer."

"First things first, Victoria." He kissed her navel, her pelvic bone, then trailed his mouth all the way down.

She'd fisted her hands against the huge cushions. He switched his weight against her and knew immediately they were both going to topple off onto the rug. When they did, neither of them struggled. They only giggled as they fell like delighted children. And, to his immense pleasure, Vic ended up on top.

"There you are," he said, smiling, reaching for her breasts again. "Right where I like you. Right where I can play with these and see us doing it all at the same time."

"I don't want to do it this way. Let's roll over."

He eyed her face for the first time in the past several minutes. "Why?"

"No reason why. I'm just in the mood for the other, is all."

"You sure?"

She nodded eagerly. "Yeah. I'm sure."

He knew it when she was lying. He knew why she wanted to be on the bottom. The OB-GYN in Jackson had told her chances were better she might conceive that way.

"Can't roll over," he said. "Coffee table's in the way."

"Shove it across the room," she said.

He kicked the coffee table three feet in the direction of the stairs. She rolled off and positioned herself on the Oriental rug beside him. He knew she would wrap her legs around his back. Wordlessly, he raised himself over her, gathered her close, entered her.

3

Everyone around knew that Aretha Budge down at the Wyoming Driver's License Bureau was the worst old battle-ax in Lincoln County. Seemed like she'd lived twice as long as anybody, and she knew twice as much as anybody, which was due—in large part—to the fact that the sheriff's department had to make a lengthy report to her every time somebody local got caught driving under the influence. Residents didn't dare let their driver's licenses lapse for fear of having to run up against her.

She waited now, bifocals low on her nose, while Victoria Roice made Charlie sit in a chair and wait while she stood in line. First thing she said when Vic reached the front of the line was, "Shouldn't've brought a kid in like this, Mrs. Roice. I have students taking driver's tests this morning."

Victoria glanced toward the long tables lined with

coffee cans full of pencils. One fellow, and one fellow only, was scratching his head and staring in bafflement at a half-dotted computer card.

"You know he's a good kid, Mrs. Budge. I'll take him outside if he gets rowdy." She dug inside her backpack, her purse of choice ever since she'd married Jim and started carrying around diapers for Charlie. She pulled out a white prescription slip from the optometrist. "Just need to take care of this, please. I failed the eyesight test and need to have you okay my license now that I've got this from Dr. Lovercheck." In truth, the whole idea horrified her. She'd never needed corrective lenses before. She'd stared with both eyes into the square glasses on the machine and she'd only been able to locate the dot on four road signs along the bridge. Didn't help that the entire test was black-and-white. She saw things better when they were in color. "Guess I'm getting old," she said, feeling it but trying to make light of the entire ordeal.

"Guess you are," Aretha Budge said. "Eyes are usually the first to go. I see it all the time. Pretty soon you'll wind up in a pine box just like old Will Hayden."

Vic didn't answer. She leaned on the counter, waiting for Mrs. Budge to process the prescription and issue her a duplicate license.

"You'll have to take the eye test over again," Mrs. Budge said, still not smiling. But, then, she never smiled.

"Yes, I know."

"You'll want to take it with your corrective lenses. Where are your glasses?"

"Contacts." Vic pointed to her eyes. "You can't see them."

"Proceed with the eye test, please," she said. "Look at each road sign along the bridge. Indicate the direction of each arrow where you see the dot. Now, sign number one . . ."

". . . arrow's to the left."

"Sign number two . . ."

". . . arrow's to the right."

"Speaking of old Will Hayden," Mrs. Budge mentioned nonchalantly. "Saw you and Jim at the funeral. Nice service."

"Yes, it was a nice service."

"Sarah's aged a bit. I remember when she came in to get her first driver's license. Blond hair all pulled back in a pony tail. Wouldn't even take the time to sit still and concentrate on the questions."

Victoria wanted to complete the test and be gone. "On sign three, the arrow's pointing right."

"Folks are wondering if it bothers you at all, having Sarah back in town and all."

"Don't see why it should bother me. On sign four—"

"She was going fishing with your Jim the day she got her license. I remember he always took her up on the creek when the tourists were gone and Miller let him borrow the boat. Missed four questions on her driver's test that day, she was in such a hurry."

Victoria glanced toward Charlie, wondering if he might be listening. He'd taken over a coffee can and was rolling at least five yellow number two pencils flat beneath his palm.

"Seems like there's one in every generation who just up and leaves the valley like that. Won't be satisfied until they've conquered the whole world and proven everything's second class here in the process."

"People have a right to the lives they choose," Victoria said.

"Never could figure out why that girl up and ran away like she did. Because that's exactly what it was, Mrs. Roice. I was one of five members of the Daughters of the American Revolution who voted to give Sarah Hayden our annual scholarship in 1984. That child concocted some sort of essay, I'll tell you. Planned to get a business degree at Central Wyoming College starting in the fall. Next thing we knew, she'd transferred, scholarship and all, clear down to Laramie. Takes nine hours to drive down that far even when the roads are good."

"May I finish my eye test, Mrs. Budge?"

Aretha Budge changed screens inside the machine, and when Vic looked she saw another bridge like the first, with different signs.

"She graduated one day and took the Greyhound bus the next. Strange, too. Neither your Jim nor her daddy saw fit to go down to Jenkins' Building Supply to wave her off. Only Blythe went, standing in that gravel driveway shivering even though it was early June, waving a full five minutes after the bus had disappeared down the highway toward Afton. Sarah came home once later, when Blythe died. She stayed for a week. That's the last any of us have seen her . . . until now."

"On sign three, the arrow's pointing up."

"That's fine. That's fine." Mrs. Budge removed the second bridge from the screen. "You passed the test long ago, Mrs. Roice. Step to the rear where you'll see footprints on the floor. Place your feet inside the footprints."

A burst of light illuminated Vic's face even as she adjusted her Sorels inside the footmarks. The woman hadn't even warned her to smile. "Next," Mrs. Budge said. She definitely stamped "Duplicate" in the margin of Victoria's application and pitched it into a pile of others.

Once, when he'd been young, Jim's father had asked him when he'd first started to love Sarah. Jim stood in the wooden barn, hanging on to the socket wrench while his father fiddled with the crankshaft on the old boat-hauling truck, counting back months, years, a decade even, and still . . . still he couldn't find the beginning.

He didn't remember meeting her. She'd always been in his life, always been the girl who lived down the path across the sageflat and through the trees, the one who'd slugged him and whom he'd teased and who'd helped him catch mud beetles to take to show-and-tell when he'd been in second grade.

Somewhere during their middle-school years, perhaps when he'd been thirteen, he remembered watching her one day while she fished, watching the skein of dandelion-down hair that blew across her mouth, and thinking she was beautiful. Not long after—while they walked—he'd reached out and grabbed her hand. He didn't take it gently, or weave his fingers through hers in possession. He darted at her hand the way a swallow darts at mosquitoes, catching it so tightly in his own grip that she couldn't have pulled away if she'd made an attempt. They'd walked along together that way, swinging arms, never mentioning it.

And that, Jim supposed, had been where the beginning came, where he quietly began to love Sarah Hayden.

"You gonna kiss me ever, Jimmy Roice?" she asked one night as they sat with knees bunched up beneath their chins. He remembered not looking at her, instead seeing the moon waver like nickel silver on the pond.

"Don't know. Haven't thought much about it." But he was lying through his teeth and he figured she knew it. He thought about kissing her all the time.

"How am I gonna know what it's like if we never try it?"

"That's just like you, Sarah Hayden. Always thinking you've got to try something in order to know what it's about."

"Doesn't seem like such a big deal as all that. All I asked is about a kiss. I'm fourteen years old, Jimmy, almost fifteen, and never been kissed."

He let out one whistle of humorless disdain. "Pshaw. Ought not to kiss anybody until you're thirty-two. That's what I've always thought. That's the only way to stay safe about such things."

"You scared?"

"Of course I'm scared."

"Me too."

He finally looked at her. "My dad says—" But then he stopped, never able to look away from her, and not able to bring out the right words.

"Being scared is a hard thing to admit," she said.

"Yeah."

"Look at the stars. Must be a million of 'em."

"Yeah."

But he wasn't looking at the stars. He was looking at her. He could see the outline of her upcast face against the night and the timber, the line of her lips and her brows backlit gently by the moon. His throat seemed to close and blood coursed through parts of his body that had no business coming to life. He sat staring at her. Suppose he kissed her—a simple kiss, just once—what harm could come of that?

He reached for her face. He bracketed her chin with his thumb and forefinger, rubbing gently, feeling her face warm and firm beneath his fingers. There could be no mistaking his touch for what it was, a prelude of sorts, a lingering, brave answer to her question.

She turned to him and he could see she sat with bated breath, waiting for him to move closer, to go one step further and take her into his arms. "Okay," he whispered. "Okay." He gathered her against him, opening his patched-up jacket so she could fit inside with him and, as her developing breasts pressed against his shirt, he thought he'd never felt anything so good in his entire life.

They backed up and looked into each other's eyes and started laughing, the sound of childhood joy and grown-up mystery rising like compline prayers into a spring nighttime sky. Then both fell silent again for a dark space, moving close, feeling the remarkable tug inside their vitals.

Finally, it was Sarah who spoke. "It's getting warmer," she said. "Pretty soon the frogs'll be—" Her lips fell open and his eyes dropped to them.

"What'll the frogs do?" he asked as he put one big hand in the shallow of her spine and pulled her toward him. His heart stuttered with the uncertainty of everything new, everything untried and promised.

"Hm-m-m. Frogs? Who said anything about frogs?"

They stared at each other as if they'd never seen each other before, marveling at this joyous mixture of expectancy and fear. He lowered his mouth to her open lips, his heart pummeling like the pistons in his dad's old, rattling John Deere tractor. He kissed her fast, brushing his lips against hers in one simple, inexperienced movement that left him feeling winded and off-center.

When he backed away, she touched his hand, a gesture as uncomplicated and candid as their adolescence itself. At her unconscious bidding, he kissed her again, feeling her heart clattering offbeat against his buttons and his breastbone. She looped her hands over his shoulders and he brought her closer, turning his head now to fit his mouth more perfectly against hers.

Still, how many kisses do you partake in when you sit by a pond and succumb to the dizziness of your first embrace? They pulled back from one another, watching each other, wondering how much of this headlong desire could be permittable. But, in moments, their eyes connected again, her arms raising, his arms encompassing,

their mouths joining, until Blythe Hayden came onto the
front porch and stood back against the screen, her face
uplifted as she dried both hands on her apron.

Jimmy leapt away from Sarah like a scalded cat.

"It's just Momma," Sarah whispered, almost giggling.
"No need to jump like that. She cleans the refrigeration
cases every night and then comes out to see the stars."

"Oh, then." He bunched his knees beneath his chin
and grabbed them with his arms. Anything to keep his
arms from where they wanted to go, which was right back
around Sarah Hayden's body. "If that's all it is . . ." He
hesitated, then asked in a whisper, "You don't care if she
sees us kissing?"

"What if she does? It doesn't matter. She knows I've
got to grow up sometime. We've even talked about it."

"You have?"

"Sure." She reached one hand out to him then and
they braided their fingers together, waiting. "Although I
didn't know it would feel as good as all that, Jimmy. I
never guessed that part."

"Oh, Sarah girl," he whispered and, in his remembrance, it was the first time he'd called her by that name.
They sat side by side again, their knees gathered beneath
their chins, their faces inclined toward the daisy field of
stars, as the night became mystic around them. A beaver,
sleek and well-fitted, waddled past them and slid noise-
lessly into the water. Despite spring coming on, winter
held, the cold air coaxing mist that hovered low against
the pond. The full moon had arched from the east toward
the west and now hung poised behind a lodgepole pine
atop the ridge, peering from behind needled branches
like a giant cat's eye scrutinizing them.

"Will," Blythe said from the porch where she stood
half in darkness, half illuminated from the plate-glass
windows of the store. "You oughtta come out here and
take a look at this broad Wyoming sky."

Through the window, Sarah and Jimmy saw Will take his hat from the hook beside the cash register, coming to seek solace with his wife in the place he loved the best. He held the screen and lay it gently back against the logs, not letting even the slamming of a door disturb the stillness. "Just look at them," Sarah said in an undertone. "You can't imagine how many times he's stood out here with Momma like this, Jimmy. You'd think a night sky was something they've never seen before."

Miller Roice's barn stood halfway into a copse of quaking aspen, its green-metal gambrel roof almost hidden from view in the summer after the trees in the grove came to full leafing. Where generations of Roices had used the barn with its stalls and bins to house, feed, and milk holstein cattle, Miller Roice used the place now to accommodate his Mackenzie fishing boats. Every summer, as in this particular summer, he kept them freshly painted and poised to use in Caddisfly Creek, each bow and stern arcing toward the corrugated ceiling like a giant's cradle, each yellow Troutfitters logo brilliant in the sun that beamed through the high, old wheel of glass.

Sometime during the past seventy-five years, one of the more industrious Roices—a great-grandfather, if account told it right—had hoisted himself by the hay pulley and cut a circle just beneath the gambrel's overhang. Into it, he puttied the one remaining wagon wheel from the Studebaker supply wagon that had brought his ancestors into Star Valley, and added angles of glass to raise a window. It was there—in the splays of light that filtered from the glass wagon wheel and illuminated the boats and the haymow—that Sarah Hayden and Jimmy Roice first became lovers.

In the haymow, they'd learned tongues together,

trusting one another, playing with one another, as Jim carefully wet the periphery of Sarah's willing mouth in enduring, guileless strokes. They'd grown up and they'd grown together as they filled out and ripened like pods on milk vetch. At sixteen, they'd explored possibilities of touch and their maturing bodies answered in full orchestral score. They learned together how a lover can be brought to life, even as a violin awakens to its sweeping chord, even as a woodwind comes alive to its rush of breath.

There came the day when Sarah first followed Jim's instructions and lay gentle, cool hands against his belly on the inside of his sweater, running her fingers higher, higher, where they tentatively nestled upon beginnings of chest and hair and nipple. Came, too, the day when Jimmy parted Sarah's coat at the zipper, spreading the bulky down jacket apart and slipping both hands against her thin turtleneck to feel the rise and fall of breath and left breast.

"Don't do more," she whispered when he'd favored that one side over the other for the longest time through the fabric. "That poor one's getting sore."

"Is it? I'm hurting you?"

"Yes. Try the other side, Jim. Maybe it'll be better."

He'd trailed his hands across her, feeling her tense when he cupped his palm around the second breast, the right one. She'd never know how desperately he wanted to slip his hand beneath knit and lace into the place that was mysterious, the place next to her skin that was warm and forbidden. "There," he whispered. "Does that feel good? Is it right?"

"Yes. Oh, yes."

From then on, they talked to one another as they mastered each other's bodies. "Here," he'd whisper, guiding her untutored hand to the places he needed to be touched. "Do this here."

"There," she'd whisper, gently moving his hand against her skin to show him. "Kiss me there."

"Just like this," Jimmy'd tell her, holding her softly against him if she became scared. "That's so right. Oh, Sarah."

And, as they learned of each other, they learned of themselves.

There came—at last—one summer's evening when Miller Roice and his wife drove across state to Tensleep, an expedition to inspect a fellow's handiwork with custom-carved handles and woven trout nets. "What's he need with new trout nets anyway?" Sarah asked, sitting on the ledge above the barn floor and letting her bare, dusty feet dangle over.

"You've gotta keep ones that aren't old and brittle. They hurt the fish if he fights too hard and gets stuck out of water."

"Whoever heard of a net hurting a fish, anyway?"

While she'd talked, he'd been milking the one holstein his father had purchased, mostly to use for table milk, and he set the pails in the cooler before he clambered up the split-pine ladder and knelt beside her. "It's the same thing as you, Sarah. You're always talking about leaving, about seeing something bigger or different. I know you. The tighter the things are that hold you here, the harder you're gonna fight to get away. The new nets'll be as flexible around a fish as the water. Even though those cutthroats'll know they've been scooped, they won't flop about nearly as much when Dad goes about freeing them."

"So they'll be safer."

"Yes, safer." He'd hesitated, not knowing if he should say the rest of it. But, above all, they cherished each other's honesty. "It's what I want to be for you," he said. "Something safe. And comfortable and gentle as water."

"Jimmy," she'd said in a voice that did not sound like her own. She reached forward and encompassed his face with cupped fingers. "You are all those things for me."

"You know already I don't want you to go, when the time comes."

"You know already, when the time comes, I can't promise."

"Sarah, I—"

"Will you kiss me now?" she'd asked. "Will you kiss me the way you taught me best?" Because, by now, they'd both learned kissing in great detail.

Jimmy Roice removed his white canvas billed cap and lay it beside them in the hay. He took her hands in his and rubbed the backs of them with each big grimy thumb, holding her away from him, just looking at her for the longest time before he pulled her forward. He tilted his head to fit his mouth entirely upon hers. And, when he did, Sarah's every feminine impulse came into play. The child disappeared, the woman emerged, as her own lips parted in acceptance of his tongue.

His hand roved down her ribcage to settle at her hips until they'd kissed fully, then his hand roved up again, fingering the fabric and wrapping his palms around her sides. He felt the welling of her breasts against the shirt and suddenly, suddenly, it seemed as if the inches that separated them might be a fathomless space, so desperately did he want to be closer, so ungainly did his legs and their knees and her elbows keep them apart. "I want you," he whispered.

Her blue eyes never left his brown ones as she nudged his hand upward, toward the top button at her collar. "Undo my shirt then."

He couldn't speak. He leaned toward her, slowly, shakily going after the top button, as she'd bid him.

The thing was tiny, as humped as a beetle's back and painted to resemble a pearl. He fumbled with the button, his blood clamoring, feeling as inept at this unfastening as anything he'd ever tried. When Jimmy'd been scarcely eight, his father taught him the craft of tying flies. Certainly, he'd mustered a good amount of dexterity in wrapping minuscule, golden-eyed hooks with chenille and feather. Why, then, did this single button perplex him, stubbornly refusing to slip through the narrow, pink-stitched hole with which it had been matched?

Sarah waited for him, her chin uplifted and barely brushing his knuckles. She gripped his hand suddenly, holding it tight against the hollow at the base of her neck.

"Confounded thing," he said in frustration at the tiny button. "Why won't it—?" But, just as he said it, the thing gave way and popped open.

"You're shaking, is why," she said. "Try another." She released him and his hands moved down.

His Adam's apple bobbed once, first up, then down. Disengaging the next button took almost longer than the first. Only when it finally let go, only after he exhaled in a rush, did Jim realize he hadn't been breathing. Eager now, he freed the next button and the next, becoming more certain as he went, until each opened and the expanse of her skin that waited before him seemed as vast and continuing as the sweeping Wyoming tableland.

She sat with eyes closed, obviously anticipating him. He rocked back on the heels of his Tony Lama boots and waited, watching her, wanting her, but willing his pulse to slow.

Sarah opened her eyes again. "What is it, Jimmy?"

"Just want to make certain is all. Just want to make certain everything's gonna end up right."

"You worryin'? You thinkin' somebody might come up here and find us?"

"Only living thing that could find us is Barley, and I

can send that pup hightailin' it back to the house with just
one word: Git."

"You think it's wrong or wicked, us doing this the way
we are?"

"No," he told her. "I think it's more like magic."

She shivered once, the movement tremoring down
through her body as if she felt cold much deeper than
skin or bone. She hugged herself with her own arms.
"This is different though," she said. "Different than anything we've done before." And, as she said it, she gazed at
him as if he was dear life to her.

The expression in her eyes told him all he needed to
know. With fingers splayed, he opened her collar where
it lay askew against her throat. He touched her shoulders
inside the open garment, prodding the fabric first off the
left side, then the right. She helped him, shrugging out
of her sleeves, as linen fell in folds around her waist.

A woman's brassiere was not something Jimmy'd
looked upon closely before. Sarah's was made of white
lace with a little knot of ribbon right in its center, with a
tiny pink satin flower the exact color of her lips. Through
the lace, he could see the welling of her flesh and, in the
gaps between two patterns, he glimpsed the excruciating
sight of rose-dark nipples.

His hand moved toward the dainty ribbon and the little pink bud. "No." Her eyes were wide, he guessed with
pleasure and a little fear. "Not there. That part's just
decoration."

"Then how do you get the confounded thing off?"

"It unhooks in the back." She reached behind, her
elbows awry, and proceeded to free each clasp.

The undergarment sprang forward like a Wrist-Rocket
sling released. It loosed her bosom before it came to
rest, dangling innocently by its straps, from the crook on
each of Sarah's arms. A breeze stirred gently through the
gray, weathered planks of the old haymow as he saw her

waiting for him to take the apparel from her. The zephyr on his flesh felt both cool and searing, and he knew he'd turned red as a peony from the clip on his bolo up to the combed division in his hair.

"Sarah," he whispered. "Never seen anything like this."

"It's a good thing. I wouldn't like it if you already had."

He was afraid to touch, now that he'd come so far. "You're so . . . so smooth."

She reached across and slid the turquoise clasp clear down the leather thong of his tie and began to muddle through some buttons of her own. His own shirt open, she placed shaking hands against the heat of his chest. In one fell swoop, he ducked out of the bolo tie and yanked himself viciously out of the grubby-rough flannel shirt. He encircled her with his arms and braced her against him, feeling the hard knots of her growing breasts. He kissed her again, urging her backward a little at a time, until she listed from the coercion and flopped with him onto a musty tumble of alfalfa hay. Her arms twined around his back, but still they could not get close enough, could not press together enough, until he purposely, perfectly, matched his length along her body.

They responded to one another, not because of what they knew, not because of what they'd read or what they'd seen. Indeed, they'd been growing up in a life much hidden, much shielded, from urbane and carnal things. But what they felt now for each other was so visceral, so otherworldly, that to deny it was to disavow every pattern of the earth itself, the wheeling flight of the hawk, the living light of fire.

Sarah's fingers wove into his dark hair and she held him against her as she'd hold a tight rein on a mare. His knee came up to part her legs, their jean-clad limbs meshed together like willowy poplar boughs. He raised himself above her, not wanting her to bear his full weight.

She lay flat-shouldered against the hay, which still smelled the faint green of last year's harvest. "What're you gonna do now?" she asked him, finding humor. "You've still got your boots on."

"We've both got jeans on, too," he said, a hint of levity in his eyes. "Had enough trouble with that bra of yours. Sure don't know whether I want to tangle with a pair of these Wranglers."

"How do they do it in picture shows?"

The last movie he'd seen was *Any Which Way But Loose* when it came for reprise at the Spud Drive-In across the pass over in Idaho. He'd sat in the back seat, craning his neck between his parents, eating Tater Tots with fry sauce and drinking a purple Nehi. As he recalled, he hadn't cared much for the part where Clint Eastwood got Sondra Locke at the end, but he'd thought the stuff with the orangutan was hilarious.

"I don't have any idea."

They tread a fine line between adolescence and adulthood, their burgeoning sexuality taking the place of anxiety or qualm. He sat up beside her in the hay and unbound the rivet at her waist. She lifted her pelvis off the plank floor, peeled the denim away from her hips, and pointed her toes so he could tug them the rest of the way.

He turned from her to wrench off his boots, then worked hip-to-hip, bringing his own jeans down before he turned to her wearing nothing but a pair of utilitarian cotton shorts with an elastic band and a snap around the middle. She grinned up at him. "So that's the kind of underwear you use."

He didn't stop to laugh with her this time. He knelt beside her. "Sarah? Haven't you ever wondered what my body feels like? Haven't you wanted to finish exploring me with your hands?"

Oh yes, indeed, she had. She'd dreamed of it at night, pondered what it would be like, as she turned and tossed in the single white bed beneath a cornice board lined with dolls. She nodded, her eyes round as quarters.

"I'd like you to find me. Comes the time when a man needs to be touched by a woman's hand."

She sat up beside him, propping herself against the floor with one arm. For one short moment, she stared at her own small hand and heard his words echo: *"Touched by a woman's hand."*

He waited on his knees and guided her hand over the cotton until she found the crook between his legs and he helped her form a gentle fist over the ridge there. The moment her hand closed, she met his eyes and was amazed to behold, to actually *see*, his pulse throbbing at the base of his throat.

What she felt beneath her fingers seemed gargantuan, much larger than anything she'd imagined or had managed to see when she'd been snooping at infants. As he reached for her now and began to pull down her panties, he wore an expression she'd never seen on his face before.

"Oh, Jimmy." She was horrified to realize that, between her legs, the panties had grown damp.

His voice was weak, his lips dry. "It's okay, Sarah. It's all the way it's supposed to be."

"What is it? How do you know what it's supposed to be?" When she spoke, he could tell she was honestly afraid again.

"The beasts in the field, Sarah. Haven't you seen them? Don't you know what they do?"

Despite everything, she'd trusted Jim Roice for as long as she could remember. "You want us to do something like that?"

He reached for her, taking both her hands in his now, recognizing the trust in such a question. "No. People are very, very different, Sarah girl. They lay down naked. And they hold on to each other."

"Show me," she whispered. "Show me what people do."

And he whispered back, "I want to hold on to you, Sarah. For always."

4

The morning after old Will's funeral, Sarah's first consciousness was a sense of the dry, light wind blowing in beneath the crack in the window, bringing with it the fragrances she remembered most of the mountains; the acrid tang of pine, the dusky-warm heaviness of smoke, the sweet purity of autumn-cured sage.

She rose from the bed and peered out the window, enjoying the quiet sense of place, for the moment a youngster again, forgetting all the circumstances that had brought her.

The black-capped chickadees out this morning kept mostly to areas of protection, the tiny white-masked birds darting from bough to bough in flighty, banditlike shifts. Occasionally, one would grow brave and play hopscotch along a row of well-seasoned buckrail fence posts, pausing in the crystal sunlight to warble, *chick-a-dee-dee-dee chick-a-dee-dee-dee,* before flitting quickly back to refuge in the ancient evergreen forest.

She could tell by the chill that the woodstove fire she'd started at midnight had long-since burned down to ashes. Padding around barefooted in the kitchen, Sarah searched for something to light one burner on the propane stove. She found the red-and-blue box of Diamond matches and struck one, turning the gas to a steady medium-low, then waited for the pop that would ignite the circle of tiny blue flames.

Her parents never believed in using automatic coffeemakers. Sarah dug through the cabinets and came up with nothing better than Will's old aluminum camp percolator, blackened from years of use. She pried the top off the metal coffee canister and peered inside. Empty.

Sarah gathered her robe high above her ankles and climbed downstairs to the dark store below. Still barefooted and drifting through the daybreak, she paused before the selection of locally roasted coffee flavors and stared out the downstairs window. What met her sight would stay with her ever afterward: the profile of a boy, his hair unkempt and tow-headed, playing an early-morning balance game on the dilapidated wagon bed that lay twisted in the meadow.

The old wagon didn't have axles left to be broken. What remained of a shattered doubletree harness lay propped sideways against one end. Even though Sarah couldn't remember it, the thing looked as if it'd been rotting in the dry tufts of wheatgrass forever.

The boy played beside the building without seeing her, leaping back and forth between the sideboards with much the same motion and levity as the chickadees hurrying back and forth into the trees. He sprang from one to another while Sarah held her breath, hoping he wouldn't fall. Then, as if he sensed her watching him, or maybe because he caught a glimpse of movement behind the glass, he jumped down with both feet and came barreling—with a large portion of white hair sticking up like duckfluff from a cowlick on his forehead—toward the long, low porch of the store.

He opened the front door, which was never locked, and poked his nose inside. "Hi. Store open now?"

"No. The store won't be open today at all. I'm sorry."

Disappointed, he halfway looked at her and halfway looked around her, as if he expected someone else to come up behind her and tell her she was wrong. "Been wantin' to buy Momma a present," he said.

"There's lots of places you can buy your mother a present. Hunter's Floral downtown has two rows of gifts."

"This is the only store close enough to walk to. Got some birthday money left over and there's somethin' she wants and I really want to surprise her. Been waitin' for Will to open up for almost a week now." He'd backed away, and now the screen closed between them. When he pressed his nose up against it, his skin poked through in a checkerboard of little squares.

"You come here to the store a lot?"

He nodded.

She just stared at him a few moments, her resolve weakening, thinking what a handsome child he was, and wondering to whom he belonged. "What did you want for your mom?"

"One of those scarves old Will keeps hanging by the register. The blue-and-green ones with the maps of all the different places in Grand Teton National Park."

She glanced over her shoulder and saw them hanging there, exactly where he told her they'd be. "Tell you what," she said. "I've got to run upstairs and make coffee. You come on in and look around."

"Gosh, thanks."

"What's your name?"

"Who? Me?" She nodded. "Charlie."

"Okay, Charlie. Pick out your scarf. When you're ready, call me and I'll come back down to ring you up. But don't tell anybody else. Don't want to be open for business today. I'm trying to get things organized."

He didn't even wait for her to step away from the door and receive him. He shoved his way on through, banging the screen and making a beeline right for the register as if he'd done this same thing a hundred times before. "Don't know which one she'd rather have," he said, fanning one out with his hand and squinting his eyes to read: "Signal Mountain."

"There's also Jenny Lake and Colter Bay," Sarah said, thumbing through them, too, for the first time.

"Guess I'm just gonna have to look," he said. "I've gotta figure out which ones are her favorite places."

"Call me," she said, smiling. "I'll be upstairs with my coffee pot."

A few minutes later, after Sarah dressed and the coffee began perking merrily on the stove, she heard him tromping up the stairs.

"I'm done," he announced when he reached the top.

"Which one did you pick?"

"Jenny Lake. Momma loves Jenny Lake."

"Good."

He craned his neck around the corner. "Where's old Will?"

She faltered. "He isn't here."

"Why not? He's always here."

Sarah stooped down before him, not knowing exactly what she should say. "Oh, sweetie."

"Why isn't he here?"

What were the correct words to explain this to a boy who looked to be about ten years old, who looked to have his whole life in front of him? "He was my dad," she said quietly, as the sorrow inside her seemed to twist, tighten, and take hold the way it hadn't before. To this one small boy, she had to admit everything she'd given away or lost, and words didn't come easy. "He got very sick. He was in the hospital but the doctors couldn't make him better. A few days ago, he died."

"How could he be your dad? I've never seen you playing around here."

"I used to play here. A long time ago when I was a little girl. Used to fish in the pond, too. Dad kept it full of fish all the time."

"I caught one last weekend," he said, his eyes brightening as if they'd found some sort of kinship. "It fought hard as a whale and I thought I was gonna lose it, but Dad scooped it up in a net. My dad's real good with nets. Then we measured it. Darn fish was six inches long."

"Very good," Sarah said. "A trophy fish."

"Had to set it loose," Charlie said. "Dad said it still had some growin' to do."

"Guess it did." She took the coffee off the burner and poured herself a cup. "You ready to pay for that scarf?"

"Yeah."

She followed him downstairs and rang up the total, her fingers finding correct placement on the register keys without her even having to think. "That'll be $8.39, please."

Charlie reached into his pockets and tugged out all the change. A number of quarters. A wad of dollar bills. Several pennies. He unfolded the bills and began to count them out to her. "One . . . three . . . five . . . seven. There you go. Eight." To that pile, he added one quarter and the remainder of his change. He'd clearly budgeted for this.

"Great," she said, sliding the change into her hand and counting it out into the open register drawer.

"Can you gift-wrap it for me please?"

"Gift-wrap it?"

"Yeah. So she can open it like a present. Old Will always gift-wrapped things."

"He did?"

"Yeah."

She looked around under the counter, momentarily confused. "I don't see wrapping paper under here. Don't think he ever carried wrapping paper."

"He didn't. He always just used *The Thrifty Nickel*." Charlie held up a pile of last month's giveaway want ads, published all the way over in Idaho Falls. "He wrapped 'em and tied 'em up with twine, then I took 'em home and colored 'em with crayons. Always made for a real fancy package."

"All right, then." She took one issue from him and unfolded it. "For Sale. Ashley wood and coal-burning stove, ideal for shop." "Wanted: British or German motorcycle, 1960–1972. Must be clean." "Idaho potatoes. fifty pounds delivered to your door." She began to tape this paper over Charlie's scarf, all the while missing Will Hayden more. She'd missed so much of the things he'd enjoyed at the end of his lifetime. And he'd certainly enjoyed this little boy. "Is it your mother's birthday, too?" she asked as she perfectly creased each corner and made a flap to fasten up over each side.

"Nope."

"Well." She cut a piece of twine, then stopped to gaze at him, her eyes almost watery. "Your mother is certainly lucky to have *you*." She finished tying the bow and handed him the gift. He took it in both hands.

She waited for him to head out the door, but he didn't. He just stood, looking at her for the longest time. Finally, he asked, "You sad because your dad died?"

She nodded. "Yes, I am."

"I had a dog that died once."

"You did?"

"Yeah."

"What happened?"

"He just got real old. Dad says there were parts of him that just didn't work anymore. You know, inside parts like his belly or his liver or something. We took him to Tuck Krebbs at the veterinarian's office. That fellow knows how to make animals better by giving 'em medicine. But Tuck couldn't make our dog better. Even the medicine didn't help."

"Were you sad when your dog died?"

"Yeah."

"Sometimes the sad takes a long time to go away."

"We buried him in the willows just past the barn, out by his favorite skunk hole. Dad says people all have their minds set on going to heaven, but dogs are just as happy staying out in a field with things they chase, like rabbits and skunks. Sometimes I go out there and just think about that pup. We put a big rock marked with his name so we could remember him. Dad let me write it out with a permanent marker all by myself: Barley."

Mention of the dog's name made Sarah's heart dance a quick stutter. Memories flowed. "I had a friend with a dog named Barley once."

"It's a good name for a dog."

"You live around here?"

"Sure do." He pointed out the window, past the run-down wagon, toward the top of a gambrel barn Sarah had always been able to see through the aspens. "That's my house there." The Roice place.

"Guess I should have known it," she said. "You're Jim and Victoria's boy."

"Sure am." And, here, he squared his shoulders with pride.

She thought, *See? See, Jim? See?*

"Wish you'd open the store back up." He stared up at the assortment of Coleman canoes hanging directly over their heads. "What're you gonna do with all this stuff if you don't let people come in and buy stuff?"

"Don't know," she said, remembering the realtor for the first time today. "I have an appointment with someone who's going to help me. Guess I'll decide those things this morning."

"I think this is the best store in the whole world." Charlie still held his precious package in both hands, his little fingernails black deep into the quick. "Well . . . thanks." He raised it a bit toward her. "You did a good job at wrapping. Almost as good as old Will would've done himself. See you."

"Yes," she said, "see you." And, as he ran out across the meadow toward the timberland, Sarah thought he seemed like a September child, with his skin still bronze and his hair the same ageless color as the bleached, autumn wheatgrass. It reminded her of dried stalks left at pond's edge after a wondrous gathering of cattails. Struck her interest, though, seeing him so fair while his parents both had hair and eyes of a much different hue.

She watched him go, taking joy in him, taking joy for Jim's sake, before she tucked her own wheat-blond hair behind one ear and went inside to make ready for the realtor.

Rita Persnick parked her black Suburban in front of the store and climbed out, stepping back to examine the building's exterior before she shut the door to reveal a gold-emblazoned panel: "Teton Valley Real Estate. If we can't sell your places, we won't show our faces. (307) 555-5498." The realtor picked her way over parking-lot gravel to the back double entry of her vehicle, where she procured two aluminum black-and-gold For Sale signs and a black leather valise. She thrust one into the dirt at the edge of the highway before she dusted off both hands, carried the second sign to the porch, and made ready to inspect the premises.

"Miss Hayden." She announced herself as she slammed her way in through the screen. "Rita Persnick. Teton Valley

Real Estate." With no further ado, she set down the sign and the attaché she juggled, *sproi-i-inged* the briefcase open, and began to arrange upon the counter, in descending order according to size, a goodly number of business papers and contracts.

"I can answer any questions you might have."

"How many acres?"

"Seven."

"Square footage of the building?"

"The store is eighteen hundred square feet. Living quarters above it are the same."

"Hm-m-m." Rita Persnick scratched her head and turned completely around, doing her best to take in the multitude of shelves jammed with merchandise. "What would you guess the inventory is worth?"

"I have no idea. twenty-five grand, maybe?"

"I'd like to see upstairs."

"Go ahead. Please."

The entire time she trounced up the steps, the realtor asked questions. "How many bathrooms? How many bedrooms? How many closets? How did they heat the place? Were those asbestos shingles on the roof? When had the kitchen last been updated?"

"The kitchen?" Sarah asked, trying her best to remember. "Think they relaid the linoleum and got a new Servel refrigerator in 1963. The stove was my grandmother's, brought over Teton Pass in a supply wagon in 1939."

"Oh."

It certainly seemed a relief when the realtor got smart and stopped making inquiries. Rita Persnick sauntered through the upstairs rooms without so much as another comment, scribbling on a yellow legal pad as she went, stopping ever so often to punch numbers into her calculator. Sarah didn't know why it bothered her suddenly that everything seemed old and in disrepair and that the realtor she'd hired was making note of it. She'd always seen the store that way herself. She figured it was the same story people with siblings told, how you could make fun of your brother all you wanted, but let somebody else try to do the same thing and you were there with fists curled, ready to bloody noses.

She didn't know exactly what it was, but she felt the need to stand up for something. "This old place has historical significance, Ms. Persnick."

"Oh, I'm sure it does. When was it built?"

Sarah counted back the years, applying what she knew of her great-grandparents. "1917, I think. It was homesteaded the same year the valley was first settled."

Ms. Persnick looked up from her notes. "This place hasn't changed hands since it was settled?"

She shook her head. "No."

"That could pose problems. If we're dealing with Wyoming homestead laws from the turn of the century, it could take months before we're actually given clear title."

"I wasn't aware of that."

"On what type of foundation is this structure built?"

"Foundation?"

"Does it have a crawl space? A substructure of concrete?"

"Don't think they made concrete back then. Certainly not in Star Valley."

"Could it be brick?"

"Don't figure it *has* a foundation, Ms. Persnick. I believe it just starts at the ground and goes up."

"That will certainly make it difficult for any buyer to get financing."

"If you don't want the listing, I can always find another realtor. A friend in New York suggested I contract with someone in Jackson Hole." Marshall had told her he thought she'd stand a better chance at regional advertisement if she listed the place with an aggressive resort company. But she'd followed her instincts this time, knowing how it would nettle if she came back to Star Valley to engender property sales with an out-of-town, big-bucks realtor.

"Oh, I want the listing." Rita Persnick's fingers began to fly on the calculator keys. "Let's come up with an asking price. Let's see . . . land per acre . . . the pond . . ."

"And water rights," Sarah broke in. "We have water rights from Caddisfly Creek."

"What about that old waterwheel? Any chance it could be gotten up and running again?"

"I don't know. Don't know much about waterwheels."

"I'm going to have to take at least twelve percent off for obsolescence. Anybody who wanted to move in and make the place liveable would almost have to gut it."

"What do you think about the inventory?" Sarah asked. "Should I offer to sell it complete? Or, would I be better off to hire an auctioneer?"

Rita Persnick stared off for a moment. "Let me give that one some thought. You might end up ahead by selling some things individually. The stove upstairs for example. It's an antique, that's for certain."

"Yes."

"And the canoes. You should sell those. Don't know about the pac boots or the Woolrich sweaters."

"I just thought, if somebody wanted to come in and keep going with the store, they might be thankful enough for what's already here."

The realtor made one last quick turn around the room. "I doubt that, Miss Hayden."

"I went through my father's files last night. Didn't find much, but there are some sales figures that might be pertinent. I've got them right over here." She'd carefully sorted everything, leaving the boxes of personal files she'd found upstairs in the attic.

"That won't be necessary. I've seen what I need to see." Rita Persnick scribbled an asking price onto her pad and began to work to complete the contracts. "It's a shame the place isn't fifteen miles closer to Jackson. Someone could build a deck out by the pond, get the waterwheel going again, and turn it into a restaurant. That's the only way I see this place having much value."

5

In Star Valley townfolks' eyes, Sarah Hayden
was an insider, a child of the privileged few, blood ascen-
sion from cowboys and crazy-headed fools who thought
they could brave Wyoming winters and live their days and
carve an enterprise from this unrelenting range of high
land. Sarah's greatest sin—as people saw it—wasn't in
wanting to leave the valley. The sin, several decided as
they sat around George Peart's barber shop watching Judd
Stanford get his hair trimmed, was in being a *Hayden* and
wanting to leave the valley. Just shouldn't happen, they
said. Shouldn't happen to a family that had been here since
Star Valley first started up.

Sarah found it impossible to define how desperately
she'd wanted to leave this place. She also found it impossible to explain how desperately she'd loved and trusted
Jimmy. Even though he was one of the kids she'd known
forever, it seemed as if he gave her a sense of herself
that felt far-reaching. She'd lost count of how many

times she'd clobbered him or how many times he'd chased her and pitched her into a wheelbarrow full of dirt clods and stickseed before their fresh, prospering bodies took over and made matters all the more importunate. He bound her to this place; he released her to the burgeoning part of herself that longed to take wing and inherit the earth.

Living life in this town gave Sarah the sensation of slowly settling to the bottom of a dark, deep, water-filled well. It was the most boring place she'd ever been. And she'd never been anywhere.

From the time she'd been ten, Sarah'd realized people in Star Valley thought about things all wrong. They figured events happening to themselves or their animals were the only important things happening anywhere. Never mind that Jimmy Carter was running against Gerald Ford and that his contention looked strong. Star Valley was 98 percent registered, voting Republican, would've been 100 percent if not for the Ben Mitchums, who moved in from Illinois over at the old Johnson place. So how could anybody in the rest of the world think anything different?

In Star Valley, nobody'd cared much when Nixon resigned. They knew folks in Washington would find another Republican fellow who could do just as good a job, probably better. Democrats didn't exist. Neither did the Big Thompson flood that year, or a girl from Romania named Nadia Comaneci, or a war overseas that had gone on longer than ought to be humanly tolerable. People in Star Valley cared and talked about only their own.

"As soon as I can, you know I'm leavin'," she told Jimmy one day as they tromped through the timothy grass to launch one of Miller Roice's boats onto Caddisfly.

"Don't like to hear you talk about that." And, in his heart of hearts, Jimmy thought she wouldn't go. How could she, with everything they felt between them? Together, they shoved the dory across gravel and pushed it into the creek. Jimmy held on while Sarah flopped over the side. He hurried then, splashing with big flat steps, to catch up and jump in beside her. "Seems like a leave-taking, going off to CWC the way you are. But I figure you'll be back helpin' your dad out at the store just as soon as you get your diploma."

"What's the sense of getting a diploma if all I'm gonna do is come back and hang it on the wall of the store? It's more than that, Jimmy. You know that."

"You're warnin' me again." Slowly, luxuriantly, the Mackenzie boat pirouetted and began to slip downstream into the current. He reached for her, knowing that as soon as they passed the next clump of catkin willow he could begin to undress her. "You've warned me since the first time I knew you. And I don't even remember when that was."

In 1984, the spring of their senior year was a good one. The creek ran briskly, muddied by melting snow high above the timberline. The days grew longer, leaving lingering hours of backlight, the shining clouds hanging to the west behind the mountains like tattered gauze hanging in a window. During one of those evenings, the Spud Drive-In across the pass in Idaho opened for its warm-weather season, showing second-run movies and selling barbecue burgers Thursday through Saturday nights. The senior play, *Bye Bye Birdie*, played to a sell-out crowd two nights in a row. Friends drove clear to Jackson Hole to shop for prom dresses. Dora Tygum served a prime-rib dinner at Caddisfly Inn to every member of the Star Valley High School graduating class. Trout season began. Sarah's menstrual period did not.

She knew only those things about her body she'd heard in speeches from Blythe, or read in the six-week health class, or discovered during her explorations with Jimmy. She counted eight days past, even wore a Modess pad just in case. The only books she knew to read were Will's ancient brown copies of the *Encyclopedia Britannica,* the ones he'd kept ever since his own grandfather boxed them and said he was saving them to use as firestarter, since none of his children felt the urge to go off to college. Using the topic and cross-index, Sarah searched through every subject that might apply: Pregnancy, Menstrual Cycle, Mammals/Reproduction, Gestation Period.

She knew she could never go to Doc Bressler for a pregnancy test. Will offered home-pregnancy kits in the store, but she didn't dare buy one.

In a Jackson phone book, she found listings that offered free tests and confidential appointments. She waited another month before she got brave enough to pursue it. But one Wednesday two weeks before they were scheduled to graduate, Sarah borrowed Will's Dodge Power Wagon, cut classes at school, and drove to Jackson. She felt difficult to live with, inconsistent, moody. And, an hour later, a smiling volunteer named Mary Hardeman confirmed her worst suspicions. "Yes," said Mary, still smiling, always smiling, although the smile seemed sad. "You're going to have a baby, Sarah."

"I thought I might."

"We suggest you make an appointment to see a licensed obstetrician right away."

"Yes."

"We have some literature we'd like you to read," she said. "Information that will help you make your best decisions. Would you like that?"

"Yes."

Mary handed her a two-color brochure from an elevated pile. *How many of those would they need?* Sarah wondered. *How many girls do they know like me?* She opened the pamphlet accordion-style and read:

> *The Wyoming Parenting Society maintains a statewide list of families waiting for adoption, with an average deferral period of nearly four years. The babies, when the blessed few of them come, go to the top name on the list unless the birth mother has serious objections.*

"Don't know what to do," Sarah whispered, laying the brochure into her lap, still clutching it in both hands.

"You're young," Mary Hardeman said. "Decisions like this are difficult to make."

"Yes. They are." Sarah sat staring at the woman a moment, trying to read her face, trying to decide what it was she must be thinking. After a long silence between them, she handed back the leaflet.

"I have a family in Rock Springs at the top of the list right now. She's a nurse. He's a loan processor at Rock Springs National Bank. They may already have found a baby by the time you have yours, Sarah, but maybe not. In seven months, anything can happen."

Sarah stood and donned her coat. Yes. Seven months. In seven months, she was supposed to be halfway through her first semester at Riverton. "I'll come by in a few days to let you know."

"Fine. We'll be expecting you." Sarah turned to go, but Mary stopped her. "We have our ways of helping, you know. Maternity clothes, vitamins, prenatal care, baby clothes. I could show you some of the baby clothes."

"I'd rather not see them today."

She hurried out into the frigid air, leaning slightly into wind that didn't offer even a hint of May, clenching her parka closed against her middle. The entire time she drove down the canyon in her father's ancient Dodge, she thought with calm deliberateness, *There's something inside me. Someone we've made because we've loved each other.*

She drove back without ever even turning on the radio. Sarah parked the truck in front of the store, something Will frowned upon, and set forth down the footpath she and Jimmy'd kept trampled open since they'd been children. She called out as she approached the old log house. "Jimmy Roice? You around?"

A gray tabby cat stood on the doorstep to stretch. His mother held open the door. "Come in, Sarah girl." And, when she did, the house was filled with the delicious hot fragrance of yeast rolls baking for supper. "Where have you been off to this afternoon? Everybody's been wondering." Thankfully, she went back to shelling peas into the huge bowl in her lap and never paused in her prattling for an answer. "Jimmy's out helping his father with chores," she said. "If you've got time, come sit."

"Think I'll just go out the barn and see Jimmy," Sarah said, doing her best to keep her voice regular. She ran up the path toward the barn and its haymow, once again clutching the coat against her, as his dog Barley bounded through the trees and fell in behind her. "Jimmy?"

He came forward, hurrying through light and shadow, stirring up dust motes as he kicked through the hay. "Well, Sarah, it's good of you to show up. Want to help out with the milking?" he asked somberly as he met her and took her in his arms. "Thank heaven Dad runs fishing boats instead of a dairy farm. I'd never stay sane if I had to pull teats for a living."

For one sacred moment, the bright fact of their youth, of their being together, overrode the news she'd come to tell him. "Pulling teats?" she laughed, drawing nearer to him. "I thought that was something you could do quite nicely."

He glanced in both directions for a sign of his father. When he saw none, he used both milky hands to go in search of her breasts beneath her sweater. She laid her head against the broadness of his chest and gently let him find her. "Hmmm," he said wickedly. "Teats, yes. Pulling them, no."

Sarah looked into dark eyes that were intent and powerful, eyes that showed feeling as openly as anyone she would ever know.

He said, "I've already been over to the store to find you. Why weren't you in Hardaway's class?"

"I had an appointment." The graveness in her eyes was the first sign he saw of trouble brewing.

"What sort of an appointment, Sarah?"

She didn't answer. She couldn't. Because the implications of what she'd chosen to do would force a reckoning between them. She buried her face against his arm.

"Come on, Sarah. You can tell me, of all people. What?"

For as long as he let her, she stood against him like that, hiding her face, overpowered by the intensity of her dreams, overpowered by the familiarity and the safety of Jimmy.

"Sarah. I've lost patience. You've got to tell me." And, here, he took his hand and lifted her chin gently, seeing for the first time hot tears splayed out across her cheeks.

"We've made a mistake, you and I," she told him. "A terrible mistake."

He tightened his arms around her. "Nothing we've done together has been a mistake, Sarah."

But she was shaking her head, the regret in her eyes so palpable that it frightened him. "Don't say that. You don't know."

"Tell me, then. Tell me what it is that I don't know." He stared down at her, never guessing what could be so horrible. "Sarah. You're scaring me."

At last, she said it. "I'm pregnant, Jimmy."

"What?"

"I'm going to have a baby."

"You are? Sarah!" His first reaction was to grab her in his arms and whirl her around the barn, so great was his relief. "A baby? Sarah, it's remarkable."

"Jimmy," she whispered, her eyes sad. "Set me down. We've got to talk about this."

"This isn't a problem. It's *wonderful*. I don't care if my parents know we've been fooling around in the haymow. Everybody already knows how we feel about each other. They talk about us down at the barber shop even. Dad said last time he went in there to get his beard trimmed, George Peart himself says, 'There go those two kids. Young and in love.'"

"Jimmy. I'm only seventeen."

"You'll be eighteen next month. Old enough to marry me without anybody's consent. But they'd all consent to it, anyway. You know that as well as I do."

"I just got that scholarship from the DAR. It's my first real chance to go to a university."

He stopped talking and noticed her face. Her expression hadn't changed during his long tirade. The regret remained. And suddenly, suddenly, that scared him all the more.

"Sarah girl." He swept her into his arms again but, this time, he wasn't quite so certain. "Say you'll marry me. We'll do it this summer, out in the meadow by Greybull Pond, after we've both graduated. This baby'll be the first of . . . how many? Three? Four?" All the while he talked, he tried to convince her, tried to make her see she didn't have to be sorry.

"You don't understand, do you?" she asked.

"Of course I understand. I understand everything perfectly."

"I don't think you do."

"You'll marry me—"

She gripped his forearms and, holding him there, backed away. "You're saying words you think I want to hear."

"I'm saying words I mean."

"Even if you mean them, maybe we'd both be better off if you didn't tell me those things right now." She took a deep breath, taking another step back from him, releasing him. "Don't ask me to marry you. Because I won't. Not now."

"Dear sweet heaven. You won't? It's what we've talked about for a year. And the baby—"

"It's what you've talked about, not me."

"Good God, Sarah."

She said it again, softer this time. "I'm only seventeen."

"I know that."

"This is my chance, Jimmy. My only chance."

"But I always thought . . ." He trailed off. For as long as he'd known her, he'd supposed she'd quit hoping to see the world after a while. He'd always thought she'd figure out she had life fine right where she stood and that, one day, she'd decide to stop seeking. It had been the one thing, the only thing, that kept him thinking their future was safe. "You wouldn't trade a child's life for your own dreams, would you?"

The moment he asked it, Sarah knew that she would. "Who's to say what's more important?" she asked him. "One life? Or another? It's my turn."

"It isn't as easy as all that."

"I didn't say it was easy. I never thought it would be easy." She saw the world outside Star Valley as some people saw heaven—unfathomable, beautiful, its routes bedecked with promise. Her only chance of tasting that promise, of escaping the store and becoming someone *different*, was to earn a ticket out of this place. "My scholarship, remember? I've worked so hard for it." And she didn't tell him now but, after she finished her degree, she wanted an MBA, too.

It was everything he could do not to shake her. "Where do you think you want to go, Sarah? Where do you think out *there* is gonna be so much better than *here*?"

"Don't know. Haven't figured that much out yet."

"What about you and me?" he asked. "What about how much we've loved each other?"

It was the first time the resolve on her face eased at all. She touched his coat sleeve. "You could come with me, you know."

"If I come with you, what do you expect me to do for a living? I've spent my whole life around this place. I'm not running off to college."

"You could work somewhere."

"Who would my dad pass the business down to? Who'd run Roice's Wyoming Troutfitters if I took off with you? Best training I'll ever have is to spend summers with Dad out on Caddisfly showing tourists how to hook up with a big one. I'm meant for the fishing business, Sarah. Couldn't survive doing anything else. The minute I start earnin' wages is the minute I've given everything I am away to somebody else."

"I believe that," she said. "I believe in what you need to do, too." Even so, she wouldn't bargain with a baby's life. "And so we've made our decision then. Both of us."

The enormity of the situation welled up and overtook him. "What will we do? What will we do with my baby?" In his heart of hearts, he knew if she suggested abortion he would fight her. But he knew so little about it. And, beneath it all, beneath the veneer of composure he kept, his own soul felt fragmented, maimed, because she wouldn't accept the future he offered her.

"There's a lady in Jackson who'll help me. The state has a list of people who want babies to adopt. A long list. They're good homes, every one." She began crying again, her own fortitude dwindling as she admitted it at last to him. "I never intended it to be this way, Jimmy. I never intended to have to choose between you and everything else I've needed."

"Stay here," he said. "Don't go."

"Jimmy. If you ask me to stay, you're asking me to give up everything I've ever wanted."

"And if I let you go, you're asking me to do the same. Think about it, Sarah. People'll hear stories about a baby. Jackson's only thirty-five miles away." But he didn't care much if people heard or not. He didn't care much about anything, except losing her.

"I'll do it a different way then. I'll transfer my records this week. If I go as far away as Laramie, no one will know what's happened. I'll start classes early. People are just gonna have to talk, that's all. But nobody'll ever know for sure. I'll make certain of that."

"Not even your parents, Sarah? You aren't gonna tell them something about it?"

She shook her head and, with her denial, went Jimmy's last vestiges of hope. "Something like this would just hurt them too much to know."

"What about me?" he asked. "What about me and how I'm hurting?"

"You've been a part of my life, Jimmy," she said through her tears. "A very special, blessed part. But I'm not willing to give up the portion of myself that would perish if I stayed here."

"You coming back after it's all over?"

She didn't even hesitate. She met his eyes, knowing this would be the final, devastating answer. "No."

"All you've ever wanted is to grow up," he said, not quite crossly, as if the idea had just dawned on him. Even so, his voice broke as he said it now. "It's all you ever wanted me for, wasn't it, Sarah? You wanted me so I could help you grow up. Because the faster you could grow up, the faster you could leave us all."

She didn't answer. She didn't tell him he was wrong.

"Folks around here aren't gonna take kindly to you just up and leaving your family like this. They won't understand why you don't come back in a few months. Your father needs you to help mind the store."

"I can't make anyone understand, Jimmy. You're the only one who knows all of it. You've gotta make them see that my leaving isn't all that bad."

"But Sarah, isn't it, though? Isn't it the worst thing you could do? If you'd stay here, we could start out right with a wedding and a family. You'd be happy after a while. Everything would find its rightful place."

"Everything would find its rightful place," she said resolutely, "except me."

6

Two days after graduation, Sarah's transfer from Central Wyoming College in Riverton came through. Both she and her DAR scholarship had been accepted at the University of Wyoming in Laramie. That night, upstairs above the store, in the only home she'd ever known, she began to pack her belongings into boxes.

"Don't leave like this," Blythe begged. "Sweetheart. At least give yourself the summer."

"I can't, Momma. Summers are too long around here as it is. And I'm impatient. I've always been impatient." More than that, she knew the longer she stayed, the harder it would be when she left Jimmy.

"At least give us the chance to get used to the idea of you being so far away before you're gone."

"You'll have to get used to it now, Momma," she said, giving Blythe a vague, dry kiss. "Summer school classes start next Monday. I aim to be there."

Once she made the decision to go, Will wouldn't even

talk to her about it. While she packed, he stayed down in the store, scouring counters or wrapping links of hot-spiced sausage. She found him that night dusting an old set of cast-iron pans that had been sitting on the shelf for well over a year.

"What're you doing down here?" she asked.

"Never do know when somebody'll come along who's wanting to buy these."

"Dad," she whispered. "aren't you even gonna come upstairs so we can *talk* about it?"

"Don't figure there's anything to talk about," he said. "Your bags are packed."

"I'd like to do this with your blessing."

"You aren't gonna have it. You already know that."

"Figured when the time came, you might change your mind."

"Won't be so. A man never likes to think that what he's spent his whole life providing for his children won't be enough to satisfy them."

"It isn't what you've provided, Dad. It's me. I feel isolated from everything real." *And I have to go because I'm having a baby*. She couldn't tell him that.

"It is easy to undervalue whatever is close to home." He crammed the pans way back onto the shelf, where it would be at least another year before anyone found them. He turned to her, stiff as a sandhill crane, looking as if he could find no place to put his hands. "I'm not coming to see you off when you go, Sarah girl. Couldn't bear standing at that bus stop, waving you into the distance."

"Didn't figure you'd want to be there," she said.

Although she heard no more denunciation from her father after that, she heard plenty from Jimmy. "Stay, Sarah," he said. "Stay, even if it's only for the summer."

But she knew what he was trying to do. He thought with an extra two months he could convince her.

"Won't be any easier in August than it is right now, Jimmy. If I stayed," she said, "somehow I think they'd know. I think they'd look at me and see that something was different."

He turned from her, staring up into the dark, ancient trees. She knew he didn't want her to see his face. And, when he turned back, his skin glistened with his tears. "What're you gonna do with the baby?"

"I'll take care as best I can, Jimmy. I promise." Unconsciously, she placed one flat hand upon her stomach, where an existence grew, an existence—a life—that would always bind them together.

"You'll take naps? You'll drink milk?" That was all Jim Roice really knew about being pregnant. He knew you had to drink homogenized milk. Gallons of it.

She couldn't keep her hands from his face. She had to touch him, had to seal their parting by acknowledging his tears, his pain. When she drew her fingers away, they were wet, too.

"You won't get an abortion. Promise me you won't get an abortion."

"Something's alive inside my body," she said. "Someone's there who I already know. I talk to it sometimes. Only, don't know if I'm talking to something that hears me or if I'm just hearing me myself."

"Promise me."

"That's what I'm saying. You've got my oath, Jimmy. I'm promising."

"You'll find a doctor that'll take care of you?"

"I will. And I figure he'll give me vitamins the size of horse pills. That's what Mary Hardeman told me in Jackson."

"And a home? You'll find him a good home?"

Him. Jimmy'd said *him.* It was the first time either conceded that the something inside could be boy or girl, darkheaded or light, blue-eyed or brown. "People don't get on those adoption lists unless they can provide the right kind of home. I'll read about the parents and select someone you'd like, too. Be sure of that."

The two of them stood together amidst sagebrush silvered by moonlight, knowing the time to say goodbye had come, never daring to admit that either might be in the right or in the wrong. "Well," he whispered. "Guess this is it, isn't it?"

"Yes," she said, her heart breaking. "I figure it is."

"Don't know what I'll do if I ever see you again, Sarah," he said, taking her shoulders in hand one last time and possessing her. "Don't think I'll ever be able to *talk* about this. And I won't be feeling amiable should we cross each other's paths."

"It's okay if you slight me," she whispered. "Maybe we'll never have to face each other again at all. Maybe God'll know that some part of it would just hurt both of us too much."

"Maybe," he said, just before she left him. "Maybe so."

Blythe alone drove Sarah to the bus stop the next morning, the dusty forest service–green Dodge arriving at Jenkins' Building Supply just before the noon rush should have begun. Blythe led her inside, clamped open her old purse, and pulled enough cash out of her billfold to buy Sarah a round-trip Greyhound ticket to Laramie.

"Round-trip?" Richard Jenkins asked, his solemn articulation radiating waves of disapproval. "You'll be coming back then?"

"Sure she'll be coming back," Blythe jumped in to answer. "She's gonna keep this ticket where she can find it and, when she needs us, she'll be able to hop the same bus she took out of here to come home."

Sarah knew those words represented a digging in, a

sprightly attempt to hedge off the inescapable. She left her mother at the counter, took ticket in hand, and went back outside, scrutinizing the highway as far up as she could see it, squinting into the sun until the white-painted dashes formed one watery line that led away. She couldn't see a bus coming.

Strange, how empty the road and how quiet the lumber supply yard this time of day. But then, really, such a thing wasn't strange at all. Sarah knew the folks of Star Valley, knew them and knew them well. Somebody interesting came into town on that bus and sales at the Jenkins place would triple. People came out of the woodwork to buy doorknobs or grubbing hoes or toilet seats or new kitchen sink disposals. Some invisible signal always brought out folks to inspect a newcomer, exactly the same way vict- uals brought out buzzing flies to inspect a picnic. They stayed away, though, feigning nonchalance and pretend- ing no one cared much, when someone from nearby became full-pressed to travel. The crowd's very absence bespoke its objection. People all took it quite personally that a girl of such pioneer stock would seek to find fortune elsewhere.

From far up the highway came the faint, turbulent hum of a multi-wheeled conveyance, its two headlamps piercing the heavy daylight in tinny, wavering pinpricks. "Momma!" Sarah called. "Bus is coming!"

As Blythe walked out, she was still talking to someone behind her, her head turned toward the darkness inside. As she finally came forward, she exhaled, flipping each hand mightily against the hem of her skirt as if she was trying to dislodge something.

"Momma," Sarah said. "I've got to get into the truck and start unloading boxes."

"Bus driver'll wait until you're loaded up."

"All the same, don't want to take too long gettin' situ- ated."

"Sarah girl." Blythe stood perfectly still, with that serious ease everyone had come to expect of her. "I've got something to say to you, child. Wouldn't be right lettin' you go off like this if I didn't."

"It's okay, Momma. I know how you feel. We've done enough talking."

Blythe put up one hand to stop her. "No, we haven't."

Sarah pulled away and climbed up into the bed of the truck to heft the first cardboard box over the side.

"Folks around town, they all know Jim Roice is in love with you. Folks around here are saying you're acting high and mightier than Moses, leaving your family and that boy the way you are."

"I know what folks are saying." The first box landed on the gravel. Plop.

Blythe took a second box from her daughter's grasp just as the massive Greyhound bus pulled into the gravel parking lot, popping rocks, its rippling silver sides reflecting the same in each one of Richard Jenkins's front windows. "Don't know what it is in your soul that makes you need to leave us like this and wander. But I don't figure I have any right to pass judgment. Don't figure anybody else in this town has that right, either. Makes no difference that they all think they do."

The bus emitted an immense hiss as the driver applied the brakes and climbed down rubber-stripped steps to take Sarah's ticket. "These boxes yours, ma'am?" He dusted off pants which were so wrinkled at the folds of his legs, they looked as if they'd been accordioned beneath his knees for the width of three or four good-sized western states.

"Yes. I've got another in the truck. And one suitcase, too."

He opened the cargo hold and began sliding Sarah's belongings into the bus's belly. "You a student goin' all the way to Laramie?"

"I am."

"We'll be leaving in three minutes. You'd best find a seat and get comfortable. You're lookin' at a ride of ten hours or so."

He walked inside Jenkins' Building Supply while Sarah turned her attention to her mother. "No matter that I bought you that round-trip ticket. It only means that we're here if you need us. This departure has been the desire of your heart since you were a child," Blythe said. "God doesn't give us those desires for no reason."

"You really think that?" Sarah asked, now finally needing the reassurance.

"I know that. Something'll come of it, child. Something that'll make all of us proud, even your father. Sarah—" And, here, a mother gathered her daughter one last time into her arms. "You don't always have to see things to believe in them. It's the opposite that's true. You have to believe in things in order to see them."

"Oh, Momma. This is funny," Sarah said. "This is funny that you want me to prove everybody wrong. Because I'd prove that you and Will were wrong, too."

The bus driver walked out of the lumber store, climbed the steps in the bus, and motioned for Sarah to follow. "It isn't so much that," Blythe said with great simplicity, still holding her daughter fixed. Her pronouncement was all, but yet was everything; confidence, gratitude, invocation. "It's that I love you. Has nothing to do with what others think. Has to do with what's inside you. You can prove yourself different, Sarah. You can prove yourself right."

The day Sarah Hayden rode a bus across Wyoming, it seemed as if all summer rose up to see her go. The high sage-desert tableland stretched in a wide lace of green naperies against the sky. The air Sarah breathed came saturated with the smell of rich earth and sunlight. From somewhere in the far distance, a flock of bronze cowbirds rose from the dust, advancing, then dissolving into the sky in a whirlwind of gleaming wings.

Sarah slept some of the way, stared out the window some of the way, and read an *Outdoor Life* magazine she found left on the seat. She basked in the bittersweet sensation of aloneness, of leaving loved ones behind, of risking something known for something unknown. And still, because of the baby, she didn't feel solitary throughout the journey.

At twilight, the bus stopped in Rawlins for supper, and she ate sparingly, only two dry biscuits and a tumbler of milk she had to pay way too much for, knowing she had to make her meager savings last until she found a small apartment and paid a damage deposit. Long past nightfall, the bus rolled across Wyoming. Passengers wadded coats or jammed soft baggage behind their heads, each doing his best to find an acceptable makeshift pillow. A few kept overhead lights on, but the majority snoozed in the darkness, the miles of interstate droning past beneath their feet.

Some thirty miles out of Laramie, Sarah began to see lights, a smattering here, a smattering there, a farmhouse, a filling station, all orderly and snug, with pale smoke rising from the chimneys and windows glowing amber from the lights inside. The town itself could be seen for what seemed like forever, a dull ginger glow laying low against the horizon. As the bus rounded another hill, a conglomeration of lights came into view, almost like star lights, stretched in a mammoth, fistlike shape across miles and miles of black, upland prairie.

The bus driver's booming voice interrupted Sarah's meditations. "Laramie," he hollered, doing his best to wake everybody up. "Next stop."

People began to rustle through their belongings. Lights snapped on. Several rose to bend over their seats or to stretch and yawn. The bus exited the highway and entered town via a well-lit ramp, passing between pools of illumination from each street lantern. It pulled to a halt and opened its doors; the driver waved them off. And so began Sarah Hayden's new life, in a station empty except for the few stragglers who chose to disembark in this college town. Down the way, she could see the high-rise dorms of the University of Wyoming campus, and a tower with a clock that extolled the hour of eleven as she conveyed her suitcase across the thoroughfare toward a sign that flashed: Motel. Motel. Low Rates. Low Rates.

She'd pick up her boxes at the station tomorrow. The agent had agreed to keep her effects in the luggage area until she found a place to settle. Last week, she'd sent away for a copy of the *Laramie Daily Boomerang* and she'd already found three possibilities, two room-in situations and one tiny apartment just across Ivinson Avenue from the Animal Science Building.

First thing in the morning, Sarah walked to the campus grounds and stood quietly on the manicured bluegrass, circling with chin raised to take in the full canopy of sky, absorbing the magnitude of everything she'd accomplished. She signed a lease and made a small deposit on the second property she viewed, a downstairs one-room apartment with a single bed that made out from the couch and only a hot plate and small sink for the kitchen. Her new landlord, a sunburned, lanky fellow from Nebraska, helped transport Sarah's meager possessions to her household, a small favor to pay—or so he said—for finding a tenant during these student-scanty months of summer. In three days' time, she registered for available freshman classes at the registrar's office, bought books at the UW bookstore with money Blythe had slipped her, and made an appointment to see Dr. Levy at the Office of Student Health. But her busyness couldn't ward off her pangs of missing Jim Roice. With Jimmy next door, life had been regular; without Jimmy, life seemed flimsy, close to breaking, unendurable.

Never wanted to just be regular, she lectured herself. *Always wanted something much more.*

Even so, on the night of her third day, she called home from a pay phone in Ross Hall. "Hayden's General Store," old Will bellowed.

"Dad? Dad. It's Sarah."

"Who is it?"

"It's Sarah!" she hollered back through the static. "How are you?"

She heard a humph, then silence on the line. She knew once he'd heard her voice, he'd presented the phone to Blythe.

"Hello. It's Momma."

"Will wouldn't talk to me."

"I expect he'll talk to you soon enough. He's got his own pride to get over, and healing to do."

"Can't make him understand," Sarah shouted, " even though I tried so hard!"

"Don't guess he'll ever understand, Sarah girl. You two both need to learn that there's times you just have to love each other without understanding."

Sarah had called to tell her folks about the trip and the apartment and her new classes. This she did, then asked, "Momma? Momma? How's Jimmy? Have you seen him?"

"That boy hasn't been around, Sarah. Saw Miller Roice, though. He came to the store just yesterday, out buying a tin of chili powder and some sage sausage to take with him on the river. He's got a whole carload of folks just in from Minnesota. He's taking 'em up all the way to the national park, then floating with them all the way down. Been trying to talk Jimmy's mother into meeting them along the way and cooking 'em pot roast and cobbler in her Dutch ovens."

From behind Sarah, someone started rattling the huge

volume of Yellow Pages. "Better go, Momma. Somebody's back there needing to telephone."

". . . love . . . you . . . Sarah, take good care . . ."

"Take care, too, Momma. Tell my dad—" But she didn't finish her sentence. The connection between Sarah and home had been broken. She suspended the receiver from its cradle, turned, and walked away.

August dwindled on the brink of September and, inside Sarah's womb, the baby grew. By early autumn—the time the customary arrival of fall-semester pupils began—Sarah'd already earned nine credits toward her bachelor of science degree, and she could only affix each of her two skirts with one large safety pin lengthwise. She'd long since felt the baby move. Each day, the butterfly maneuvers inside her vitals became stronger and more frequent. Doc Levy had given her vitamins, and she stayed careful of what she ate, but still, often in the afternoons, she got so sleepy she thought she might pass out right in the seat of her rigid classroom chair.

Sarah'd told the doctor she'd decided to give her child up for adoption. He'd started the required paperwork, told her he'd locate Jimmy, and already, the State of Wyoming had assumed responsibility for her prenatal treatment and care. As the season settled in, so did a certain amount of excitement on campus. Friends returned from far places. Wyoming Cowboy football games began in the obelisk War Memorial Stadium. Now, even if she'd wanted it, Sarah could not go home. Everybody with eyes could look at her and see she was carrying a baby. One morning as she thumbed through her business management text outside Coe Library, a familiar-looking girl with green eyes and a pretty smile stopped and announced, "You're the one in my business analysis class."

Sarah looked at her. "Yes."

"Don't mind me asking, but I sit there sometimes during Tuttle's boring BANA lectures and watch your stomach move around. You're pregnant, aren't you?"

"Yeah." Strangely, it felt pleasant to finally say the words aloud to someone. "I am."

"You married?"

Sarah shook her head.

"Some people who go to UW are. Married, I mean."

"Well, I'm not."

"Did you want to be?"

"No."

"Does it hurt when the baby moves like that? Sometimes I see you grab your stomach right in the middle of lecture."

"Doesn't hurt. Tickles and pushes other parts of my insides out of the way sometimes. But mostly it just feels . . . interesting . . . like something's there that's more than me."

Her name was Kirsten Simpsen, she'd lived in Burntfork since the day she'd been delivered, and she'd never had a boy so much as kiss her. She tended to view Sarah's growth and pregnancy as something fascinating and exotic, a mystic rite of womanhood that so affected her, she became friend, apprentice, adorer.

Each afternoon they toted textbooks to the apartment on Ivinson and studied together, after Kirsten's baby questions were over, quizzing each other on probabilities and marketing strategies and management techniques. Together, they imagined big cities where they would work—Boston, New York, San Francisco, or maybe even just Denver. They talked about things that seemed glamorous, like Boris Becker winning Wimbledon and Dr. Ruth Westheimer's television show and the captors in Beirut feeding the American hostages cake before President Reagan brought them home. They listened to David Lee Roth, they ogled over Tom Cruise in his new movie, *Top Gun*. And, on Thursday nights, if Kirsten didn't have much reading to do, she'd accompany Sarah to the childbirth classes Doc Levy had recommended. There, they'd sprawl across the floor on a big foam pillow from Woolworth, following breathing techniques with puckered lips and giggling at the nurse as she demonstrated how a plastic doll could move through the plastic replica of a pelvis.

A blue norther blew in the last week of October, sending crumpled cottonwood leaves skittering up the streets and shivering students digging to find parkas and mittens. Sarah couldn't close her jacket around her voluminous middle. She found it a titan effort just to waddle to classes. Kirsten went with her when the doctor requested to see her every week. Again, she examined the state list of adoptive parents. "Unless something changes," Dr. Levy said, "these people in Rock Springs are still top on the list. They know about you and are waiting for the phone call from the Wyoming Parenting Society when you go into labor."

"They look like a fine family to me." She read over the listing carefully, committing every detail to memory. A bank loan officer, a nurse, in a sprawling brick house with a cedar fence and crimson verbena growing in pots on the porch.

"You'll need to stay close by," he told her after the exam. "Your cervix is already almost totally effaced. Unfortunately, I can't advise travel over the holidays. You'll have to tell your parents you won't be able to have Thanksgiving dinner with them this year."

"They aren't expecting me," Sarah said.

On Wednesday, the first snow of the season blew in, or at least some would call it snow. As they walked across campus, pelting ice fretted their skin like stitching needles, this nothing like the storms in Star Valley, nothing like the moving tapestries of gentle snow that came to the mountain highlands.

"Come with me to Burntfork for Thanksgiving," Kirsten said as she shook ice droplets off her hat. "Mother always cooks a massive turkey. They'll be eating it for weeks."

"You've made me welcome," Sarah said, "but I can't leave Laramie."

"Turkey Tetrazinni. Turkey soup. Turkey enchiladas. It'll go on clear into December."

"I can't."

"They'll be lucky if they get finished in time to cook another one for Christmas."

At odd, drifting times, a keen sense of loss entrapped her. That sense came now, came with all its bitter intrusion. She'd cut herself off so completely she didn't expect to see Blythe and Will at Christmas, either. And she knew, dear God she knew, how difficult it would be to face Jim Roice this soon after the baby was gone. "Can't go any place, Kirsten. Doc Levy says I've got to stay close."

"Our house is just three hours away. If you went into labor, I could drive you back here. I heard the nurse at your class say how long it could be after the contractions started. Besides, we've got a fine doctor in Burntfork. He'd be nearby if you had an emergency."

But Sarah shook her head. She'd grown accustomed to Doc Levy. She didn't want a stranger tending her during labor and delivery.

"I hate the idea of you being here by yourself for four days."

"I'll manage. I'm grown now, you know."

"What if something happens? What if you can't get to the hospital? You don't even have a car."

"I'll be fine." Then she laughed. "If my own mother knew about this, she'd sound just like you."

"Good. I wish she *did* know about it. Then I wouldn't feel so awful about leaving. Sarah, what if you get snowed in?"

"I've been walking everywhere I go for the past six months. I'll walk to the hospital if need be."

Kirsten scribbled the Burntfork number on the corner of a notebook and tore it off. "Call me, will you? If anything happens, or if you just get lonesome, or if you get scared or something. I'm not that far away."

7

The twenty-eighth day of November dawned
cold, a gray day of perpetual motion, the wind blustering
as poplars and water ash bobbed to its rhythm and clouds
raced across a winter sky. What remained of the snow
blew like scattered ribbon along the school grounds,
weaving a filigree of white throughout the coyote mint
that lined the lawn. Even though classes were still fur-
loughed, Sarah'd been studying, making good use of the
quiet library. She'd piled the volumes partially against
her hip and was starting for the door when a tightness
gripped her, a pain so fleeting that it caused her to stop
and incline her head. She backed up to the glass door and
pressed gently, easing her way out into the gale.

The draught took her hair and tossed it across her
face, setting her slightly off balance. When the next pain
began to rise, it came deep and warm, an entrenching of
body so complete that Sarah stopped, waiting, astonished
by the intensity that came so unbidden from within.

"No matter about that," she said aloud to her books and the overcast sky and a pavilion of ice-encrusted grass that only one month ago had been green. "No matter at all. Doc said it'd be hours still before anything happened."

She hurried home and stood looking out through the tiny window, her breath fogging the glass, her forehead propped against one wooden ballast. By the time she'd counted twenty-seven cars gone by and six contractions, she decided to gather her things and make her way alone to Ivinson Memorial. If she arrived too soon for a nurse to admit her, she'd wait in the lobby.

As she hefted her backpack over one shoulder, Sarah felt a rush of fluid gush from between her legs. Liquid soaked the inseam of her pants. She set the pack against the wall as a pain enveloped her so thoroughly she had to grip the round of a chair to support herself.

Sarah tried to remember everything the nurses had taught her. Relax your lips. Think of a focal point. Breathe yourself through.

Only after the contraction waned did she realize the futility of her plan. She couldn't walk through something like this. The pains encompassed her entirely, filling her, taking over. But walk she would. Sarah had no choices. And, looking back, the journey she began that day as she closed the door behind her would be, perhaps, the longest journey Sarah Hayden traveled in her lifetime.

The baby kept coming. The wind pirouetted around her. The contractions hit her often, fully, savagely. Each time her body compelled itself against her, she stopped to lean upon whatever she might be passing—a brick wall, a cement step, a signal post. She'd stopped to count and breathe over a dirt-filled planter when a woman stopped on Ivinson, leaning to open the door to her GMC and to holler at her.

"Honey? You okay? You sick or something?"

Sarah tried to say the words loud enough for the

woman to hear her out in the street. The contractions sapped her strength totally. "I'm having my baby."

"Good Lord." The woman looked at Sarah with interest. "Today? Now?"

Sarah nodded. She didn't speak. She couldn't.

"You out walkin' along this sidewalk like you're out for a spring stroll and you're on the way to the hospital?"

"Trying . . . to get there . . ."

"Good Lord," the woman said again.

Sarah leaned over the planter, focusing on the brittle remains of last summer's flower vines, once more counting breaths. The woman left her truck parked in the middle of Ivinson—the very middle—and ran around the front fender to help Sarah. "They're coming real close, aren't they?"

Sarah nodded, tears in her eyes.

"Honey, between you and me, we're gonna hoist you up into this truck and we're gonna make it to that hospital. We'll get you there in no time."

Strange, the negligible details Sarah remembered later. A red frayed seat behind a windshield with a crack the shape of Kentucky. The truck lurching forward as the woman reclined against the steering wheel to frantically grind its gears. The jutting nose of the intern at the emergency room door who stopped and held her while she counted again and pursed her lips to breathe.

"How close are the contractions?" a nurse asked from behind a glass partition.

". . . don't know . . . been . . . walking . . ."

"Let's just get you into a room and check to see."

". . . help . . ."

"Seven centimeters. Almost total dilation."

". . . they've been bad . . . a . . . long . . ."

"Sweetie, just hang on. You're having a baby, fast."

". . . this baby . . . hasn't . . . been . . . fast . . ."

After telling her she couldn't depart Laramie, Dr.

Levy had gone off to celebrate Thanksgiving with his own family instead. He couldn't possibly be notified in time for her delivery, a nurse informed her. She'd have a different doctor today, one who hadn't attended her before.

An admittance clerk stood by her bedside and asked any number of questions. "Do you have insurance?" "Have you notified anyone?" "Is a family member coming?" "Where is your labor partner?"

"I wanted my doctor," Sarah said.

She never knew the woman's name who parked her truck in the course of traffic and saved her. Years later, she would scarcely recollect the obstetrician's face. But the baby arrived at 5:12 P.M. on Thanksgiving Day, 1985, and Sarah would never forget one moment, one small inkling, of the time she shared with her child. From the last drowning pushes and the first appearance of his tiny head, still covered with blood and vernix, she treasured him. "Hello," she whispered. Nothing more. Just, "Hello."

Her son did not cry when he saw her. But Sarah cried when she saw her son. She kept bleeding and the doctor kept pinching as he stitched tightly where her skin had torn. Nothing of that mattered, nothing, only the baby, as they placed him in her arms and she felt the heaviness and life of her firstborn.

After a nurse cleaned him, she found that he already had hair, plenty of it, soft and fine and not far from the color of her own. At this time, giving up her son became a much different sort of decision. This child, this boy, became a person in his own right, bone and flesh. Sarah's thoughts became, at once, more personal and more reaching.

"You going to breastfeed him?" one of the nurses asked.

"He'll be adopted," Sarah said.

"Oh. I didn't know."

"It's in my records. If Doc Levy had been here for the

delivery, he might already have phoned the Wyoming Parenting Society."

"It's why you're alone, then. We've all been wondering why you're alone."

"I suppose his father would have liked to see him once."

"You think so?"

"He wanted us."

The nurse stepped over to the bed and watched over Sarah's shoulder as she swaddled him closer in the faded flannel blanket. "He's a beautiful child. Adoption is an unselfish choice."

"Am I being unselfish?" Was her leave-taking totally worth this price? Perhaps it would always be for her. Perhaps it would never be for Jimmy. "Is this an unselfish choice?" She saw her own motivations now for everything they were. She was exactly like so many in the world, bored, talented, and young, chasing after a terrifying, beguiling unknown. She'd been born for it. As surely as she held this boy, Blythe had held her once and, even then, her future had been destined, her soul had already decreed to fling out to the world just as a sail flings out to catch the wind.

"His new parents will be lucky," she said, "lucky and blessed to have him."

The nurses treated her differently after that. They took better care of her as she mended, treated her like an honored guest. And she noticed they cared for the baby now, too, changing him themselves instead of asking if she wanted to try, feeding him themselves instead of presenting her a bottle. They took better care of him. They brought him to her less.

Dr. Levy stopped by to visit early the next morning. "I missed it all," he said lightly as if it had been a slightly amusing joke. "I missed the whole thing."

She played with a fold in the blanket.

"I've phoned his new parents. They're driving over from Rock Springs. They'll be here by noon."

"You haven't missed anything then. You'll get to see it when he meets his parents."

"You shouldn't feel insignificant, Sarah," he said, touching the hand that plucked tufts from the blanket.

She lay the fuzz on her knee, watching it while it rolled off.

"You ready to sign the relinquishment papers? We'll need them from you now." And, after that, she still had six months to change her mind, but he didn't want to speak of that now.

"Yes. I'm ready. Everything else is done?"

"Everything. You want some time with him before he goes?"

"Not much time. I couldn't stand much time."

"I'll bring him in for you, if you'd like."

"Yes," she said. "Please." She held out her arms.

"We'll be right back," he said.

Sarah never saw Doc Levy again.

When a nurse brought in the baby later, Sarah sat on the bed still waiting, clenching her gown against swollen breasts that had just begun to ooze. "I love you," she said when the nurse left them alone. "I love you even though I'll never know you."

His round blue eyes never wavered from hers. His face was red, wrinkled, beautiful. She ran one finger along the mat of hair, remembering it as weightless sheen beneath each stroke.

"Could be a feather," she whispered, "no heavier than it is."

In that instant, as all girls do when they first bear children, Sarah understood how deeply she'd been honored and loved by her own mother. *Thank you, Momma,* she thought, *for your loving of me.*

She shut her fingers firmly over the miniature hand

that, someday, would grow to be like her own or Jimmy's. "Just look at you." She wagged her head back and forth at him, her mouth forming an *o*.

He watched, seriously entranced. With his own mouth he made his own circle, every bit as round as Sarah's, perfect.

Blythe Hayden died one bright April midday while she stood in the yard hanging clothes. Will was working at the tall wooden counter, cleaving an immense round of cheese when he heard her stop whistling.

"Don't you quit that trillin'," he bellowed as he gave the muenster one final whop with his huge knife. He knew she couldn't hear him out the door, but he wanted to give the words voice anyway. He did so often. "Blythe, you sound prettier than a songbird when you sound off like that in the yard."

When she didn't start right up again immediately, he walked to the window to look at her. There she stood, at her clothesline, her willow basket beside her and still full of wet laundry, her face raised fully to meet the sun. She held a bedsheet to the line with both hands and rested, the sun streaming through white, woven cloth the same way as it streams through a swan's translucent wing. The sheet flapped full against her, its hems whacking the length of her legs.

One minute she waited there, just savoring the sun. Next minute, Will watched her topple over straight into the willow basket.

"Blythe!" he hollered as he threw off his apron and ran. "Sweet Bejesus. Blythe!" He knelt beside her in the grass and gathered her into his arms, smelling everything of the day, the damp textiles, the remnant of soap, the molten sun so bright and unexpected it made his body throb. "Dear sweet heaven."

Doc Bressler told Will later it was because she'd gotten an aneurism, that a vessel had burst free in her brain.

Sarah hadn't gone home for Christmas. She'd run out of scholarship money and had started a job as night hostess at a Village Inn. She hadn't gone home for spring break, either. With the giving of her son had come a new, bleak knowledge of herself, a knowledge that had gone past the ego and felicity of her youth to something baser, something stronger. She'd done a selfish thing, done it because she'd had to do it.

She missed the baby, missed being two persons instead of one. And now she'd missed her momma, too. She came home from Laramie that night with the second half of the ticket Blythe had bought her, bypassing a whole week of classes and two midsemester exams. Together, they strode out by Blythe's clothesline, Will's hands tucked into each of his pockets, while Sarah walked beside him and cried.

"Life happens fast, Sarah girl," he said. "You're missing it."

"I'm not missing it," she said. "I'm trying to find it."

They stopped where Blythe had fallen and Sarah fingered a wire. "Just look at this rickety old thing."

"I know," he told her. "Used to tease her how I wanted to hitch up my mules to her clothesline and give the kids a ride on my flying jenny. She used to swat me on the rear every time I talked about it."

"Wish she wouldn've used the dryer in the summer, too." Sarah backhanded tears from her face like a four-year-old. "Maybe it wouldn't've happened if she hadn't been outside working so hard."

"Your momma wouldn't've picked any other place to die. She greeted God on home ground."

"I'm going back to school in a few days, Dad," Sarah said. "Nothing good ever happens around this place."

*   *   *

"You know she came home once," Beulah Hardaway mentioned as she selected two choice cuts of sirloin from the cooler at Happersett's Roadside Market. Happersett's was newfangled, its neon sign and gleaming glass a put-off to those who'd shopped for years at the general store. But with old Will gone and the place closed, they'd had to resort to second best. "Only times she's been back is because of people dying." Beulah dropped two steaks into her basket. "That oughtta keep Ed and me fed until I get the chance to drive to Jackson Hole."

"How long do you suppose she'll stay, now that old Will's gone?" Becky Farrell asked, leaning forward over the red plastic handle of her shopping cart.

"She'll do the same as she did before. She'll be here long enough to close things down and then she'll be off. Only difference is, when she finishes out her father's business, she'll be finishing out everything she's known here as well."

"What happened when she came before?" Becky asked.

"Well, she didn't even *see* Jim Roice, that's one thing. After all those years spent snipe hunting and borrowing Miller's boats and kissing at the lockers, she stayed one week, closeted upstairs with Will going through her momma's things, then she was gone again."

"'Course there's those who say he wouldn't've let her in his front door if she'd tried," Becky butted in, eager to give her version of the story. "Folks say he would've left town himself rather than swallow his pride enough to ever let that girl set foot in his life again. He's a proud man, Jim is. Staunch."

"Tell me, Beulah." Ardith Haux stopped beside Becky's cart, her arms filled with milk gallons. "You've had just about every kid in this county go through your senior English class. Are any of the other valley kids as interesting as Sarah Hayden?"

"Of course not." Beulah snorted exactly like the prized holstein bull Silas Braxton trucked in to mate with his heifers. "No one's ever done what she did. No one's ever gone out like that, totally alone, and made so much of a life. Boys neither. Will told me about her office once. Up there on Madison Avenue, just as highfalutin as anybody."

"What is it, really?" Becky helped herself to a yellow Pick o' the Chick. "What is it that makes everybody still talk about this after so many years?"

"I know what it is. It's what happened on that boy's face the day she took off out of Star Valley." When she had something of importance to say, Ardith Haux played each word full volume and in four/four time, like the notes on the antique pump organ down at Morning Star Baptist Church, where she sat in the front row each Sunday. "You know what it's like for a young man, don't you? Everything is in front of a young man. He can own the world if he wants. That's the way it was with Jimmy then. Only all he wanted to own was a little corner of his father's land and two or three fishing boats so he could bring along the family business."

"Well, he got those things, didn't he?" Becky said.

"It's hard to guess what'll take the light of youth from a man's eyes. Never know what'll take 'em to the point where all expectancy is gone, like nothing's gonna be either joyous or horrible anymore."

"I've seen it happen," Beulah said. "Saw it happen the night Vern Chappell's barn burned down. Lost his favorite pig in that fire. Could hear that sow squealing all the way over into Mac Johnson's pasture as she burned. After that, seemed like Vern just lost all sensation of good and bad. Didn't change even after everybody went over and helped him build his barn back. Never did enjoy anything much again. Never did waver under affliction, neither."

"Did Jim Roice get callused the same way as that?" Becky asked.

"The day Sarah Hayden stepped on that bus, all the light just went out of Jim Roice's eyes," Beulah informed them. "If he'd have been a lesser man, or an older one even, he might've let it embitter things. But he didn't, you know. Went out and found a life for himself despite all the hurt Sarah Hayden caused him. Watching his face when he started to court Victoria was like watching a sunrise. First you saw the pain there, and then you saw the healing. Never been so happy to see something happen in all my living days. Victoria did it, and that boy, too. They saved Jim Roice. Brought him back to himself from the brink of something awful."

Victoria Tayloe Roice learned to parallel ski about the same time she learned her numbers in nursery school. Her mother began by toting her—short skis and all—up the tow rope on the beginner's slope at Sun Valley. By the time she was in third grade and her father had moved them to Wyoming so he could manage his father's dairy farm, Victoria had mastered starting gates and a slalom course.

Vic loved Star Valley. She loved it because Star Valley was only thirty-five miles away from Jackson Hole skiing. While Sarah felt cut away from the world, Victoria skied and felt the world moving toward her, bringing with it a delicious sense of freedom and experience that filled her with adolescent authority.

Once, in the spring, the entire high school took a Lincoln County school bus and skied Teton Village. She'd been a sophomore then, old enough in town to know people, new enough to still seem exotic to kids who'd lived in the valley forever. She had in mind to cajole one sturdy girlfriend to ski outside the groomed boundaries with her. But, by the time they'd finished discussing it on the bus, a whole group of girls had decided to come.

Even high on the mountain and off trail, Victoria didn't find much fresh snow left to carve a turn. She led them off the lift to a place on the Divide called Upper Rock Springs and, from there, she began to lead them down.

"Where are we?" one of them asked.

"You're at the top," Victoria answered.

"This is harder than I thought."

"I told you it would be hard. Go back to the trail if you're scared."

"I'd be scared on the trail. Rather stay with you. At least you know where you're going."

A group of Star Valley boys got off the lift behind them. Wyllis Fox turned around and hollered up at them, mostly because they were boys, mostly because they appealed to her, "Get over here, somebody. We wanna go down with somebody else."

As if the sound itself had jarred her loose, Laurie Carver began to slip sideways, her skis suddenly freed from their edge. Laurie dug in but kept sliding, her skis circling slowly, then faster, then pinwheeling out of control.

"Laurie!" Victoria shouted. "You're aiming toward the cliffs."

Laurie Carver flipped backward. She kept going.

"Grab her poles."

"Get her."

Throwing a sharp rooster tail of ice, Jim Roice skied between the girl and the rock ledge, catching the edges of her skis and stopping her. "Laurie," he said. "Hang on to me." Together, they stood on the rim for a moment, staring down at the granite crags several hundred feet below.

"Why'd you do it? Why did you bring them up here?" he asked Victoria after he'd gotten Laurie back.

"I know how to do this. I wanted someone with me."

He skied away after her answer, following his friends and the group of girls that went with them, and Victoria could see he wasn't a good skier.

"He'd be better at this if he'd spend more time practicing and less time fishing. Spends all his time with his father or with his girlfriend."

"Who does he go with?"

"A junior. Sarah Hayden. You know her?"

"I know who she is. I've seen her at that old store."

"Far as anyone else is concerned, it's the *only* store."

Years later, Victoria often teased him about saving Laurie Carver's life. "It was her time to go and you stopped it," she said that night as they sat watching flames roll inside the front glass of the woodstove.

"How do you know? You're the one who took her where experts ski. How do you know it wasn't her time and you almost made her go?"

"You tell me. You're the hero. What if she'd gone over? It would've marred me the rest of my life."

"You wouldn't've let it, Vic. You never let yourself get out of control."

She sat back on cushions, not speaking now, watching Charlie come down the steps with another of his oddly packaged benefactions. "Brought you a present, Momma."

Victoria took it from Charlie and balanced it on her knee without realizing the significance of its trappings. Jim, however, recognized it immediately. This gift was wrapped exactly the same way Will had wrapped the others.

"How long have you had that, son?"

"Just since this morning."

"This morning? Where did you get it?"

"Hayden's General Store."

"But the store's—"

"Closed."

"Yes. Closed."

"The lady there let me in even though old Will's gone. Had to talk a lot to get her to let me shop, but she did. Did you know she's old Will's kid? Said she used to play here herself when she was little."

When Jim's voice came, it sounded gritty, as if he'd swallowed sand. "So you've met her."

"Told her just how I wanted her to wrap it, and she did everything I said. Told her all about how Will used to get the *Thrifty Nickels* and tie 'em up with twine."

"Charlie. Chickadee." Victoria started to unfasten the ties, but, at the worn, pale expression on Jim's face, she stopped.

"That store's closed," Jim said to the boy. "Don't go there again."

"I love the store. It's the best place on earth. And she's real nice."

"Charlie—"

"It's the only place close I can buy Bubble Jugs."

"Bubble-gum jugs don't make a difference."

"Yes, they do. They *do*."

With a small frown, Victoria laid the parcel by. Her hand still on the gift, she hesitated, feeling suddenly as though some danger was lurking, waiting for them outside. "Jim, I—"

"Don't enter this, Vic. It isn't your decision."

"You're scaring him. Why can't you act as if—?"

"Vic."

"First time I heard anyone mention her name was the day you saved Laurie Carver. You were skiing off and I asked, 'Who does he go with?' and someone said, 'Sarah Hayden.'"

"That was her name," Charlie piped up happily. "Sarah."

"Charlie, you are not to visit the store again."

"What I hate," Victoria said, "is that you're acting as if it matters."

"You'll be grounded if I find out you've been there," Jim said, "grounded from your hockey stick."

"But Dad—"

"Let us stop, please. This is enough," Victoria said.

"Promise me, Charlie. Promise me you won't go again." As he said it, he thought, *I sound like God, asking this of him without explaining why*.

"Don't like promising," Charlie said. He went to his room, not waiting for Victoria to open the bundle.

8

Jim Roice worked as a guide and doryman during his senior year summer. Proud and tanned and angry, he stood in the middle of a boat each day, oars in hand, legs bare, his brown hair scorched dry from the sun. While Jim rowed, pushing Caddisfly Creek back with great winnowing strokes, his father showed novice fishermen the nature of the water, pointing to the riplets that played along the shallow rocks, the white foam and the backwashes, the quiet, sheltered currents beneath mossy overhangs where trout slipped in silence beneath the surface of the stream.

The tourists always asked him questions, as tourists are prone to do. "Is this your first try at something like this?" "Where's home?" "What will you study in college?"

With each question asked, Jim's resentment centered deeper. "No need for college," he'd say. "It's a waste of money to learn what you already know." Or, he'd tell them, "Worked this river since I could walk. And I'll work it until I'm ready to quit, which oughtta be when I'm about ninety years old." All the while he showed Star Valley visitors the otter dens and moose feeding and the places where ospreys nested in the trees, he thought of Sarah, thought of her life and her leaving, realizing how like these travelers she'd been.

"Are most kids in this valley like you?" folks would ask before they passed their final judgments. "Do most of them graduate high school then stay to run the family business?"

"Some stay," he'd answer, "and some go."

By the end of the day, after they'd caught and released plenty of trout and had selected several to take home in their creels, they'd say, "If I could make a living at this, I'd do it, too. You're lucky. Richer than you know."

Am I lucky? Jim wondered. *Am I lucky because this is the life I choose? Or would it be better to have gone with her? Would it have been better to be like them?* "Riches are where you find them," he said frankly as he unloaded tackle boxes and life jackets over the side of the Mackenzie. Occasionally, they'd shake his hand, tell him to look them up if he came to the city, and pass him a five-dollar tip.

In late July, by the time Caddisfly Creek ran low and clear, Miller Roice booked a group of locals to make the trip downstream. They arrived early one morning, a morning that had already revoked its chill, one that hinted of heat to come. As they climbed into the boat, a familiar-looking girl settled between bow and stern, right beside his feet, where she made him wary.

"You like to fish?" he asked, not expecting much of an answer.

"Fishing makes me forget about things I don't like to remember," she said. "It keeps my mind busy."

Doesn't keep my mind busy, he thought. *For me, there's no forgetting.*

"So this is what you do," she said.

He stared down at her again, considering how he might know her.

"We go to the same school," she said, without him even asking. "You've seen me there, but I'm pretty new. We moved here from Sun Valley."

"Jim?" Miller shaded his eyes and motioned toward the gear they provided. "You want to rig those poles, son?"

"That wasn't a question," Jim said to the girl at his feet.

"I didn't figure so either," she said, duly impressing him. "I'll rig my own pole."

They didn't talk again until they'd headed out past the log jam that jutted out from the east shore of the creek. As Jim rowed, she cast her line before his father had instructed anyone else in the boat to do so.

"You're showing off," he said.

"I wanted you to notice me," she said.

"I've noticed you before."

"But not how I wanted to be noticed." She jogged his memory. "I'm a skier, remember?"

"I know you. The one who almost killed half the girls in high school on Upper Rock Springs."

"They didn't have to come if they didn't want to. Besides, I didn't almost kill everybody. Only Laurie Carver."

"It was a stupid thing to do. You shouldn't have been up there yourself."

"I'm good. I could ski it."

"You were showing off then, too. You can't expect other people to be good at the same things you are."

"Oh, really?"

"What's your name?" He didn't have to tell her his name. Miller had introduced him when the fishermen boarded the boat.

"Victoria Tayloe."

"Nice to meet you. Is that what everyone calls you? Victoria?"

"Call me Vic. Vic Tayloe. I shortened it myself when I was twelve because it was a name that sounded good for the Olympics. I always wanted to ski in the Olympics."

"That's surprising."

"Wanted it from the beginning. Mother kept my old crib mattress in the closet until I was in kindergarten. I pulled it out one day and stood on it and slid down the stairs."

"That's the day you decided to be an Olympian?"

"No," she said, laughing. "I decided the next day when I watched my dad try it. He hit every stair on the way down because he was so heavy. He wasn't any good."

"Will you do it, then? Will you compete?"

"No. Some people are all talk," she said. "Perhaps I'm one of those."

"You aren't. I know that already. Is it because you lived here? Is it because you missed out because you're stuck in this little mountain town?" He asked it point-blank. He wanted to hear her say that it wasn't.

"Wasn't that at all," she said.

He smiled. His face was cracked, broken, because of the summer sun.

"You should grow a beard. Then you'd look like a river man."

"Maybe I'll do that," he said.

"I tried out for the Olympic team last year," she told him. "Came within a half second of qualifying. Sometimes I think if I'd been training on the mountain longer, I'd have done better."

As he asked the next question, he grinned wider. He sounded like all the tourists who'd been quizzing him. "You gonna be a skier when you grow up?"

"I am grown up."

"Good answer. That's what I tell everybody, too."

"So." She peered out over the water, away from him. "How's your girlfriend?"

He looked at her, startled, and missed a stroke. In the months since Sarah had left, nobody had dared ask him about her. Everybody'd been talking about it for two months, in the barber shop, at Dora Tygum's Caddisfly Inn, on the steps at Hayden's General Store. But nobody'd gotten brave enough to talk to him about it. Seemed like nobody, least of all Will and Blythe Hayden, wanted to admit she'd ever been around.

"She's gone."

"Where?"

"Off to school. Off to real life."

"From what I've seen, when you leave this for real life, you don't come back."

"She's not coming back."

About noon, with the sun overhead and the water meshing to make golden coins on the water, Victoria Vic Tayloe snagged a cutthroat she couldn't release. She'd been fishing with barbed hooks and, as she stooped over the side of the Troutfitters boat at a hilarious angle, she couldn't bring the barb around without injuring the fish.

Jim lay the oars aside and yanked his needle-nosed pliers from the pocket of his open khaki vest. He kept everything he needed in his pockets these days—extra line, extra flies, clippers, swivels, weights. He even carried a tube of Gink, to keep an errant dry fly cresting high on the water. "Move over."

"I can't move over. Don't want to let him go. He might get hurt."

"He's in the net. Fish won't get away."

"I've got quite a grip on him."

Indeed, she did. She held the lashing cutthroat lengthwise in both hands, keeping it low and facing the current, so the living thing would survive.

"Here. You've got to make room for me." Jim slid his

hand over the body of the fish. Together they held the fish there, a quicksilver slickness writhing to escape, the draft rushing past as their fingers intertwined, their purposes engaged.

He held two hands over hers as the thing within their grasp fought for escape. The creek sluiced through their fingers, rose in plumes around their wrists. No man-made scents came to them, only the damp pungency of the willow glade they passed, the rich weedy smell of wet ground.

As Jim gained purchase of the fish, Victoria leaned against his shoulder and made the transfer awkwardly, releasing the trout just enough so his hand could gain entrance, could advance with hers. He moved his thumb rhythmically, meaning to massage the creature's sides, but skimming the girl's knuckles instead. She turned to him and gave him a meager and knowing hint of smile.

They waited, their faces a breath away from one another.

He tilted his head, making no fathomable response, the bill on his white canvas hat shadowing his face.

She made no particular effort to gather the line closer.

He watched her for a while, then lifted one arm, as if to let the fish go now, teasing.

"Ah." She fell forward and gripped tightly with both hands again, sending spray in every direction.

"Tough job, this," he said. "He's hooked in a net and yet you can't catch him."

"You said you'd help, didn't you?" She felt as netted as the fish, as frozen into place by the woodsy, grain scent of the country they passed through as by the hardy, sun-raw youth at her side.

A dorsal fin breached the surface beside them, bronze, illuminated from behind, aloft. Next came the tail, a scissorflash of mottled amber, throwing forth whips of water.

"Turn his head up so I can get at it."

She did as he asked.

He crimped the end of the hook, disarming the barb so it would nick back through the trout's mouth without tearing much of its scales and skin. "There now," Jim said.

When they let it, the fish skittered away, swimming in frantic, wriggling commas for distance. "I've had my fill of fishing," she said not long after. "I'd rather just talk."

"So talk." He'd begun rowing again, his back toward their fathers, oar and motion cutting the current, pushing them on.

"Why do you have hair on your toes?"

"All guys have hair on their toes."

"Not like yours." She made to pull some.

"Hey!" He jumped, jostling the boat.

"Just checking."

"Checking what?"

"To see if they're attached."

Jim tried his best to look mean. He couldn't do it. She made him forget to be angry. He liked that. He also liked the way she looked, all dark eyebrows and red glints in her hair, all contrast and color, so different from Sarah.

He waited until they'd reached the length of the trip, until he and his father beached the boat at Crazy Woman's Bar, before he told her what he was thinking. "You ever go out or anything?" he asked abruptly, hearing his own words in his ears as if someone else had said them.

"Sometimes." She sat on a rock, examining fly casings that had washed ashore. She looked up at him sideways. He could only see her curtain of hair, one eye, the side of her nose, one gold stud earring in the lobe of her ear. "That depends."

"On what?"

"On if the person who asked me expected me to play second fiddle or something. I wouldn't ever want to take second place to an old girlfriend who had left and gone away from home."

"You never would."

"You sure?"

"Of course." It felt good, damn good, to finally deny the influence of Sarah Hayden. "That was nice, but it's over." He didn't allow himself to think that she was alone somewhere in Laramie, bearing his child. No matter what Sarah chose to do, he chose to save himself. "She was just a girlfriend, you know."

"Then it depends on something else, too."

"What else? What other stipulations could you possibly name?"

"I only go out if the right person asks me."

"So, I'm asking."

"You've got a lot of nerve. Just assuming like that."

"I'll take you to the Spud Drive-In. Or we could always drive to Jackson and walk around the town square and eat ice cream."

"Let's do both," she said.

Different folks have different ideas these days on why and how it's good to share one's life with a child. For Jim Roice, the profusion of logical questions had only one true answer. He wanted to share Caddisfly Creek with Charlie. He wanted to share the way his father had shared with him.

When Charlie had been scarcely a toddler, father and son spent hours at stream's edge, holding hands, exploring the banks together, the rocks of every color, the debris-gray waterline that marked the high flow of the season before, the fascinating assortment of flotsam brought up onto shore. Together they'd decipher water stories, pointing across the way to roots dangling from carved hillocks of dirt, growing through the earth and worrying the lustrous surface like gnarled primeval fingers.

"How come those underneath plants don't wash away?" Charlie asked.

"They're bottom rooted, buried in the rocks. Won't be swept away by anything, son," Jim answered.

"Why does the water wiggle some places and sit still in others?"

"It all depends on what's underneath," Jim said. "Where he creek bed's shallow and filled with rocks, the water ances. Where the bed drops off deep, water runs mooth, doesn't have reason to hurry."

"What makes Caddisfly Creek go one way and not the ther?" Charlie asked. "Why doesn't it ever change its ind?"

"A river has to flow downstream, Charlie," Jim explained. It always goes from the mountain land to the places elow. Creeks can change their course but not their irection. Same thing as people and their lives."

From the time Jim and Victoria married and moved nto the small rental cabin down the road from the Roices', making a life that way wasn't easy. During the summer, Miller was able to pay his son a good working wage. Winters, they survived on the teaching fees Victoria made on the mountain. A snowy winter meant higher pay. It also meant their long, furrowed driveway drifted closed every time the wind blew. In Wyoming, in winter, the wind blustered every day.

One Sunday afternoon such as that, Miller Roice drove up to their drafty old place and stomped in the front door, wiping his ice-encrusted beard dry best he could, leaving clumps of packed snow on the mat where he doffed his boots. "Well, hello you all," he said, pulling a corked bottle of his homemade hard-crack cider from the inside of his coat and setting it down on the center of the table.

"What's important?" Jim asked, raising his head from his tying vise and his finishing whip. Miller Roice made hard-crack cider every Christmas for the Roice relatives. About drove Jim's mother mad, having all those bottles aging in the bathtub in early fall, never knowing when one might pop a cork and send the deadly thing ricocheting toward you while you sat innocently on the commode. She always breathed easier after mid-November, when Miller boxed them up and moved them all out to cold storage in the haymow. After that, except to give as gifts or to celebrate an occasion, he didn't bring them to light again.

"The occasion of our new agreement," Miller announced as Victoria, interested now, laid the tea towel by and came to the table.

"What agreement?" she asked.

Miller didn't answer her at first. He hung his coat on the rack. He made himself at home as he was prone to do, opening and rummaging through the junk drawer, bypassing the chewed Pronghorn Hotel pen, the length of chain Jim used to hang the hummingbird feeder, the carpet tacks, the plumber's putty Jim'd used three times and still hadn't been able to stop the leak behind the washbasin.

He found the corkscrew and went about opening the bottle.

"We're going to drink that stuff?" Charlie asked, standing nose high beside the table.

Victoria brought glasses to the table, not wine-stemmed ones, but the closest thing in her possession, juicers with pedestals and orange go-go flowers from the sixties.

Ceremonially, Miller held the bottle to the light and turned it, waiting for the yeast to filter to the bottom. As the mixture cleared, he began to pour, filling each glass halfway, even Charlie's. The crack cider shone amber clear, the same opulent color as a cutthroat's fin. "Here here," he announced as he raised his own glass, gestured to all of them around the table, and drank.

"We'd know better what to say if we knew what we were hereing to," Jim reminded him.

Miller's beard had begun to melt. It dripped in dark plops over the placket of his workshirt.

"We've proven something to one another over these past two years," Miller said simply. "We've proven Roice's Wyoming Troutfitters won't support two families, yours and mine."

"We've proven nothing of the sort," Jim said. The glass waiting at his nose made his eyes burn. "We'll get by, Dad. You're doing fine by me."

"I could do better."

"What are you trying to tell us, Miller?" Victoria asked, scarcely able to conceal her eagerness.

"The land, the business," Miller said. "Your mother and I have decided to pass the place off to you now."

"The house?" Victoria asked, even though Jim put up one hand to stop her. "Will you pass off the house as well?"

"Everything. The house is certainly an important part of the holding."

Jim set the glass down and stared at his father. He knew neither what to say about the revelation nor what to feel.

"That's terrific," Vic said for him. "Wonderful."

"Thought you'd think it that way."

"What about Mother?" Jim asked. "What does Mother say?"

"Exactly the same thing."

Jim had long established in his mind that he'd run Roice's Troutfitters one day. He'd long pictured the waning days with his father, spent retracing routes they'd always chosen along the waterway, finishing things. He'd thought of the two things separately, never together, as if they marked different passages in his life, not coinciding. He found it impossible to imagine not sharing the great canopy of branches, the sky over the water, with his dad. He'd never once thought of working Caddisfly Creek these next years without Miller.

"Dad." He tugged at his father's sleeve as if he was a child again. "This may not be the right time."

"It's right," Miller said. "This will give you a chance to really have a go at it."

"What will happen to you and Mom?" Jim couldn't imagine his father's life without the house, the land, the boats loaded and ready to set forth.

"We'll work some way for you to buy me out. I'm not short on thriftiness, you know. I'll buy a small travel trailer and we'll be able to retire nicely. Got to take your mother to Arizona next winter so she'll get a good look at the warm country."

"This will be wonderful," Victoria said again. "We won't have to rent this place any longer. We'll have two bathrooms. And we could buy a horse for Charlie if the mood ever struck."

"You're not tired of fishing," Jim said.

"No, I'm not. Never thought to retire from it so soon." Miller retrieved his coat from the hall and handed Jim the contracts from his pocket. "Never knew I'd have a son like this, either, one who deserved so much."

"Dad." Jim rose from the table, jostling the liquid in his glass and Charlie's. The boy had taken one sip of the stuff, screwed up his mouth, and departed. Victoria had drained hers to the dregs. "Dad."

"No need to say anything. It's in the natural progression of things."

Jim read the contract his father slipped into his hand. "Purchase Offer & Agreement," it said. "We wrote it up as best we could for the both of us," Miller explained. "Tax man down in Afton advised us."

"How can you retire?" Jim asked again. "You're doing what folks want to do after they retire."

"Had the place appraised so we could get everything set right. You'll have to pay interest on the balance to make everything legal. We'll forgive a portion each year until the balance is gone."

Jim looked up from the figures, astounded. "Dad. You don't have to do this."

"No, I don't," Miller said. "But we want to."

Early next spring, before the aspens had leafed out enough to shiver in the breeze, Jim, Victoria, and Charlie moved into the old stone house by the creek, within eyesight of the gambrel-roofed barn, within earshot of—as Charlie called it—wiggling water. Charlie settled in with his sports paraphernalia, his bears, and his trunk in the loft room that, before, had only been his place to stay when he came to visit Grandma. Victoria hung new lace curtains in the kitchen. Jim had new brochures printed, ones that said: "Roice's Wyoming Troutfitters. Jim Roice, Proprietor."

After his parents left for different parts, Jim worked a plan to pay them interest on the amount held against him, then added a small amount, a principal payment, that he thought would help his father get along. "Why do you have to do that?" Vic asked one night. "That'll put us in a bind."

"It'll be harder on us than Dad intended it to be," he conceded. "I want to help them, though. If they aren't working off this river, they deserve enough off of it to relax in style."

"Wanted to put new linoleum in the bathroom."

"Be satisfied, Victoria. Be satisfied because what we have now is better than we had before."

In the end, it was the annual tax assessment that began to do them in. The yellow bill from Lincoln County arrived in Margaret Cox's mail truck the first part of September, and Jim stared in horror at the amount they'd have to pay. Half was due by November 10 and the other half by May 10 of the following year. "Dear sweet heaven," he said, sitting beneath the pool of light at the kitchen table, a pile of envelopes on one side, where he'd paid the month's invoices. "We can't come close to this."

Victoria sat beside him and stared at it, too. "What is that?"

"They must have reassessed the place after Dad had it appraised."

"Can they raise it this way in one year?"

"If the property changes hands, they can."

"Jim. This is ridiculous."

"I agree," he said, but he should have expected it. Any land within commuting distance to Jackson Hole had gone sky-high. The appraiser had added more for the river frontage, the commercial zoning, the barns, and the house with historic value. "Dad couldn't've anticipated this, not when he's lived here all his life, when everything's been the same for so long."

"Maybe this is why they gave it to us, Jim. Maybe they couldn't pay it, either."

He stared up at her, unable to keep himself from slightly resenting her, from taking offense at the way she suspected others' motives. "The money will have to come from somewhere."

She hated to say it, but she knew they had to consider their options. "We could sell, you know."

Jim looked at his wife as if he'd never known her. "It isn't ours to sell, Victoria. I still feel as if it belongs to Mother and Dad."

"It's in our names. And it's worth so much, Jim, we could already list it for more than its appraisal. We could pay off your parents and they could live in high style. It's what you've been worried about, isn't it? That they wouldn't have money to get along? Plus we'd make enough extra to give us a better start."

As he said the words, his body rocked like a strong pine in the wind, a silent sway, anguished and deep. "Why do things always look better to you when you don't have them, Vic?"

"It would just be so much easier sometimes." And,

when she spoke, he found her miserably, utterly sincere. "In the winter, we could take trips. You could work for someone else, guide where it's warm, in South America, or Australia, or Belize."

"This place will pass to Charlie some day," he said ightly. "It will pass down to him the same way it has ssed down to me. I give it up and I become nothing ore than a wage earner, a slave to someone, to have thing, to be nothing."

"All the worrying gets to me, Jim," she said quietly, ming him. "We've never had a time, since the begin- g, when we didn't have to worry. Sometimes I think t's why I'm not pregnant yet, because of all the worry."

He looked at her, dark eyes simmering, accepting her me with painful, rigid-jawed pride. "I'm not worried, toria. I'll never be."

He couldn't pay the first half of the taxes on time. In cember, the county began tacking on its eighteen per- t interest penalty. Jim drove to the Lincoln County urthouse in Afton late one Tuesday afternoon and pre- ted his case to Kathy Gwilliam in the assessor's office, t she only shook her head. "It's terrible, isn't it? Same ng's happening to plenty of people around. Me and ck, we had to sell off a parcel last year, just to keep ings reasonable. You can still manage it, though, Jim. If u pay the full amount by December thirty-first, the county waives the interest."

"What happens if we don't?"

"Same thing that happens to everybody else. Second half's due May of next year. If it isn't in by the fifteenth, county starts running legals and advertising for a tax sale."

"It'd be put up for auction?"

"Auction's always July 1. You can pay everything off right up until the day of the sale, but that means interest and advertising charges, too."

"I'm not worried," he said.

Where others did worry, Jim worked. Where others might've given in, Jim tried a different tack. He gave up fly tying for a while and took an early morning job laying tilework. He did part-time work as a mechanic down at the Star Valley Sinclair. He drove from farm to farm, finding boats in dry storage, offering to repair them for a fee. He mailed brochures to the entire client list from Lester Burgess's Pronghorn Motel and offered to hold a space for their entire party on a full-day fishing trip, campfire meals included, if they'd send a deposit.

Trout season officially opened on April Fool's Day that next year, almost before the ice came fully off the water. Roice's Wyoming Troutfitters stayed wonderfully busy until mid-May, when temperatures rose and snow run-off muddied Caddisfly Creek and all its tributaries. By the time Jim Roice had enough to submit the tax remittance, the Lincoln County Tax Assessor's Office had already started advertising a sale.

He paid it off, interest, advertising, and all, with enough left over to slip Mr. and Mrs. Lester Burgess a small commission for their trouble. He'd booked longer days throughout the summer, a sunrise trip, a day trip, a sunset trip when his fishermen would be more likely to view elk bolting among the trees and moose grazing on willows along the marshy bottoms.

"I suppose," Victoria mentioned one evening while he rinsed his fishing waders in the faucet then hung them upside down to dry, "this is the first I've known how much all this means to you."

He stripped off suspenders, socks, mud-caked britches. "It isn't simple, is it?"

"You're going to kill yourself, just hanging on to the place."

"Worth it," he said. "Everything's worth it."

"You'll have to do this all over again next year."

He stopped and turned toward her, wanting to reassure her, wanting her to acknowledge his capabilities. "We'll know what we're up against then, Vic. We'll plan ahead. The taxes won't catch us off guard again the way they caught us this time."

Eventually, Jim was pleased to see that Victoria came to believe him. He worked hard at the house on the high ridge, often until midnight, cleaning and gearing up for each new day. He slept well. Charlie learned to handle life jackets and a tackle box. Even though he still loved fishing with worms, Charlie learned fly knots. He could tie line to leader to tippet to fly using the blood knot, the surgeons', the perfection, the improved clinch. Every so often, when Caddisfly Creek stayed calm, Jim allowed Charlie to row. Jim watched him closely, loving him, seeing himself, teaching him, taking joy in the ways the boy grew.

9

Marshall Upser attended Sandlin and Bonham's Thanksgiving get-together alone. Employees met in an enormous tower suite at the Waldorf-Astoria on Park Avenue and, at midnight, staff members brought in a supper. The usual clients attended; champagne flowed.

"When is Sarah coming back to New York?" everyone asked.

"In two days," Marshall said. "She'll be home by Thanksgiving."

"That's surprising. I would've thought it might take longer to put things in order."

"She says there isn't much to put order to."

Marshall left early. The taxi smelled like old cars always smell, the dry, biting stench of sun-rotten leather and dust. He gave the driver an address three blocks from his apartment and, when they arrived, he angled his hat against the oncoming flood of lights and pulled his jacket tight around him.

He needed the walk, needed it worse than anything in a long time. All the time spent reassuring others of Sarah's return, and he struggled with such reassurance himself. Something about her voice yesterday, something about the way she'd said his name when he'd only repeated what she'd told him, made him suspicious.

He'd long since known of Sarah's restlessness. "I've gotten everything I wanted," she'd told him one day as they sat corner to corner at a table in a board room, wrangling ways to ship United States–constructed satellite dishes to China.

"I'd like to see you happy then."

"I'm happy. Of course I'm happy."

Because he loved her, he'd often noticed her ambition and her grief. "You've sacrificed."

"No," she said quietly. "I haven't."

Marshall poked both hands into the pockets of his overcoat as he walked, his chin low inside his collar, his gait heavy. He passed a grate and heard water rushing far below. At his own brownstone, he trudged upstairs, reminding himself as he climbed that she was thousands of miles from him, in some Godforsaken western place where only fishermen, cowboys, and coyotes would go.

She'd stayed with him often enough to make him expect her. When they hadn't been together in the evenings, they'd been in some pigeonhole at Sandlin and Bonham, taking notes across a desk. Perhaps, in his thinking, he'd discovered the singular problem between them. Only their lives bound them together, nothing more. They'd expected everything of each other, they'd expected nothing.

Maybe he should phone her again, just to check on her and make certain everything stayed on schedule. And maybe he shouldn't. Maybe she'd think he wanted to push her.

He reached around the corner for the light and, when

it went on, Marshall winced. As his eyes adapted, he envisioned Sarah standing before him, wrapped in the Grecian goddess nightgown he'd given her not long ago, clasping it around her middle, folds flowing down her legs like milk. He remembered now, when she'd spoken, he wasn't surprised by her words. He'd only been surprised she wasn't melancholy when she said them. "I had a baby once, Marshall."

"Did you?"

"Yes. A boy."

"Do you think about this often?"

"No," she'd said. "Not often. But sometimes."

He kept a vase of dried statice on the mantel and she peeled one off, stripping the flower down fiber by fiber the way he'd seen children fringe bermuda grass during a boring summer day. Piece by piece, she fed the threads into his fire, watching as each curled or arched into a red, glowing filament.

"Sarah." He'd stepped toward her then, wanting to take her into his arms.

She turned her back fully against him, firelight shining through her gown, highlighting her skin the way sun shines through a cresting wave. "No, Marshall. Don't."

"If you'd let me closer, perhaps things would be better for us."

"No," she said, flipping the last of the statice in and watching it flame. "I can't."

"Love is different than you think it is," he'd said. "Love isn't entangling. Love is freedom."

"Only people who've ever loved me have tried to make me less of *me*."

"Maybe not. Maybe that's only how you see it."

"I loved my baby," she whispered. "I loved him and I let him go."

"Yes."

"They said it was unselfish. Everyone said I was doing

right. Giving up that baby for adoption was one of the most selfish things I've done in my life."

Now, finally, she turned to him. "You're beautiful, Sarah," he said.

"Help me, Marshall," she said. "Please, help me."

"Mrs. Roice," called the receptionist at the OB-GYN clinic in Jackson. Victoria rose, lay the *Skiing* magazine on the counter, and followed the nurse to an examining room. "Dr. Barkley will be with you in a few minutes."

"Thank you," she said.

Victoria scooted herself up onto the examining table and felt the paper crinkling beneath her weight. She swung both feet where they dangled and looked at the poster on the wall that showed the nine-month progression of a healthy pregnancy.

She was starting to hate this place.

"Mrs. Roice." Dr. Barkley opened the door and stepped inside. "Good morning."

"Couldn't they have put me in a different room?" She pointed to the shiny-flesh billboard of the distended womb. "You shouldn't put your infertility patients in with your OBs."

He lay her charts on his stool, calmly walked to the wall, and removed the thumbtacks. The placard tumbled down onto the floor and he poked it into a drawer. "There. Is that better?"

"No," she said. "The damage is already done. All these healthy Wyoming farm kids. You don't have many people with this problem, do you?"

He ignored her question. Instead, he said, "Victoria, things haven't been going well for you."

"No, things haven't been going well. Things haven't been going at all. Nothing's happening," she said. "We're . . . I'm . . . trying so hard all the time."

He hiked his pants up at the knees and settled on the stool, charts opened.

"I never should've fooled around all that time just going to Doc Bressler. But he's been my family doctor for so long down in Afton, and, until that first year went by, it never crossed my mind that I would need a specialist."

"Frankly, I don't know what you need," Dr. Barkley said, scratching his head. "All the tests have come back negative. And none of the ultrasounds show any sign of endometriosis. It could still be some ovarian problem I've overlooked. But, until we do exploratory surgery, I won't know the answers to that, either."

"Is this our next step then? Exploratory surgery?"

"No. Not quite the next step. We need your husband to come in, Mrs. Roice. I'd like to conduct a sperm count on Jim."

She shook her head. "He won't do it."

"He isn't as committed to this as you are?"

"He doesn't know how much I'm doing. I haven't told him much because Jim's just more"— she hesitated — "satisfied."

Barkley closed the files and laid them aside. "Victoria, perhaps you should be satisfied, too."

She stared at him, unable to believe he'd say such a thing after all the time and money she'd spent in his office. "It's different for a woman," she said, annoyance in her voice. And, despite her anger, she felt dangerously close to tears. "A woman wants to bear her own child. It's just part of . . . who we are."

"Don't lump yourself with other women, Victoria," he said. "So many of those who cannot bear children never get the chance to raise a son as you have."

Victoria slid off the examining table and straightened her skirt. "I don't have to listen to this."

"I'm your physician. You're paying me to look after your well-being."

"I'm paying you so I can have a baby. I'm paying you so you'll find out what's wrong. I want the scientific aspects from you, doctor, not the emotional ones."

"My nurse and I will be back with you shortly, after you've gotten into your gown."

He turned to go, but she stopped him. "I've been dreaming about this, you know. I've been dreaming that this is something I've done to myself, that I've torn something loose with my skiing. Could it be that? Will you check to make sure nothing's just . . . loose?"

Dr. Barkley smiled. "I've checked already, Victoria, but I'll check again. That's the puzzling part of it. After all the scopings and tests, you look healthy as—"

She finished it for him. "As a Wyoming farm kid."

"Yes," he said. "You do."

Victoria looked Dr. Barkley right in the eye and finally admitted it to someone. "Sometimes I resent Charlie," she said quietly.

"You do?"

"I love that boy so much, Dr. Barkley. He's everything to both of us. But I get the feeling Jim'd do things I asked if we'd never adopted that boy. It's easy not liking myself for that. It's torture loving somebody and resenting them, too, especially an innocent child. But I know what'll happen. I know I'll go home today and say, 'Jim, I've been going to Dr. Barkley and I've checked out fine. Doc wants you to come in for a sperm count.' Jim'll just look at me with those eyes of his, then he'll turn right back and look at Charlie. Then he'll say, 'I don't need a sperm count, Victoria. I've got everything I need right here.' I swear to you, Dr. Barkley, sometimes you'd think Charlie was Jim's own kid right from the beginning."

"You want to opt for the surgery?" Barkley asked. "It's obtrusive, painful. There may be no reason for it. I don't like doing things that way."

"I'll do anything," Victoria told him. "I'll do anything to have my own child."

In Star Valley, native cutthroat season traditionally ended the twenty-fifth day of November. "Won't let snow stop *us*, will we?" Jim grinned across the Mackenzie boat at Charlie as they tugged it once more toward the water. "We've gotta go after those trout while we can, kiddo."

"This'll be the last time, won't it, Dad?" Charlie asked. "The last time for fishing before winter sets in."

"I suspect so. Creek's gonna ice up down at Long Draw any day."

Jim clapped his white canvas cap on his head and took the boat into the water first, sloshing into the current until Caddisfly Creek rippled just below his knees.

"Jump in!" he hollered to Charlie. "I'll pull us out."

For a moment, the boy hesitated, his reflection wobbling as the river parted at his shins, then came back together in rivulets. He did his father's bidding, tumbling head first into the Mackenzie boat, sprawling out across one seat and flipping a good amount of creek water into the tackle boxes.

When they reached mid-river, Jim hoisted himself into the dory. Neither of them spoke. Father and son sat looking to the southeast, admiring the trees that passed them, the great clumps of reddening willow, the aspen thickets already stark and leafless from the cold. The waterway ran clear and fast, gamboling against its banks like any of the spring-melt creeks that fed the mountainland.

Charlie flipped the lid off a Styrofoam container and poked around in the black dirt to find a worm.

"You fishing off the bottom?" Jim asked him.

"Don't know what I'll do," Charlie said. He pulled one lanky worm from the soil and held it so it shone, opalescent, in the slanting afternoon sun. "Look at how skinny this worm is. Sorriest excuse for a fish bait I've seen."

"Son."

"Should've known they'd be this way coming from that ice cream cooler at Happersett's. Betcha they don't even feed 'em there or anything. Old Will used to give his worms coffee grounds every time he'd empty a pot. Then you got to pick the best ones because you went out with a tin can and dug 'em up yourself. They were so fat and there were so many of 'em back in his worm garden, you had to be careful not to cut them in half when you went in after 'em with a shovel."

"Maybe Tom Happersett will let you care for his worms, too. You've gotten to be quite an expert."

"She would've let me dig some, Dad. Even though old Will's gone, Sarah would've let me have my pick of the worms."

Jim finished his improved clinch knot, pulling the line through the eye on his fly, then tightening it with his teeth. "You never know. That real estate sign went up awful quick over there, Charlie. She's probably already negotiated the worms in on the deal."

Something in the father's voice made his son turn and take a look at him. "You know her when she was a girl, Dad?" The worm still hung lamely from Charlie's fingers, dangling straight and thin while he searched for an appropriate hook.

"Yeah. I did." This time, Jim spoke carefully, his words meaning a great many things. "We used to tell fairy tales together."

"You don't like her much, do you?"

Jim cast his line. "No. Not anymore."

As the trip progressed, neither of them worked too hard at fishing. Jim cast occasionally, when they came to a still, deep place, and Charlie dragged the worm for miles, trolling behind them. The afternoon was more a

relaxed act of departure than an energetic search for
cutthroat trout.

"Momma opened my present after I went to bed last
night," Charlie stated at last.

"Yes, she did."

"She came up and made me open my door and told
me how much she liked it."

"I'm glad." Jim didn't turn from the river. "Vic was
sure mad at me, Charlie. Told me I'd ruined everything
for you."

Charlie sat sullenly for a moment, not speaking.

"I'm proud of you, you know. Not because of anything
you've done, but just because of who you are. I'm proud
just because I'm your dad."

At that precise moment, a fish struck Charlie's bait.
"Whoaaa!" he shrieked. "I got a bite."

"Is he still on there?"

Charlie pulled the pole forward and felt the jagged
animation of a trout struggling in strokes to break free.
"Yeah. I've got him."

The trout swam furiously, skewering the line off to
the right-hand side of the drift boat. Charlie watched the
cutthroat flash copper-slick beneath the sun-heightened
surface. "He's going sideways."

"That, he'll do. I'm going to get the net. Hang on."

The reel clicked with each turn of the handle, sending
a spray of water droplets up Charlie's arms. "I've got a
question."

"What?"

"Do you like it better this way? When it's just us? Or
do you like it best when we have paying customers?"

Jim was still rifling through the pile of supplies, trying
to reach his net. He turned and grinned back over his
shoulder. "I like it this way, of course. I like it when it's
just you and me."

The trout surfaced.

"Dad. Hurry."

"I've got it. Here it is." With one swoop, Jim Roice dipped the net into the water and captured the fish. The wooden oval of the net came above the creek at an angle. The backbone of the cutthroat stayed below. "You reach down there and unhook him, son."

Charlie fumbled about for a moment before he found the fish's mouth. He plied the thing open with one finger and looked straight down the trout's gullet. "Isn't good news here. He's swallowed the hook, worm and all."

"Well, let's bring him on into the boat then. No use trying to save him. We'll have to clean this one and take him home for supper."

"All that trouble trying to reel him and keep him on the hook, and he was caught straight through the whole time."

"It was good practice for you, Charlie."

"Once we get him clear, I'm gonna tie on a dry fly," Charlie said sadly. "Only reason I ever wanted to use those confounded worms was just because I was mad about 'em coming from Happersett's."

10

They'd just pulled the boat out of the water at Crazy Woman's Bar when they saw her walking where a hiking trail wound along the southeast shore. "That's the lady from the store," Charlie said, proudly dangling his one fish from the stringer so she'd be sure to see it.

Jim still stood hip-deep in Caddisfly Creek, his hands veed on the keel of the Mackenzie. He heard the front end dragging on the rocks. "Charlie. Keep the boat up. We're not to shore yet."

"But she's there."

"Makes no difference. We've still got our work to do." Certainly she's there, he thought. She wouldn't come to Star Valley without coming to this spot. It had always been one of her favorite places.

They'd landed in a bosk of shuddering, white-skinned mountain alder just past Long Draw, a small wood out of rank in the towering evergreens, one that guarded the perfect, shallow expanse of stones and an unfrequented, boggy meadow. How many of their own floating trips had they ended in just this place, in just this way, with Sarah sloshing along through ankle-deep wheatgrass, dipping low in her skirts to pick the clumps of wild purple huckleberries.

"Halloo!" Charlie called, arching the stringer high over his head in a wave.

"Get the boat up," Jim said.

She turned and saw them. Jim watched her recognize, watched her react to, the Roice's Wyoming Troutfitters logo painted merrily on the boat's hull. She halted. Her neck suddenly took on the jutting incline he knew so well, the one of mild annoyance.

Charlie practically dropped the boat onto shore and ran toward her. "Had to keep this fish," he bellowed. "Dad made me fish with worms from Happersett's and the dadburned trout swallowed the whole thing."

"Hello, Charlie." She glanced over his head at Jim, who was still angling his end of the boat into the shallows. "Let me have that fish. We'll hang him from a tree. Looks like you left your father needing some help with his boat."

"You know about boats?" Charlie asked, astounded.

"A little."

Together they ran back to shore, and Sarah went in with her boots on, hefting the drift boat high so Jim could swing his end up onto the bank. "Nothing like getting deserted in midstream," he said coolly to his son as he carried the thing and began to strap it on to the trailer he always kept hidden there.

"It's her," Charlie said again. "She's here. My mom liked the scarf from the store. She thinks it's real pretty, doesn't she, Dad?"

"Yes." Jim adjusted the bill on his white canvas hat, pulling it low over his eyes for effect. Only then did he allow himself to meet Sarah's gaze. "She likes it. Guess we oughtta say thanks."

"Wasn't me doing anything." She met his eyes straight on, boldly. "Charlie told me what he wanted."

"I suppose he did."

"Now," she asked, rumpling Charlie's hair. "What is it with the worms? Why did you buy some down at Happersett's when you could've walked over and dug some up for free at my place?"

"Didn't know that for sure." The little boy shoved his hands in his pockets. "Dad says you probably wouldn't care much about sellin' worms now. Dad says you probably negotiated the selling of worms right along with some real estate deal."

"Jim, he could've walked over—"

"Sarah," —he raised a hand to stop her— "don't encourage this."

They stared at each other in silence for a good half minute.

"I see," Sarah said finally.

No, you don't, he wanted to say. He was heartsick just thinking Will might've left some record somewhere, something on paper that Sarah could find.

The sun disappeared to the west, sending tapers of light sieving across gaps of mountain rock.

"Get that fish in the cooler," Jim told Charlie. "We'll come back with the truck and bring everything home."

"How are you getting back to the truck?"

"Same way we always do, Sarah. We'll hitchhike." Somebody they knew always came along who was willing to drop them off at the bridge.

She hesitated, knowing she should let them go alone. It wouldn't do for anyone in Star Valley to see them driving together. But perhaps she thought too much about it. Perhaps so much time had gone by that it didn't really make a difference.

"I could drive you," she said. "I've got my rental car from Jackson."

"Let's go with her, Dad." Charlie jumped down from the boat trailer and dried his hands off on the grass. "Then we won't have to walk at all. We'll be home in time for supper."

Jim Roice thrust his hands into his pockets and jiggled the items there: keys, pennies, a Leatherman do-all-things tool. He hesitated for every reason she had hesitated, too. *How long are you going to be with us, Sarah Hayden?* he wanted to ask. *When are you leaving us alone and going back to the life that you chose?*

"Come on, Dad," Charlie said, dancing around them.

In his heart of hearts, Jim did not want her near any portion of the life he'd managed to build for Victoria and their Charlie. But in this meadow, at this moment, with Caddisfly Creek cavorting by, it seemed suddenly silly to say no. She was only talking about a car ride, after all.

"It's okay, Jim," she said, seeing his misgivings, knowing they echoed her own. "I just thought—"

"I know what you thought."

"I couldn't just *go*—"

"Dad, please. Let her take us back."

Victoria had stopped after work in Jackson for another of her examinations at the Jackson Hole OB-GYN clinic there. He knew from experience she wouldn't be coming along the highway for at least another hour. And it sometimes seemed dangerous to him, making such a big deal out of this in front of Charlie. Sure the townspeople would talk, but they'd been talking for ten years already.

"It's all right, Sarah," he said. "We'll take that ride with you, if you don't mind."

She halfway smiled at him, then motioned toward the car. "Okay. Hop in, you two."

They'd fished a suitable part of the afternoon, traveling down the canyon for a number of miles. As they wound their way upstream toward Star Valley, he finally asked her about the store.

"We saw the For Sale sign go up yesterday."

"Yes."

"Are you selling everything, Sarah? Are you holding on to any part of the land?"

"I've got to get back to New York as quickly as possible," she said, never looking at him. "I'm selling it all."

Jim settled back into his seat, scrutinizing the treetops where the road wound along the river shore. In time, he came to realize that Charlie had slumped upon his lap and was faintly snoring. He shored the boy's head against one of their jackets and brushed his hair behind the one shell-like ear that lay toward them.

Sarah glanced over from the steering wheel, both hands gripping leather, watching while he enjoyed looking upon the face of his son. "He's special, isn't he?"

"Yes."

She turned her attention back to the road, drove for another mile, and chewed her bottom lip before she found the courage to say the rest of it. "I'm glad you and Victoria have a boy."

He didn't say anything to her. He couldn't.

Finally, after they'd passed the cutoff toward town and turned toward the bridge, she said, "It does me good to see you."

When he asked her the next question, he asked it abruptly, as if the words had just come upon him. In truth, he'd been wondering about her lifestyle for days. He often wondered if she regretted what she'd done. "Sarah? What about you?"

She smiled again, this time fully. "What about me? There's nothing much to tell, Jim. New York's wonderful. And this is our busy season at Sandlin and Bonham.

You ought to see the orders for purchase we're taking in from China. And now, with NAFTA going through—"

He stopped her. "That isn't what I'm asking."

"It isn't?"

"No."

She glanced across Charlie's lolling form at him. "What is it, then?"

"I'm asking about *you*. I'm asking if you've ever let anyone close enough in your life to love you."

Her expression went cold. When she spoke, her brevity came with ice. "This is no time for condemning."

"I'm not condemning, Sarah. I only want to know. I suspect your answer will be important to both of us."

"Will it be? Or are you only wanting to make me struggle?"

"Perhaps that's it," he said, his tone instantly cryptic and hard. "Perhaps I need to see you struggle the way I struggled once."

She'd been clutching the steering wheel so firmly, her knuckles rose as white knobs beneath her skin. She signaled her turn and navigated the gravel curve that took them down off the highway. Jim's hauling truck waited there, in the same spot she knew, two hundred yards south of both their places. As always, he'd left it parked beneath the crumbling overpass where he liked putting in the Mackenzie.

"Nothing much has changed," she said.

"No. It hasn't," he said.

She had in mind to tell him about Marshall Upser. She nearly began to describe their grueling hours at the office, their wild contingency plans that often came with foreign dignitaries, their walks from his brownstone through Central Park toward Saint Patrick's Cathedral early in the mornings. But something stopped her. Something told her he couldn't fathom it. And she wondered if that answered the question he was asking anyway.

"I got to where," he said, "I couldn't remember your face. I got to where, when I was thinking of you, I didn't see you anymore. I was only picturing a photo, one of those silly ones the tourists used to take of us each summer. What is it about that? What is it that allows us to remember images from photos but not people as we've regularly seen them?"

She turned toward him, her eyes brimming with pain. "You never once asked me about the baby, Jimmy. Didn't you ever want to know?"

He stared out the window, not moving for fear of waking Charlie, not daring to turn so she could see his face. "Maybe I didn't want to know, Sarah. It almost killed me, seeing that our baby didn't matter to you. Maybe, to keep my sanity, I had to fight to keep it from mattering to me, too. Maybe it would've hurt too much if I'd have let myself care."

It was exactly the same thing she'd thought of her father. The files came to mind, the ones she'd tucked away in the attic that first night because she'd known they'd be too painful to read.

"There were times I prayed you'd write me and ask," she said almost angrily. "There were times I thought I'd die if I couldn't just tell it to somebody. And you were the only one I wanted to tell it to. Didn't you ever think about it? Didn't you ever want to know whether it was a boy or a girl?"

Between them on the seat, Charlie stirred. He sat up, his face indented from the car seat on one side, and scrubbed his eyes open with fingers still covered with worm dirt.

"When are you going back?" Jim asked instead.

"Day after tomorrow if everything goes according to plan," she answered. "I'd like to be there"— she almost said "with Marshall" —"by Thanksgiving."

"That isn't long. You never stay long."

"No, I don't," she said. And, secretly, he was relieved.

He reached for the door handle, turned it, and gathered Charlie into his arms. He groaned as he tried to push his way out the door. The kid weighed a ton. Jim Roice had vowed years before that he would tote and fetch his son just as long as his own physique allowed him the privilege.

"Jimmy," she whispered. "Goodbye."

"Yes, Sarah. Goodbye," he said. "Thank you for the ride."

Rita Persnick didn't get the bad news until after she'd already telephoned three prospective buyers for Hayden's General Store. Down the street, at Paul Arthur's Title Insurance Office, three faxes came in from the county clerk's office at the Lincoln County Courthouse in Afton.

"This is unfortunate," Rita said when Paul Arthur dropped them by her office. "I guess we should've expected something like this, given the nature of the property."

"Yes, I suppose so," he agreed. "But it's impossible to anticipate everything, isn't it?"

"I've got someone driving up from Denver to view the old place tomorrow. And somebody else is coming in Friday from Utah."

"You'd best have them hold off and handle this quickly, Rita. Or you might lose a sale. There aren't gonna be too many buyers interested in such a white elephant."

"You never know, do you?"

Rita Persnick called Sarah at the store immediately. She'd learned that past week to let the number ring on forever, that the only phone at the store was a black rotary contraption that sat on the counter downstairs. But when Sarah answered, she did so after only three rings and she was breathing hard, as if she'd only just run inside.

"Hello?"

"We've got a problem."

"What problem, Rita?"

"Long time ago, before your great-grandfather's homestead patent was filed, a man named Dab Burch lived on a portion of the property. Mr. Burch went to Lincoln County court and filed a lien against the property, said your family'd measured their quarter section wrong, and he wanted them to pay him for the acreage they'd overtaken."

"How did they measure it?" Sarah asked. "How could they have measured it wrong?"

"Most likely, they tied a bandanna around one wagon wheel and set out to count the rotations. It was easy to make a mistake. Fact is, in those days, exceptions were when people measured land accurately. According to the records still maintained with the Lincoln County Clerk, your ancestors neither paid off nor disputed that filing."

"You're saying they moved in right on top of him and then didn't worry to set the situation right?"

"That's what the paperwork shows. Of course, as time passed, the circumstance should have rectified itself. If the place had sold and someone had reason to apply for a new warranty deed, the lien would have been discovered. And Dab Burch was taken in for horse thieving just several months after your family established their own rights. He died in jail, with no known relatives. Nobody ever found reason to clear the issue up."

"Only in Wyoming," Sarah said, laughing now because it was the only way to chase off the worry. "Real estate problems like this don't come up on the East Coast."

"Occasionally they do."

"What are you telling me?"

"I'm telling you to extend your stay in Wyoming until we can get things straightened out."

"Why? Why can't I do this long distance?"

"It will draw things out longer if you are out of state as we do our digging," Rita said. "You may have to issue a sworn affidavit or two. You may have to testify before a judge as to the known history of your family. This will cause a delay, Sarah, but it isn't something impossible to overcome. I expect we can gain clear title to the property in another three weeks." Rita actually thought it might take a month, but she didn't want to belabor the point. "I may even have a buyer for you by then."

Sarah sighed. She'd have to phone Marshall and tell him to cancel their Thanksgiving plans. "Three weeks? You think it'll be three weeks?"

"You might want to open the store up for business, Sarah," Rita suggested lightly. "It's going to look better if you're bringing in a profit during November and December."

"Damn," Sarah said. "This isn't what anybody wants."

Jim and Victoria's marriage bed had always been a place of adjournment, an encasing not so different from the insect casings that floated to creekshore, a guarded place, a place of respite, protection. They'd long since promised one another they wouldn't bring their cares here; they'd bring only themselves, their gentle vulnerabilities, their souls. Jim lay now, savoring this place, holding his wife as her hair fell across his arm in its characteristic tangle, thankful for one more lengthy evening, since Charlie had been delivered to his own room.

"Mm-m-m," she murmured, creeping ever closer to him, her breathing deliciously warm as it fretted the crook of his neck.

"It was a good day," he said. "Charlie and I had our last autumn fishing."

She kneaded his chest with one flat, pressing hand, wanting to say something now, knowing she shouldn't. Instead, she worked to rouse him again, enticing him with her fingers. She circled the outline of each nipple, smiling at him all the while as he watched her, then ran her hands down completely toward his groin. As always, she proved too much for him. He took her wrist. "What are you doing?"

"What do you think I'm doing?"

"You want more, Vic?"

"I always want more."

From outside the window, a waxing, transparent moon limned the outlines of her breast, of her legs, with light. With his own hands, he began to explore the shadows of her body, feeling the heated dampness of her breath as she sighed and lay back for him. He raised above her, fit against her, discovered her as if for the first time.

She couldn't keep from saying it any longer. This act of their loving plus the desires of her heart came so inherent to one another, she and Jim's very coupling seemed to drive the words from her mind and into suggestion. "Came from the doctor's today. Jim, I want a baby. My baby. Ours."

"Of course you do," he said, running his hands through her hair. "We both do."

"I want one worse than you," she said, meeting his eyes.

He didn't look away. Instead, he kissed her, letting her know that, at this moment, his mind remained absorbed with countless other things, not the least of which concerned her naked body next to his. "Can we talk about this later?"

"I like to talk about it while we do this. Thinking of a

baby's such an important part of this, like humming music while you're dancing."

"No, Victoria," he said, his eyes suddenly alight with amusement. "Dancing has nothing to do with the humming. It has to do with the rhythm." And, here, he began to stroke into her fiercely, while she laughed.

"Why are you always so practical?"

"Be quiet," he warned her. "You ask too many questions."

"Okay, Jim. Okay."

They made love with slow deliberateness as the moon ascended high from the east into the azure-dark vault of sky, silvering the sage, sending shadows through the trees. It was late, toward the wee hours of morning, when Victoria rolled over, sated, and, touching her stomach, said, "There. Maybe, after all this, we've done it."

He raised himself again over her, this time with just one arm. "You have a baby, Vic. You've got Charlie."

"No, Jim," she said calmly, as if she'd expected just this when they were through. "It isn't the same thing."

"It ought to be."

"No. It ought not to be. But maybe only a woman would know. Maybe only a woman would realize the difference."

"I'm trying to get you pregnant, Victoria," he said, now recognizing her desperation. He'd seen her in this mood before. These resignations, when they came, came often, unprovoked, uncensurable. He had to laugh, not at her, but at the entire idea. "I'm doing everything I know to do in that department. Think I just proved that to you."

"Dr. Barkley wants you to come in. He wants to run some tests."

"Wants to test *me*? For what?"

"Your sperm. He wants to make certain you're able to father a baby."

Jim stared at her, the relief pouring over him, soaking

in the way parched soil soaks up rain. "Why, of course I can father—" He stopped, interrupting himself, realizing the implications of the stories he thought to tell her.

"What? What are you saying?"

"Nothing." He straightened the sheets around him, tucking them in when they hadn't needing tucking at all. "I'm not saying anything. It's just that, I never thought it, *I* . . . could be a factor."

"Well, it might be. Dr. Barkley can't find anything else to satisfy him."

"So he's going to go after me?" He hated himself for doing this, hated having to find quiet ways to put her off. "Isn't this costing us an inordinate amount of money?"

"Yes," she said, "but don't you think the spending's worth it?"

"We don't have a lot of savings. What we've got has to last us through the winter, until business starts up again."

"You didn't answer my question, Jim," she said, looking at him strangely. "Don't you think it's worth everything?"

"No," he said, looking up at Victoria and catching danger, knowing that, with the question she asked and the answer he'd give her, she moved them into a standoff. "Not always."

Her composure broke. She sat up, not bothering to cover her breasts. "Damn it," she said. "How could you be so nonchalant about this?"

"I'm not nonchalant. I'm just not obsessive the way you are."

"I'm not obsessed," she said. "I'm only normal. Don't know what it is about this that makes you so defensive."

"When it becomes this important to you," he said, "you make it seem as if Charlie has no worth at all."

"How can you say that?" She got up and gathered her robe from the back of a chair, jabbing her arms into each sleeve and then belting it tight. She cast open the sliding glass door and stalked out into the nighttime on their back deck, Jim in immediate pursuit. She wheeled toward him. "I love that boy more than my own life and you know it. You aren't playing fair."

He gripped her arm. "What if you had to pick, Victoria? What if you had to choose between Charlie and a baby of our own? I almost think you'd give him up, just for a chance at your own pregnancy."

"What an awful thing to say." She was crying by now, hating him for voicing it, hating herself for the warfare of emotions within her. At times, Jim knew her better than she knew herself. She'd told the doctor as much this afternoon, and she'd meant it. At times, she'd trade anything to bear a child with her own body. Even so, she wouldn't let it go by without standing up for herself. "I do homework with him every night. I take him to hockey, I snap on the millions of pads and lace up his skates. I'm planning the biggest birthday party in Lincoln County for him next week."

"No," Jim said. "You're always away in Jackson Hole, managing skiers or teaching at Teton Village. I'm the one with calluses on my thumbs from lacing his skates. And I'll do it a thousand times more before he grows up. We both will."

She turned away again, leaning on the cedar railing as if it might give way and she could escape. "What more can I give Charlie? You know how badly I want my own baby. You want me to stumble with Charlie and, because you watch me for it, you only see what you're looking for."

"Is that what you think?" He wanted to take her in his arms suddenly, wanted to reassure her, wanted to say he was wrong, only he wasn't. "Is that how you honestly expect me to see this? That I'm seeing only what I want to see?"

"I'm a normal mother of a normal nine-year-old kid.

He makes my heart soar sometimes. He makes me furious sometimes. And I'm giving him everything I have to give."

Jim moved toward the door to go inside, knowing this conversation should never have gone as far as they'd taken it. And, in the end, he knew he owed it to Victoria to be brutally forthright. "I'm afraid sometimes," he said to her. "I'm afraid of how having a baby would change us."

11

Maudie Perkins appeared on the front porch of Hayden's General Store Wednesday with a huge bell jar of her famous crab-apple jelly. "Sarah, talk around town is that you don't have a place to eat your Thanksgiving dinner," Maudie said. "I served turkey to your papa every Thanksgiving. Don't care what all these well-meaning harbingers say. I intend to serve you, too."

"Oh, Maudie," Sarah said, sighing and not knowing what to answer. She took the jelly and held it so it glittered like a pink treasure in the sun. "Been so long since I've had any of your best crab apples." What she meant was, *It's been so long since I've beaned anybody in the head with one of them.*

"You're one of us," she said. "If you'd 'a left yesterday like you was supposed to, none of us would've been the worse for wear. But you're one of us, child. Your daddy would turn in his grave if he knew you'd come home for a while at last and nobody bothered to invite you over."

"Maudie, you don't have to do this." Sarah stood inside the screen, her hand on the jamb, not knowing whether to feel amused or sorry. Now, because she was staying, her presence took on significance to everyone. This was one major reason she'd wanted to go.

"It's a shame about your problem with the deed on this place," Maudie said. "Think it'll get cleared up ever?"

"Does everybody in town know about that?" she asked.

"Yep. I reckon so. You know how news travels around this place."

"Yes," Sarah said. "I remember well."

"I'm serving dinner at two. No need to bring anything, either. Don't figure you're cooking much for just yourself over here. Although I could use a relish tray." Maudie peered in over Sarah's shoulder. "You got any canned beets in there? Or any pimento olives? Beulah Hardaway is bringing her homemade brussels sprout casserole and some crazy concoction of hot pickled okra her aunt sent up from Alabama this summer. I could use something traditional."

"I'll bring beets," Sarah said. "I'll bring olives. And I may be able to scare up enough sweet potatoes in Dad's storage room to make a sweet potato pie."

"You gonna open this place back up?" Maudie asked, obviously determined that, since Sarah'd accepted her offer of hospitality, she could go politely on with the scuttlebutt at hand. "You gonna bring in business just like Rita Persnick wants you to?"

"You know I've never been good at doing what folks want me to do."

Maudie put her hands on her hips and let out a mild guffaw. "That, I know, Sarah Hayden. That, I know."

"You tell everybody that's askin' I haven't decided what to do about the store. You tell folks I'll settle it according to my notion, not the whims of some real estate broker." And, secretly, Sarah thought opening the store for the next three weeks might be exactly what she needed. With the exception of the times she'd go to court in Afton or sign papers, she didn't know how to keep herself occupied.

"I'll tell 'em you're saving the news for them until they see you at my dinner," she said, almost chortling with mirth. "Oh, I'll just have to buy a bigger turkey, won't I?"

Thanksgiving Day dawned like so many of those that mark the passage from fall to winter in the mountains, a morning as sharply cut and brilliant as a jewel adornment, the sky a high, thick blue, the sunlit colors so richly detailed that a painter's brush might never capture their profundity. Upstairs, in the old oven, a sweet potato pie baked, filling the store with the lavish, heavy fragrance of browning crust and cinnamon.

She'd decided to open the store and to keep it open, at least for the time being. It would give her an honest chance to take stock of her father's inventory. She could measure actual cash flow, a measurement that would help immensely when the time came to negotiate or accept any offer from a buyer.

Sarah stepped to the screen and peered out at the children playing at the pond, Charlie Roice and two others, one in faded overalls, a spare girl with hair pulled straight back from her ears with a band, and another in plaits and a dress as frothy and ill-placed as the other child's was plain. At the marshy south end of the pond grew a tangle of dried reeds and ripening cattails, a labyrinth of tall sienna pods that waved through water and air as joyfully as palm fronts waved when Christ made his exuberant entrance into Jerusalem. Two robust Labradors accompanied the children, one dog a deep mahogany, the other smaller and pure black. The dogs bounded through the water, splashing the children and making them shriek, landing with paws set wide at pond's edge, to shake spirals of prismy spray into the children's faces.

The black dog discovered the cattails first. He leapt at one, his impressive jaws clamping on to empty air. "Look. Look," the overalled girl cried. "Crazy Bean's goin' after those things."

"Can you believe it?" Charlie bellowed. "Dogs can't jump that high. Crazy."

At their pointing, the deep-brown dog took off too, barking and joining her companion in a game that caused even Sarah, from where she stood, to break into laughter.

"Look. Nelson's doin' it, too."

The powerful dogs launched themselves from the pond in magnificent thrusts, gathering their legs beneath them, springing ridiculously forward. Each time, their mouths snapped shut vainly upon thin air. But each time they came nearer, leaving the cattails waggling from sloshings in the water.

At long last, the dog named Bean found his mark, shredding into the reeds and bringing forth the first dark husk. He chomped down on it in the water, but Charlie screamed at him, "Bring it here, boy. Bring it to me."

Bean took the thing to shore, shaking and wetting them again, depositing it neatly into Charlie's grasp. "I want one," each girl said. "Charlie. Make them get us one like that, too."

"Can't do anything. You've just gotta wait for Nelson to start getting 'em."

Sure enough, on the next try, Nelson did, stripping one down, then dashing about proudly, as if he'd captured a prize. "Here, boy." Charlie clapped his hands. "Here."

In no time at all, an adequate number of cattails had been collected, and each dog and child amused himself with several. The frivolous girl pretended to juggle, tossing two pods above her head and proceeding to catch them. Charlie broke his apart and peered inside, fascinated by the delicate clocklike shapings inside. Sarah walked toward them all, unable to hold herself back from the gathering as the girl in denim tore hers apart piece by piece, sending seedtufts sailing about her head in great clumps.

"You've gotten them all in your hair," Sarah said, still laughing as she came upon them. "You're covered up."

"Oh," Charlie said, giving a start as if he'd been caught doing something he shouldn't. "We're only doin' what the dogs are doin', fetching cattails and tearing 'em up for fun."

"I can see that."

"This here's my cousin," Charlie said, pointing to the child in the OshKosh overalls. "Her name's Iris."

"Hello, Iris."

"And my other cousin, Sue."

"I'm juggling," Sue said. "See?"

"You two here for Thanksgiving dinner?"

"Yep," Iris informed her. "We come to Charlie's every year. Dad always said spending a family day meant spending a day on ground where the cousins could run."

"Not supposed to be at the pond, though," Charlie said matter-of-factly. "Dad said not to come anywhere close to a place where we might be botherin' you."

Sarah smiled, already knowing what the answer to her question would be. "Did old Will let you and your cousins do things like this on a holiday?"

"Always," Charlie said.

"Well, then I will, too."

"Look at them," Iris hollered. "Just would you look at those crazy dogs?"

Nelson and Bean had played tug-of-war with one particular cattail until it exploded, drifting clear in to snuff their licorice-shine nostrils. Nelson had given up to sneezing and Bean chewed upon the spoils, happily teething as the seeds attached to his ears, his eyes, and, most impressionably, his chin. As he went merrily along, the beard on his jowls grew longer and longer, while the four of them sat in the wheatgrass—Sarah, too, just enjoying it all—and rocked with glee.

"He's Santa Claus," Sue said.

"No he's not. Santa Claus is our dad," Iris said.

"You mean it? You mean Dad is the *real* Santa Claus? He's the one who goes visiting all those kids?"

"Shut up, Iris," Charlie said. "No sense confusing her."

"Bean is Santa Claus," Sue said. "He's got the nicest beard I've ever seen."

That morning, for the minutes—the half-hour—that cattails flew, Sarah became as a child again, remembering long-ago days spent at this very pond, watching skippers glissade in tiny wrinkles across the surface, or digging her toes into the mud.

"I've got a new shell for my collection," Charlie told her. "Dad brought it for me when he went to a fishing meeting in Oregon. It's big and curled like an ear and when you hold it to your head, you can hear the sea."

Charlie's words flung her to a time in her life when she'd possessed a shell in which she could hear the ocean. She remembered holding it against her head, remembered the roaring, remembered that, hearing it, she'd known. In the instant, she felt again her own faith as a child, the faith that asked no questions and, in its innocent freedom, knew no boundaries.

When had she started asking the questions? When had she started doubting that an ocean sound could come from a shell, or even wondering how? She sat with knees tucked beneath her chin again, laughing with the children on that morning, overwhelmed, not able to grasp the simple faith again, yet knowing its importance, knowing it to be something larger than that place, or than herself.

"Are you gonna do a pulley bone today?" Charlie asked, as if he'd almost read her mind. "We're all eating lots of turkey so we can find it. Dad says whoever finds it gets to pull it with him and make a wish."

"That's right," Sarah said. "Pulley bones do bring on wishes. I suppose we'll have wishes, too." At the thought of Thanksgiving turkey, she recalled the sweet potato pie she'd left baking in the oven. "Oh, my goodness!" she said, hefting her skirts to her knees and bounding to her feet, dislodging another cloud of cattail parachutes. "I've left something on to burn."

The cousin Sue stared toward the store. "Don't see any smoke comin' out the windows yet."

Such a large crowd came to dine at Maudie Perkins's place, Sarah had to park the car clear back on Person Street. "Who are all these people?" she asked Maudie as she handed over the perfectly arranged relish tray.

"Just plain country folks who wanted to come take a peek at you," Maudie said, sincerely amused. "Never had so many people call me up and tell me they didn't have a place to eat in all my life. About noon yesterday, I was ready to pick up and move the whole blessed event over to Dora Tygum's Caddisfly Inn. Let Dora and Kimmy Jo get *paid* for doin' all this cooking and serving."

"Maudie, if you've got too many, you should've told me. I don't have to eat a fancy dinner with anybody."

"Nonsense, child. If you didn't come, half these other folks wouldn't either. That'd leave me cooking up a feast for nobody but Harvey and me. That'd be the worse thing of all."

The table had five leaves and ran all the way from the south end of the dining room to the north end of the sitting room, where Maudie played the piano. Crockery from seven prospering Star Valley families arrayed the table, lent or brought in for the occasion, and Maudie placed serving spoons in her display of vegetables, soufflés, and casseroles, enough to provision an army. "I'll fill the glasses," Sarah said. "How many glasses do we need?"

"I'd reckon about thirty-five," Maudie said, clucking with satisfaction. "I've got 'em, though. Had to borrow glasses and plates and dinner knives from the potluck stash at Morning Star Baptist Church. Pastor Owen had to lug 'em all over here in his pickup truck."

Maudie set about cutting pies against the hour they'd be served. Prentiss Smith and Tuck Krebbs had already challenged each other to a turkey-leg eating contest and had placed ten dollars a piece on it. As Sarah broke open two ice bags and began to set about her chore, she listened to snatches of idle talk from the other room.

"Will you share your bread recipe, Beulah?"

"Did you know Harvey and Charlie Egan are driving over the pass to the tractor pull in Idaho next weekend? Did you hear they've added an extra fifteen minutes to the bus stop at Jenkins' Building Supply?"

"Remember last year when that driver took off with Lisa Jo Owens's baby asleep in a back seat? Greyhound folks say they're extending the stop because of it."

Sarah walked into the room with a tray full of ice-filled glasses and they all got quiet. Thirty-four of them stood and found their places and would've stayed tight-lipped throughout the meal if not for Tuck and Prentiss going after the legs on the turkey carcass.

"On your mark, get set, go!" someone shouted, and the two grown men began to jam meat into their mouths like fiends, snarfing competitively the way dogs do, or the many coyotes that howled from up past Taggart Point.

"Come on, Tuck!" half the folks shouted.

"Get a move on, Smith!" hollered the other half. "Eat! Eat! Eat!"

Harvey Perkins kept an eye on his stopwatch, waiting

for the first man to raise a clean bone. "Yah!" roared Prentiss as he lifted his high over his head, and Maudie's guests applauded. "You've done it. Pass the ten bucks, Tuck Krebbs. He won it off you fair and square."

The money changed hands. Crockery began to change hands, too, mashed potatoes piled high atop the bowl like meringue, cranberry relish, beans and corn, sweet crusty rolls, with squash prepared in every way, shape, and form. Sarah figured the dishes must've passed well over two miles apiece by the time Carol Mortimer stood to clear the massive table and Maudie brought in cups with coffee. "You read much up there in New York City?" Beulah Hardaway asked her. "After all the studying you did in my class in high school, I hate to think you aren't reading the classics."

"What color is the Statue of Liberty?" Prentiss Smith leaned forward in his chair, the ten-dollar bill still hanging out of his shirt pocket, enthralled.

"Does New York City have escalators in all its stores?" Francis Beery waited, mesmerized, for Sarah's answer.

"They got dairy cows anywhere near there?" Tina Ankeny asked.

Sarah answered their questions as best she could. Eventually, they moved to topics of interest they considered much more pertinent.

Beulah Hardaway, who'd gone to the Gai-Mode Beauty Salon and had commissioned a fresh permanent wave for just this occasion, sat with coffee cup balanced on one knee. "Heard about the birthday party the Roices are giving next week? Jim and Vic have a skating party planned." Red-faced, as if she'd just realized something, she glanced directly at Sarah, then pointedly turned away. "Saw Jim driving by just the other day to see if the ice was freezing on Greybull Pond. Those kids're bringing sticks, pads, pucks. Heard tell they've rented a net and're planning a full-fledged game down there on the twenty-eighth."

"We've been working for years to get the county to put up a warming hut down there," Carol Mortimer commented. "Those kids'll come in crying about numb toes for sure."

"Jim says they're gonna start a fire in a trash barrel and serve hot dogs with a whole potful of hot chocolate," Harvey interjected.

"Eric's invited," Tina Ankeny said. "He and Charlie Roice are best friends."

Of course, Beulah'd set the conversation along this course for a reason, Sarah surmised. She couldn't figure why Beulah Hardaway would comment on such a thing, though, except to gauge some slight reaction from her at the mention of Jim Roice's everyday life. The date stuck in Sarah's mind, however; there was something slightly discomfiting about that particular day for the party, the twenty-eighth day of November.

As the others candidly gave their opinions on the new parking lot at the Mormon stakehouse and the rare holstein hoof disease and Charlie Roice's new Bauer hockey skates, the date became veritable in her memory. November twenty-eighth. Thanksgiving Day in Laramie. The day she'd walked alone to Ivinson Memorial and had given birth. The day Doc Levy hadn't come.

Even as Maudie's other guests settled in for a long, relaxing afternoon beside the fire, Sarah fidgeted. Certainly, surely, she shouldn't be thinking of Jim's son's birthday, thinking this day marked the same day as her child's. She had no right to even ponder. But the files old Will had maintained began to take on untimely significance. She felt as if her heart might pound clear out of her chest.

"Tell me something," she said, interrupting about three of them talking at once. She knew her question would seem ungainly, that everyone would talk about it for weeks, but now, no matter how impetuous she appeared, Sarah needed to know.

"How long were they married before Charlie was born?"

"Who?"

"What?"

"Why?"

"Who got married? When?"

"How long were Jim and Victoria Roice married before their little boy was born?"

An entire, silent room full of folks stared at her. She might as well have asked something idiotic, like, On which side of the cow might I find its udders?

"Oh, Sarah, didn't you know?" Beulah asked. "Charlie Roice is adopted. Those two married at the justice of the peace in Afton one Friday and brought that baby home the next."

"Goes to show how long you've been away from this town," Francis Beery commented offhandedly. "Everybody talked about it for months."

Sarah gripped the side spindles of Maudie's chair and sat in bleak, white-fisted silence.

"Strange story it was, too. Even though you weren't in town, you ought to have known about it," Carol Mortimer expounded. "Those two tied the knot just a week or two after your mother died."

"They seem happy enough, don't you think?" Prentiss Smith asked all of them. "I mean, considering."

"Never could figure why that boy was so hell-fire ready to start a family," Beulah said. "Seems he would've wanted a year or two to enjoy his new bride first. Guess it's worked out in the long run, though. It's been awful hard on Victoria, not being successful at having her own."

Sarah stood, gingerly took her coffee cup to the kitchen, and set it aside. She glanced over her shoulder at her hostess, hoping Maudie wouldn't notice her hand jangling the cup. "It's been a nice holiday, Maudie," she said, "but I must go. There's work to do over at the store."

"Where are you going in such a rush?" asked Prentiss Smith as he followed her in.

"I've got files waiting on me," she said offhandedly. "Paperwork that I've laid to the side too long." She hurried to explain it so they wouldn't think her abrupt departure curious. "What with opening the store and all . . ."

Tuck Krebbs walked into the kitchen at that exact moment and rummaged around in his pocket for his pouch of pipe tobacco. "Did I hear what you said, Sarah Hayden? Did I hear you're reopening the store?"

"I am," she said, although the store was the farthest thing from her mind. "It'll still be a few days, though. I've got an amount of work to do to get it ready."

"Well, why didn't you tell us two hours ago?" Tuck jabbed his pipe stem at her and grinned. "Maudie wouldn't've had to feed near this many people if you'd just announced it first thing when you walked in the door."

12

Sarah climbed to the attic again. The kerosene lantern she'd transported nights before waited on the ledge, the match tin laying at an angle, as if she'd just left it.

She had a need, for the first time in years, to sense old Will still near her. She struck match against grain and watched the head set to spark, raised the chimney on the lamp, and adjusted the wick. She touched match to cloth and the lantern brought him to her, and living liquid light, as it set forth pools of amber across the desk where, as a child, she'd watched her father laboring.

She'd long since sorted through every file in Will's fruit and citrus crates. In her haste to procure a set of business files for Rita Persnick, she'd gotten them into disorder . The *Q*'s began even before the *F*'s.

In one particular crate, Sarah'd left personal files, items she'd decided might be of private value, as she'd categorized with her idea of making a fast departure. She dug through gardening notes and passed Blythe's denture file, all the while admitting—as resignation seized her—that she might've missed this, might've let it all be shoved over into a rubbage bin, if she'd left Star Valley upon her prearranged schedule.

She thumbed through each tab and scrawled label until she found the one she searched for. "Sarah's Baby," it read in Will's strong, slanting script.

Her dread grew. She didn't know if she dared open its pages. She didn't know why she hadn't opened it long ago. She'd assumed it contained nondescript documents, her health records from Ivinson Memorial maybe, but nothing more.

She carried the unopened Smead folder to the desk, settled into the chair, and stared at it as its flawless surface lay ringed in perfect, dancing light.

"Just suppose Will kept this file because he knows my son," she whispered, preparing herself for the idea. "Just suppose."

Hands shaking, she flipped the file open.

Even though she'd prepared herself for this, what lay inside jolted her, a set of official-looking papers from so long ago, and signed in her very own hand.

Sarah lifted the first document and held it in two fists, her eyes dry, but, still, emotion causing the letters to swim. Here they were, the health records from her doctor, the personality profile by the Wyoming Parenting Society, plus an information sheet she'd never before seen on the baby: "Seven pounds eleven ounces. Twenty inches long. Time of birth. Date of birth. 6:12 P.M. November 28, 1985." As if the weights and lengths opened a passage before her, Sarah voyaged to a far-off place, and a place that had never been far away at all, her heart's abode, the strong and tender dwelling where, still, still, she cradled her child.

The pages and facts before her mixed in bitter congru-
ence with Sarah's recollection. She leafed to another document and found it an oddity, the relinquishment paper
she'd signed under the witness of Dr. Sam Levy and his
nurse. Someone had torn the paper apart piece by piece
as if to destroy it. Someone had then bound it together
again with great attention to detail and a good amount of
tape. This job had been done so well, Sarah could read
every word of the state's legal compliance, and her own
unsteady endorsement at the bottom as well.

What would Will have wanted with this? And where
could he have gotten it?

The final credential in Will's mysterious folio answered
several questions and made her ask many more. Word by
word, she read the recount and tried to comprehend it.
Word by word, the recognition of her loss and gain swept
over her like breakers sweep then ebb upon a shore.

Sarah made her way through three times, sentence by
sentence, before she buried her face in her hands and
absorbed it, never crying, feeling the bittersweet affliction of truth. As night came on, she sat alone, picturing a
baby's face. In her mind, she saw his perfect, new-made
feet, his hands with nails like tiny quarter moons.

How long ago the morning seemed, the morning she'd
spent with Charlie Roice and the cousins and the fly-away
dandelions. How recent seemed the day she'd counted his
fingers, smelled his hair, pondered what sort of child he'd
be, and how he'd grow.

This day has changed me, she thought. *This day has
changed me forever.*

She put the papers into the folder and slipped it back
where it belonged.

She'd wait now, because the truth scared her as much
as it overjoyed her. Sarah'd wait until her soul couldn't
bear to wait more. Then, when the waiting became
unbearable, she'd ask Jimmy. He'd know. He'd tell her.

°   °   °

Seemed like all the residents of Star Valley sat around waiting for Greybull Pond to freeze clear through. Once winter set in and snow began to encrust the ground, boys from all over Lincoln County started tape-wrapping their hockey sticks and sharpening their skates. The Lincoln County parks and rec department kept two old nets back at the courthouse in Afton and, every year about this time, a mother or two would volunteer to bring them out and repair them.

The waiting was a slow process. One day, the pond would be unobstructed, visited heavily by familiar birds that flew along the watercourses. The next, a thin film of scalloped glass would appear at its edges, trapping the last of the skippers and mud insects inside gilded bubbles beneath the shallows.

The geese, mallards, and mergansers didn't sojourn in quite the established numbers that had flocked to this place before. Gone were the dark, slim silhouettes of herons that swooped low to catch fingerling trout or minnows.

Then, seemingly overnight, it happened. The circle closed. Tiny veins and rivets appeared below while, above, the ice began to glisten, its unmarred surface beckoning like a friend, almost saying, Come. Slide. Skate while I'm new, while I'm yours and no one else's.

Three days after full icing, county drivers ran a truck on the veneer, making certain, with tons of county road gravel and steel, that the ice held. The next morning, Greybull Pond was covered with skaters, young and old alike, spinning, racing, falling down. They hadn't been on their skates for three full seasons, and it showed now as they took matters in hand, stumbling out once, twice, before they got their legs about them. At one end of the pond, a stick and puck practice broke out immediately. At the other, a mother held her toddler's hand, showing how to push a plastic chinking bucket along for balance. And everybody on the ice talked about Charlie Roice's upcoming birthday party.

"Gonna play a real game!" Brad Dilger yelped as he feinted a pass across the pond.

"It'll be just like the games we played at the end of the season in Jackson last year," Joey Sikes bellowed.

"They gonna call penalties and make us sit in a box?" asked Eric Ankeny.

"Of course. Charlie's dad's gonna ref. He's gonna call *everything*."

"Checking, too?"

"I dunno. How can they call checking when there's no sideboards?"

"You check somebody, you land head first in the snow. That's your penalty."

Charlie Roice was, perhaps, the proudest boy in John Fremont Elementary School. The party, when it came, brought out Lincoln County kith and kin from thirty miles around. Parents came without planning and never left, joining in on the refereeing or cheering from the bench beside the fire.

Victoria kept treats coming—warm cocoa and grilled hot dogs, which no one wearing hockey helmets could quite figure how to eat. "Happy birthday, Charlie," everyone shouted as they munched on hot dogs or chips and heaped a vast assortment of presents on a table. "Hope you like this, Charlie." "Hope this makes you well-pleased."

"Love you, Charlie," Victoria said as he lay in the snow and she finished buckling his new set of goalie pads. "You happy?"

"Happier than anything," he said as he stood up and dusted himself off.

"Charlie. Get out here," somebody hollered. "First period's already started."

"Gotta go, Mom." He pulled on his second mitt.

"Fine. Get on out there."

"Mom." He stopped, turned toward her, and hesitated. "Thanks."

"You're welcome, son."

He glissaded upon the ice with the mastery of the past four days' practice, his stick moving fast and always opposite his forward leg. Someone pitched him the puck. "Hey, Charlie! Let's see if you can shoot this year!"

"Sure I can shoot." He hauled back and walloped the thing as hard as he could, groaning as it ricocheted off the post and slid past the outside of the net. Brad Dilger shot next, Charlie rushed in on defense, and, before they knew it, the full-fledged game they'd long anticipated had broken out.

"Pass it here."

"Way to block it, buddy."

"Get some lumber on it, Roice."

"I'd better get out there and referee." Jim did away with the last of his hot dog. "They've been waiting for this day ever since Greybull started freezing. It's easy to see they're not willing to wait longer."

Jim skated onto the ice, too, tugging on warm gloves as he went. Victoria watched him go. His neck was tan to a point, then white to mark his latest trim from George Peart. His ears shone red, lucent in the sun and cold. As he reached to pull on his polar fleece cap, she thought of how Jim's hair had thinned over the years, how she'd long loved his hair, the shape of his head, his expressions, the movements of his body.

Deftly, he jumped over someone's failed slap shot and blew the whistle that hung about his neck. "Okay. The ref's here. Side off, everybody. Let's name teams and get started the way we're supposed to start."

"We're the Blackhawks."

"We're the Lightnings."

"I'm right wing."

"I'm goalie."

"No, Charlie's goalie. It's his birthday and he just got the pads."

"Get over there, Brad. You're the center."

"We're doing the face-off, Mr. Roice."

Sticks hit the ice. Boys skated in circles. Jim dropped the puck in the midst of it all and boys, skates, sticks started flying.

"Shoot. Shoot. Rebound! Get the rebound—"

"He iced it. Call that. He iced it."

"Watch my wrist shot."

Slam went the puck and Jim vaulted over it again, skating hard to keep up with the passel of kids.

One by one, as the other parents became involved in the game, Victoria's duties dwindled. She moved next to the fire, viewing the scene on the pond through tendrils of ash and rising heat. "Great party idea," someone said. "Look at all those kids."

"The little kids or the big ones?" Victoria asked.

"Both."

"Ah, dads and little boys. They're always happiest when they're playing with one another." But she said the words without feeling them. Even at this moment of celebration, Victoria's uncertainty survived. She saw the game as if she weren't there, as if she watched it projected from some dark, primitive place.

"Shoot it. Shoot it." Brad Dilger's mother screeched.

At that precise moment, Brad shot and scored.

"Score!" Jim shouted from the ice.

"He did it. He did it." Mrs. Dilger leapt off the bench and danced around as if she'd just watched her son score in the Stanley Cup play-offs.

Victoria poured herself a mug of cocoa and stood back, where no one could see. She pulled a small bottle of peppermint schnapps from her coat pocket and saluted nobody. She kept the schnapps hidden for just these times, times of celebration, when the darkness wouldn't go. Victoria dumped a good amount of the bottle into the cocoa, pocketed it again, and stirred with one finger.

Mariah Dilger. Pat Sikes. Tina Ankeny. Victoria matched mothers with their skating offspring. In every case but her own, they resembled one another.

She coveted their resemblance. She coveted their peace, the fact that they could sit on the bench today and be satisfied. She knew herself, disliked herself, recognized her own dissatisfaction with something practical and good.

On the ice, someone else scored. Victoria held her mug high and toasted nobody. She'd taken her temperature four hours ago. Perhaps during the next hours, she'd ovulate. As she stood rinkside, watching the play through smoke and soot, she remembered a hundred other times like this, times she'd stood alone anticipating the workings of her body. She didn't see the sky, the players, the presents any longer. She saw paths, courses, possibilities within herself. For the hundredth time, as the schnapps began to warm her, Victoria's hopes soared.

She started off to walk the circumference of the pond, wanting to watch this game from a different angle, from a separate place. As she rounded the corner through the winter woods, she saw a woman settled on a log, her raggwool cap pulled low over blonde hair, her arms wrapped around her knees. "Sarah Hayden," she said.

The woman on the log turned face full toward her. "Hello, Victoria."

An awkward silence invoked itself between them. Victoria found herself annoyed by the slight sense of invasion she felt at Sarah Hayden's presence.

"Just on a long walk," Sarah said, as if she felt she had to explain something. "Couldn't help watching. It's been a long time since I've seen a hockey game the likes of this one."

"I imagine you played in a few yourself."

"Oh," Sarah said. "I did. Jimmy was always—"

She stopped; the awkward silence came again. A black-billed magpie flew with white flickering wings, as his *yak yak yak* reverberated through the ancient, creaking evergreens.

"Everybody in town's been talking about this party," she said instead, changing the subject.

"Everybody in town talks about everything."

Sarah turned away and began drawing circles in the snow with a stick. "That's one reason I left. Couldn't stand it."

"Some people want that," Victoria said. "Some people like being talked about."

"I didn't."

"You can talk about Jim if you'd like. I don't mind."

Sarah rose and dusted snow off the seat of her britches. "It's like coming back in time, coming here," she said. *It isn't Jim I want to talk about. It's Charlie.* But she had no right and Sarah knew it. "I'd better go."

"You want to know how I fell in love with Jim Roice?" Victoria asked. "It was the day we all rode the school bus to Teton Village to go skiing."

"That long ago?"

"I've always been a better skier than most of my friends. Seemed like every girl in the junior class followed me to Upper Rock Springs. One of the girls lost control and almost fell off the side. Jim came along and helped her back up where she needed to be."

"Where was I that day? I don't remember."

"Doesn't matter where you were," Victoria said. "Everyone told me about you. Sarah Hayden. The girl Jim Roice had been in love with since he'd been in dungarees."

Sarah said it again, smiling. "Everybody talks."

"He's stronger than you think he is, Sarah. You may look at him and see a man who's in the same place he was nine years ago. I look at him and see a man who's fought to the very depths of his soul for pride and simplicity. He's often surprised me. Holding on isn't without its cost, as you well know."

Two well-padded boys slid across the ice toward them, entangled.

As the boys scraped toward her, Sarah squared her shoulders, looking somewhat frightened. "I need to talk to him, Victoria. Would you ask him to come to the store?"

Victoria stared at her as if she was crazy. "You want me to tell my husband to see you?"

"It's important," Sarah said, "or I wouldn't dare ask."

"Won't tell him a thing," Victoria said. "You talk to my husband alone, you'll have to do it without me knowing."

"Checking," Joey Sikes called. "Eric's checking me." They both landed helmet down in a snowbank along the shore.

"He must come tonight. This won't keep longer."

Jim raised the whistle to his mouth and blew. "End of first period. Time for cake and presents."

Victoria turned back to Sarah. "He didn't love me for a long time after you left Star Valley. He asked me out to the Spud Drive-In all that summer and I went, full aware I was his second choice and everyone knew it."

"Vic?" Jim called out through the timberland. "It's time for cake."

Victoria didn't answer her husband. Instead, she turned to the woman, not so young anymore, who stood ready to disappear into the forest. "Told him once, right at the beginning, that I wouldn't take second fiddle to anybody. By the time me and Jim got married"— she pulled up her parka hood and tied it beneath her chin as if she'd been walking a long way—"he only wanted me. He hasn't wanted anyone else since, Sarah. He hasn't thought about you at all."

*   *   *

At Victoria's words in the forest, Sarah wished she could disappear as vapors vanish, or a spirit. Instead, she left Victoria and kept to the trees, slipping away from the babel of the party into the thickets. Sounds carried across the snow and she could hear the revelry well, a man laughing with a boy, a woman's pleased exclamation at a gift, a circle of voices raised.

"Happy birthday to you . . . You live in a zoo . . ."

She'd known when she began her walk that she would come to this place.

She broke trail now, going back to Hayden's General Store a different way than she'd approached. In her father's Sorel pacs, she plowed through deep, dry snow. As she walked, she stepped into a clearing and, to her surprise, alarmed a small assembly of Canada geese. With great beating of wings, the flock rose, each bird sounding its deep musical honk of warning. She backed up and allowed the birds distance to take flight, watching them rise higher, higher above the clearing before they circled as if to return.

In the cacophony of the geese, Sarah hadn't realized Charlie's party guests had grown silent. Now she knew it, hearing only hushed voices in the distance and the crunching of a person running toward her in the snow. Before she could move on, Jim Roice found her. He stopped short, obviously not expecting to see Sarah. "What are you doing here?"

Sarah felt at once tense and desperate, caught at something, even while an odd feeling of hope settled inside. Despite all the pain between them, when she saw him she always had the sense of finding an old, precious friend. "I'm out walking is all."

"You scared those geese?"

"Yes, Jim. Almost as much as they scared me."

"Came checking for wolves," he said as if she'd asked him his intention exactly as he'd asked hers. "Since Wyoming Fish and Game released wolves in the park, we've been careful. Didn't know what else would stir up a whole gaggle of geese that way."

"Guess a person would," she said, halfway smiling.

"Guess so." He stepped beside her in the clearing, his polar-fleece hat pulled low over his ears. He didn't look at her. Instead, he shielded his eyes with one leather-gloved hand and watched the flock's formation.

"Didn't mean to scare them into flying," Sarah said. "We surprised each other. All of us."

"It's easy to come upon things that surprise you in this place," Jim said.

"Strange." The half smile dissipated. "Never thought that way while I was here."

He shoved his hands into his pockets, looking apprehensive. "You always talk about it in the past tense. You're here now. You could think about it differently."

She bundled her coat tighter around her to ward off the deep cold and turned toward him. Indeed, now she agreed with him. "Sometimes I think it's too late for that. People don't like to let a person change."

"That's a bad excuse. It always has been."

"I'd best get on," she said.

"You've walked a long way."

"Jim, I—" She stopped to measure her words. She didn't think it fair to tell him she'd seen Victoria in the woods and asked to speak with him. She didn't think it fair to tell him she'd been denied. If she'd been Victoria, certainly she'd have made the same stand. But Sarah'd belonged to Jimmy once, wholly belonged, heart and body, first, before either of them had loved anyone else. And, perhaps, despite her leaving and all she'd given away, something bound them together now.

"I know you'll never forgive me," she said.

"Good God, Sarah," he said. "You think we're still at the point of forgiving? I've had an entire life pass since then."

"We shouldn't discuss this now," she said sadly. "You've got a party to attend to."

"We won't ever discuss this." He turned to go.

"Wait. Jim." She touched his arm, but he might've kept walking, might've stepped away from the touch until it became nothing. Instead, he paused, let her hand on his arm detain him.

"What?"

She'd realized that, in his reticence and refusal, he kept the power, kept her at his mercy. An entire life had passed since she'd deserved that, too. "I came out here because I needed to know something from you."

"Really." He made no movement, only watched her, looking grim. "What could you possibly need to know from me, Sarah?"

"Come to the store alone tonight," she said. "I'll ask you then."

"Don't know," he said. "Don't know if I'll be there or not."

"Jim. You owe me that much," she said.

He said, "Don't owe you anything." Then he stepped from her touch and walked away.

13

That night, Jim stepped in through the doorway of the old store, peering inside, smelling dust and wax, feeling as if he'd stepped through some portal into his past. Sarah stood at the register as if she'd been waiting for him, her hair tucked neatly behind one ear, her face pale.

"What is it? Why did you ask me to come like this?" It had been a decade since she'd done anything similar, but neither of them stopped to count now.

"Didn't know if you'd really do this," she said.

"You were waiting for me," he said.

"I couldn't afford not to."

"What is it then?" He didn't bother to hang his coat on the rack. He didn't intend to stay long. "What's so important that you'd do such a thing?"

"Do you have to ask? Haven't you guessed?"

He stared at her.

She waited for him.

Watching her, seeing the agony in her eyes, he did know. Jim's hopes retreated. All was lost.

He walked one pace toward her. "Sarah."

She remained where she stood, protected behind the cash register and a display of Snickers candy bars. "He's my son, isn't he?"

"What on earth would make you think something like that?"

"I found the papers, Jim. The papers my father filed away."

In the corner hung an aged pendulum clock with a face advertising the rich bold taste of Raleigh cigars. It ticked off seconds. Four. Five. Six. An eternity.

"I can't believe you're asking me this."

"Just answer me."

He raised his face to the ceiling and shut his eyes, struggling for composure. He clenched his fists into huge, muscular knots. Sweet heaven, he wanted to hit something.

She came around the counter and leaned on it, making herself vulnerable. "It's why you never asked anything about the baby, isn't it? It's because you've known all along." She didn't dare move forward. "Just tell me, Jim."

He opened his eyes again, knowing full well what his words would do to her, knowing full well the torment he'd inflict. It had come to this, then, between them. The reason he'd prayed, begged, bargained with God. She'd been so hell-fire determined to leave her life with him in this valley. Why had the fates deemed it necessary to bring Sarah Hayden back now?

"Yes, Sarah. Charlie is your son."

The clock ticked.

Outside, the night's storm began as frozen rain, pelting the store's metal roof like shattered glass. Sarah Hayden and Jim Roice stood facing each other, neither moving during the onslaught. Seemed like forever, an eternity, before the clattering dwindled. They stood until it finally began to snow, flakes whorling slowly past the window, then thickening to a moving tapestry of white.

Sarah couldn't speak. She only stood at the opposite end of the store from Jim, her face gone as colorless as the snow outside. "I've been so happy for you," she said. "I've been so happy because you have everything you wanted."

"Does it make any difference how I got those things?" he asked.

"Damn it, Jimmy," she shrieked, leaving the counter and charging toward him. "How could you have had him all this time? All this time I've been—"

He grabbed her wrists, stopped her. "What? What have you been? Feeling sorry for yourself because you remember a cute little baby? No muss, no fuss. Just give birth to a child and go on your merry way."

"I have my regrets."

"What could they be, Sarah? That you couldn't afford the fanciest apartment on Fifth Avenue as soon as you'd have liked? Seems to me you've gotten everything you wanted, too."

"Let me go." Her pain was immense. She raised her drawn face to him. He stood so close she could feel his heart pounding.

He stared down at her. "That's all you've said to me for the longest time, Sarah: 'Let me go. Set me free.'"

He hadn't shut the door properly and the wind caught it now, thrusting it open, the cold air and the snow rushing in to brace them. He felt himself go taut against her and hated himself for it, his muscles reacting to her proximity without his conscious bidding. Her breath caught in her throat. He heard it distinctly.

When she spoke at last, her words came racked with pain. "All this time you've had him." Against her, he felt so solid, so real, when reality, solidity, had eluded her for so long. She'd run from him once to find it.

He felt the keen agony as sharply as she. "Yes. I've . . . we've . . . had him." That's all he said, but in few words he clued her to everything; his regrets, his discoveries, his remembrances.

Sarah raised her face to his. "Does Victoria know she's raising my son?"

The clock still ticked its irrevocable tempo from the corner. The door remained open. Remnants of the winter storm billowed in, snow drafting in circles across the floor. Jim moved to shut the door, thanking the fates that he'd found a reason to step back from her, to put distance between them. "No," he said without glancing back. "And if she found out, it would kill her."

"Why? Because it's me?" A pretentious question to ask, but one Sarah wouldn't shy away from. The folks in town had spread an awful amount of gossip during the past years.

"No," he said. "Because it's me. Because Charlie's my son, too, and she has no child."

"Dear sweet heaven."

"I can't stay, Sarah. They'll be wondering where I've gone."

"Tell me first," she said. "Tell me how it happened."

"You read the file."

"Yes, I read it."

"I wanted old Will to burn those papers. Once, he said he would."

"The papers said someone complained. Someone thought his adoptive parents had hurt him."

"Yes. He went for his immunizations and he had bruises all over his little legs, Sarah. He was only four months old and they had hit him so hard they made bruises."

"But they were a good family." It all came back to her, how she'd picked them, the lists, the names, the descriptions: a bank officer, a nurse, in a pretty little house with flowers on the porch.

"Everything isn't always as it seems, Sarah. He didn't go to the family you picked."

"He didn't?"

"No. Doc Levy's brother was a lawyer in Colorado. They had someone else picked out altogether, a man who'd offered them a great deal of money to find him a son. It's done from Laramie, Sarah. Wyoming adoption laws are some of the most lenient. And people like Dr. Levy know exactly how to get around the laws that do exist."

She felt as if she might crumble from the burden of it all. She backed away from him and sat down slowly in an old wicker chair that had stood in the corner for as long as she remembered. "He didn't go to them. He didn't go to the people I picked. When I thought they'd be so right."

"Levy destroyed all record of the people you'd chosen. When Wyoming Social Services started looking, no one even knew who they'd been."

Sarah'd fought long and hard to keep from seeming vulnerable to Jim Roice. But this was too much. "Oh my God, Jimmy. They just *took* him. They never cared, did they? They only wanted money when I thought I'd found the best place for him."

It was the first time Jim Roice had seen her intentions, had seen how she'd prepared for the baby's future, and at what cost. He'd always thought she'd given their child to anyone who was willing. He'd always blamed her for that. As he heard her speak now, he realized they'd both been young then, hurting, set on finding their own ways, and so gullible.

"When Colorado authorities began investigating the whole thing, they traced it back as far as the hospital. A nurse remembered you. The hospital contacted the Wyoming Parenting Society and the baby"—*The baby*, he said. *When the person he spoke about was Charlie*—"became a ward of the state."

She thought of Charlie again, of how carefree he'd been as he played at the pond. Even now—just from this afternoon at the party—Sarah heard the melody of Charlie's laughter. Even now she remembered the miraculous symmetry of his little body, his tiny mouth searching to nurse, his eyes alert and blue and wavery clear like starlight through a depth of moving water.

A powerful ambiguity struck her, an emotion so all-encompassing it threatened everything about herself she'd known. She felt at once great joy and incredible pain, fire and ice—the pain to see what she might have been a part of and hadn't, the joy to see him happy, growing, and whole.

"How did they find you?" she asked.

"The six-month grace period for the adoption wasn't over yet. They didn't know whether to risk placing him in another home. They came looking for you only a week after your mother died," he said. "Instead, they found old Will."

"Dad." She whispered his name as if he stood in the room with them, amidst trappings of the store he'd kept for six decades.

"Victoria and I'd already talked about getting married. We'd been dating almost ten months. When your father waylaid me at the store one morning and told me the Wyoming Parenting Society had called him, I knew I could intrigue her with the idea of adopting a baby. She'd always been intrigued by babies, even then." Even before she suspected she couldn't bear any of her own.

"She thinks you're both adoptive parents."

"Yes. And so does Charlie."

"Sweet heaven."

"It's the hardest thing I've ever done, Sarah, next to seeing you go. I pretend I'm his adoptive father when he's my own flesh, my own blood."

"Does he ask about his parents? Does he want to know where we are?"

"Yes. But there isn't a way for him to know. When your father found out, he tore up that relinquishment paper you signed. As long at that paper isn't on file with the state, there's no record of who you even *are*."

"He taped it back together. It's in the attic." As had been his Last Will and Testament, amazingly straightforward, leaving everything to her, never mentioning anyone else. Sarah walked from aisle to aisle in her father's store, touching things, disturbing dust. "This is difficult," she said.

Jim said, "He's wanted to know about it, Sarah. He's wanted to know why his real mother would have him and give him away."

She took the wound he inflicted wordlessly. Instead, she said, "So my father became acquainted with his grandson."

"Charlie spent much time at this store. Old Will loved him as much as I do, maybe more. He was a part of you, Sarah. He was the only part your father could hang on to."

On the cereal row, she found where a mouse had chewed into a box of Cream of Wheat. She picked it up to throw it away, sending tiny white nodules bouncing across the floor.

"It was easy because I never gave up my parental rights to him. When the state investigated and we asked that doctor about it, he tried to show me a legal advertisement he'd run for one issue in *The Pinedale Round-Up*, three counties over."

"Doc Levy didn't need to run a legal to find you. I gave him your address, phone number, and all."

"Told you he knew how to get around the rules. Funny thing is, if he'd contacted me while you were pregnant, I would've relinquished my rights to any part of your baby. Then, I wanted to kill something. Ignoring him would've been the next best thing. Giving credence to a baby meant giving credence to what you'd done to me, Sarah. I would've gladly handed him over."

She found another cereal box with holes. "Dadgum mice," she said. "I'm going to have to get a cat."

Her statement gave him pause. He moved from past into present. "A cat? Why on earth would you need a cat?"

"I'm staying for a while," she said.

"How long?" he asked. "How long are you staying?"

"Don't know exactly," she answered. "I've decided to open the store for business."

They heard a dog bark, far away. The screen door squeaked and a small knock sounded. Through the beveled glass, they saw the cowlick and bangs of one tow-haired boy.

"It's Charlie," he said.

"Jim."

He watched her swallow, watched her pointedly set the cereal on the shelf. For one brief instant, their eyes met and held in commiseration.

"What are we going to do?" she asked.

"We aren't going to do anything," he said. "Nothing will change, Sarah. It mustn't. We won't act as if anything is different."

"But I don't know if I can—"

"You don't have any choice. You made your choices long ago. With him. With me."

"You're being cruel."

"I hope it's paid you, Sarah," he said, knowing she'd read the grim anger, the sorrow in his eyes. "I hope it's been worth all you've given away."

He opened the door to their son.

The snow in Charlie's hair had already started melting into diamond droplets. "Where did you go, Dad? I was looking for you."

"I came here," Jim said. He ruffled the boy's hair, making certain to smooth the cowlick.

Charlie turned to Sarah, his blue eyes filled with

innocence and joy. "Got the pulley bone on Thanksgiving. Got the longest end, too, so I got to make my wish."

"Lucky you," Sarah said, her own eyes watery. "I hope it was a good wish."

The little boy turned back to his father. "You've got to come back. Mom's upstairs doing one of her temperature tests with the door locked. It's my birthday and I don't want to watch football by myself."

Sarah moved one step forward, one step.

"I'll come along home," Jim said, glancing once at Sarah. He lay his hand against Charlie's shoulder. "Let's go."

"See you later," Charlie bellowed and waved crazily.

The two walked out into the night, leaving only blue, wet footprints in the snow behind them.

When Sarah'd been a girl, she'd loved watching out the window of her bedroom, through the darkness, seeing light from the Roices' house on the high ridge. She did the same she'd done as a child tonight, staring out the window as the pendulum clock downstairs clicked and made ready to chime midnight.

The snow clouds had moved out hours earlier. Outside, the sky had cleared to perfection, the moon shone like a beacon, the night breathlessly still. Her own window light lay upon the snow in one distorted square. Through the fishbone shapes of the pines and the bare, reaching branches of aspen, she could see Jim and Victoria's house illuminated even at this hour.

What would they be doing together in those rooms? Talking? Making love?

Inside that place, so nearby yet so distant, her child slept.

How like this midnight the one years before, when she'd lain in a bed at Ivinson Memorial, too filled with sorrow and love, too amazed by the baby, to sleep. Never would she forget the length of that night; never would she forget the miracle of his tiny fists curled at blanket's edge, his tiny mouth suckling in slumber.

"Oh, Jimmy," she said aloud to no one as she stood looking out. "He's the only treasure we've ever shared."

Each year, Jim kept a small but adequate fly-tying supply zipped into the front left pocket of his canvas fishing vest. Often, he stopped at water's edge, examining the living flies there, then took out his vice and set to work in place, copying the day's hatch with an unnamed, spontaneous pattern all his own. Other than Jim's streamside concoctions, which often came early in the season, before insects emerged in any marked succession, he didn't bring out the feathers, threads, and dubbing until the boat had been repaired, cleaned for the winter, and strapped tightly beneath tarpaulin.

Tonight, as moonlight ranged over low, snow-burdened roofs, Jim trudged through in pacs and, for the first time this season, brought his apparatus boxes from the barn. He spread the spools and small packets upon the table as Charlie wriggled into the chair beside him; Charlie, who knew most everything about flies, Charlie, Sarah's son.

He must do something with his hands.

Jim attached the vice to the table. With finishing whip in place, he began his first design, wrapping thread the color of an eggshell around the shank of one tiny hook.

"Can I do one?" Charlie asked, his eyes shining.

"You ought to be in bed," Jim said. "It's late. Almost midnight. You've had a big day."

"Just don't want my birthday to end yet," Charlie said. "I'm gonna have to wait again a whole year for it."

Jim smiled at his son. "I'll let you do just one. Watch me first so you can remember."

"Can I do a pale morning dun like you?" Charlie asked, propping his small, bony chin amidst two palms.

"These take a while. Only if your—" He stopped. He had in mind to say *mother*. *Only if your mother will let you*. How odd he should be the one, with his truth-telling, to inflict such pain upon Sarah. How odd that tonight, when he referred to Victoria, the title of mother did not come easily.

"Mom's already in bed," Charlie said. "After you got a phone call and she couldn't find you in the house, said she couldn't see any sense in waiting up."

Jim bent over the fly, working with dun-colored hackle, wrapping the feather over and over again until it splayed in every direction, capturing the shape of a fly's wing whirring, moving so rapidly as to lose all appearance of motion. He finished and scooted his son and his chair toward the vice. Jim kept vigil as Charlie fished the appropriate hook and thread from the shelved box and began to carefully wind.

Outside, the moon moved behind a cloud and, for a few moments, the night darkened. A vague, powerful notion struck Jim Roice. Just suppose, just suppose Victoria knew he'd walked to Hayden's General Store tonight, that he'd gone in search of Sarah. Just suppose she'd be jarred enough to forget the inanity of a different baby, that she'd come suddenly satisfied with the treasures their own lives had dealt them.

Would Charlie tell her tomorrow where he'd found his father?

As the child's fingers wound, Jim silently wished for goodness. His mind traveled. He thought of a day long ago, a day before he'd learned mistrust, disappointment. A time when he and Sarah had first loved each other.

"You think you're something, don't you?" she'd teased him.

"I know I'm something," he told her as they tromped

through the grassy marsh beside the waterwheel, cold
mud fingering up between his toes.

"Don't know how you think we're gonna catch fish like
this."

"That's why I'm teaching you, Sarah. There's all sorts
of things you can do if only you understand the nature of
things."

"I know the nature of things already," she said.

"Not as much as you think." He took her hand and
lead her to the irrigation ditch that ran from Caddisfly
Creek on to her father's property. "See? The cutthroat
come downstream here and then get caught up because
of the waterwheel. They can go through into the pond
but they don't know it. They stay cornered in this one
stretch of water."

"People do that," Sarah said. "People get caught, too."

Barefooted, he stepped into the water, setting up one
turbulent cloud of loam beneath the surface. "Takes
patience. Once you've gotten in, hafta wait for all this dirt
to settle." He stood, straddling the stream, while the dirt
he'd stirred filtered down and covered his feet. "You've
gotta be quiet, too, or else they'll hear you."

"Fish hear from underwater?"

"Of course."

"Do I have to do what you're doing at the same time?"
she whispered.

"No," he said, teaching observance as his own father
had taught him. "You watch."

The brook at his feet became clear again. He rolled up
his sleeves and grinned at her, this time not daring to
speak. "Here we go," he mouthed cleverly, then bent at
the waist and eased both hands side by side into the water,
cupping the current. He'd discovered this hole not long
ago, on a morning when his mother had sent him walking
to the store for some salt. The trout hid here, darting in
beneath the root-encrusted overhang and waiting until an

insect drifted by, or until it grew voracious enough to swim again upstream.

He should be watching the water but, instead, he watched Sarah. Beside the channel, she squatted low in her cap-sleeved gingham dress, peering into water as crystal and sheening as her own eyes. "Don't you see a fish yet?"

The dress was one she'd worn since girlhood, one without seams up the bodice, and her growing breasts filled it nearly to the sundering point. Her knees, brown and knobby, poked from beneath the skirt. With one finger, she hooked a strand of yellow tangled hair behind one ear and held it there. He felt the new thing happening in his stomach again, the precipitous yearning that came every time he began to think of Sarah and her body. "Can't look at fish so well when you're sittin' near. I wanna look at you instead."

She rocked back on her heels as if to rise. "You'd best not. Makes me feel all burny inside."

It'd been a good five days since they'd been alone in the haymow, and they were both beginning to feel it. Miller Roice had chosen this inopportune week to rearrange the tack room. He'd worked mercilessly there, stacking pails, looping and fastening ropes, hanging rakes and shovels in descending-size order along the weathered planks. He'd stirred up dust that hadn't been stirred up in thirty years.

Jim knelt toward the water, searching it again. "I'd about give my soul to be loving you right now."

"Can't catch a fish that way," she said, and he knew she was teasing him still. He wondered if her thoughts turned as often as his to the textures of their bodies, to her skin, that felt smooth as arumleaf to his roughened fingers, to her neck, the eloquent length of it that raised and waited, prepared for the trailings of his mouth. Her hands, oh, her gentle hands, how he loved thinking of what they could do to him. "Should've known you were kidding before today," she said. "You just brought me out to distract me is all."

"I did no such thing. Just you wait."

Wait they did and, eventually, a native cutthroat flashed upstream from beneath the shelf of roots and grass. It might've been invisible against the bottom if not for its movement, the flip of tail, the gaping of mouth, the fanning of gills. Jim waited, his hands positioned inches apart, his legs spread wide.

The fish swam between his hands. With the speed of a diving windhover, Jim closed them, clasping them around the sleek buoyancy and muscle that struggled against his hold.

"Got one," he cried, lifting the fish high above the water. Water splashed on his shorts and ran in rivulets down his legs; in great bits of diamond light it fell, spattering against rocks and grass and water.

"Can't believe it!" she hollered, rushing forward. "Jimmy. You did it."

He bent to the surface and released the fish, watching as it flipped sideways and plunged deep, to safety. "Now you come try."

She hiked her skirt and stepped into the ditch in front of him. He touched her waist, showed her where she should bend and, when she did, the whole front of her skirt soaked down into the water. "Silly thing," she laughed, gathering it up and tying it into a huge, dripping knot at her thighs.

"Stand still as you can," he said, wrapping wet arms around her middle, pulling her back against him. "We've gotta let the water settle down again. Fish won't come out to feed if it's muddy."

"Won't do any settling this way," she said. As she turned around to him, her hand fell naturally into his and he stooped to her, finding her sun-dried lips with his own and kissing her.

"Mm-m-m-m." She sighed, closing her eyes.

"It's been too long since I've had you to myself," he said. "Can't stand much more of this."

"If you'd help your father clean out the tack shed, he'd be finished twice as fast."

The silt began to descend upon their feet once more, and together, soundlessly, they waited. When he spoke, Jim watched his breath moving the hair at her ear. "When you bend, Sarah, slip your hands in the water as easy as you'd slip 'em into stockings. Fish sees your hands coming in, it'll spook for hours."

Gingerly, slowly, she lowered cupped fingers into the stream, holding them inches apart to make a passage for trout to swim through.

"Now, you've done just fine," he whispered. "All you've gotta do is stay there until he comes out."

"How long will that take?"

"Could be minutes. Could be an hour. Until one appears, you never know if one's there."

"I can't just stand like this all day long," she whispered.

"You saw me do it."

"It's hurtin' my back."

"Fish'll come soon."

"Suppose you'll make me turn it loose, just like you did."

"Sure I will."

Time passed; the sun changed slightly on the water. Just as Sarah was ready to trudge on out of the water, a long head, a gawking mouth, jutted from beneath the bank.

"There's one," she whispered.

"Okay," he whispered back. "You can get him."

"What do I do now?"

"Wait until he heads upstream. He'll have to swim between your hands. Right when he's gettin' there, grab your hands against each other. Faster than you've ever done it before."

"When? Will you tell me when?"

"Yeah." He eased his mouth up closer to her ear. "Soon. He's almost there."

"Now?"

"No. Not yet."

"Now?"

"No," he whispered. "But almost."

"Jim?"

"Now! Now! Get him. Grab him now."

He saw her hands clamp around the trout. "I've got—" But she started shrieking too soon. The fish wrenched sideways and broke free, ribboning upstream.

"Get back here, you fish," Sarah shouted merrily as she grabbed after it. But as Sarah grabbed, she stumbled and lost her balance. "Jimmy Roice! Confound—" she shrieked as she toppled face first into the water.

"Too late now," he bellowed, sloshing after her and extending a hand. "That scared 'em for sure. After a body goes crashing in on top of 'em, they won't come back for days."

"Shut up," she laughed, reaching for him innocently, then pulling him right back in on top of her.

"Sarah." He splashed full bore into the stream, vest and shirt and all. Took him a full thirty seconds to push himself back up again. "You." He spit brook water out, then shook wetness from his hair all over her.

"Ah!" she hollered once more. "Get off me. I'm drowning."

"Seems to me that's your problem. You pulled me in."

"You wanted to teach me to fish."

Together, they climbed out of the stream, each laughing, each sprawling on the timothy grass, presenting faces and young, fit limbs to the sun. They lay for a long while together, giggling with pleasure. Oh, the joys of first-seen spring, when high-mountain willow buds burst forth in fleshy, green growth. Oh, the joys of first-known love, when innocence and rarity set into play their perfect, simple sequence of hope.

Jim rolled over and sat on his haunches. "I've got an idea."

"Don't know if I can take any more of your ideas."

He crawled to all fours, then stood above her and waited for her to stand, too. "This is one you'll like. Come with me," he said, taking her hand again.

"Where?"

"You'll see."

Stepping high over knotted brambles, he led her to a willow thicket beside the waterway, the lace-edged catkins and unfurling leaves providing just enough cover for their hideaway.

"Used to play house in here," she said, laying one hand against Jim's sopping chest. Indeed, he could still see the remnants of it, an old apple crate once used for a table, a tattered cloth still hanging from a low branch, a rusty tin can filled with dirt and set aside.

The warmth of her hand soaked through to his skin. As the sun baked the ground, he smelled the pungent weediness of the creek shore. "We aren't playing now," he said. Jim held his arms out to her, as he'd been longing to do for days, and she nestled against him.

"What if somebody sees us?" she whispered.

He stroked her sodden hair, held it briefly away from her face with both hands. "No one's gonna find us, Sarah. If anyone comes looking, we'll be quiet as field mice."

"If they find us, they might think we're wicked."

"Don't see how they'd think such a thing, not when we love each other the way we do." He kissed her.

"I know," she said against his mouth, trusting him. "I don't see how they'd think it either."

Between them, their wet clothes clung to their bodies and became nothing. At last, for the first time in days, they gave themselves away to the effortless, wizened bounty of their young, newfound sensuality. A breeze sprang up and brought with it the heady scent of newly grown pine. He unzipped her dress. She helped him with his buttons. He opened his flannel shirt and took her inside it, against him, completely. "There's times I can't get close enough to you," he told her indulgently, whispering against her hair. "There's times I want to stop everything from going along at its own gait. Times I want to say 'Don't you see? Don't you see?' and make everybody in the world wait so they can know what's come into me."

"Oh, Jimmy." He felt several wet droplets roll down his chest. He had no way to know if they came from her hair or if she cried. "Loving you has always been the best thing about this valley."

She lifted her face to him and he saw that, indeed, she'd started crying. Her nose was pink as a globe mallow blossom. She made him smile. "Sarah girl." He said her name as he eased the dress and its cap sleeves down, then held on to her bare shoulders. "Are you afraid now? When you weren't afraid in the barn?"

She nodded, biting her bottom lip like a little girl. "Yes. But not of the things you might think, Jimmy. I'm so often afraid of myself."

That morning was warm, filled with the exuberance of freshly sprouting alfalfa and hawthorn. He'd stooped to his knees and tugged her along, down to the billowy grass, where she silently dropped her dress for him and they intertwined like two shadows.

Jim would long recollect the day, could almost feel it now, as he watched his boy complete the pale morning dun; the remembrance of the sun, the sanctuary, the flock of pelicans that spiraled overhead, changing color—white overwing, dark underwing, white overwing, dark underwing—each time they fulfilled a turn. He would long recall the way she'd reached for his face, her lithe, brown fingers tracing his nose, the line of his jaw, then falling still.

"Makes no difference, does it, if we don't end up like everybody else?" Her mouth fell open slightly as she awaited his answer, and he looked down to see her eyes upon him, replete with him. He lay his hands against her small, well-rounded breasts, feeling her heart, brimming with life, beating there.

"What do you mean, 'like everybody else?'"

"Like the people who always need reassurances, who never want to question if what we each must do has reason, or is right."

"You trust me, don't you, Sarah?" he asked her.

She touched his face again, and he knew she thought of a hundred different times she might've said no. "Of course I trust you," she said, grinning. "I've trusted you ever since you stopped whaling into me with snowballs." Then, with the hands he loved so well, Sarah Hayden reached for his groin, plying him with gypsylike fingers, the way they'd discovered in the haymow before.

14

Jim found Victoria's note on his bureau that night as he emptied his pockets to go to bed. "Prentiss Smith called," she'd scribbled. "Couldn't find you anywhere. Howdy Partner meeting tomorrow. Hayden's General Store."

He read the message twice, folded it accordion-style, and stuck it into his sock drawer.

Not until he sat on the bed beside his wife, untied his shoes, and thumped them on the floor, did he realize that the thermometer lay out of its box beside the lamp. At once, he remembered his son's words in the store: *"Mom's upstairs doing one of her temperature tests with the door locked. It's my birthday and I don't want to watch football by myself."*

Victoria's minutely kept daily chart stood propped on the nightstand, the information for this day scribed carefully in the box marked "November 28." He picked it up and read it.

"Damn," he muttered aloud, seeing what he'd missed. Her temperature had gone up noticeably. An ovulation day.

He leaned over her. "Victoria?" he whispered. "Victoria? You awake?"

She didn't answer.

He stripped down to his shorts, spread back the blankets, and climbed in. He reached for his wife and wrapped his arms around her, but she made no reassuring movement. Instead, she lay taut on the other side of the bed, her back turned against him like a fortress.

"Vic?"

When he heard her steady breathing, he knew she wasn't sleeping.

"Vic. Say something."

"You went to her, didn't you?" she asked from deep inside her pillow. "You walked to the store and spent time with Sarah Hayden."

Until this moment, he hadn't thought to feel guilty. "Yes. I did."

"She came poking around Charlie's party today. What on earth did she want?"

His voice caught. "I can't—" He couldn't explain it to Victoria, who wanted her own baby so badly, who was raising Sarah's son.

She blew one burst of breath from her mouth and rolled away.

"Victoria. It isn't important. Sarah doesn't make any difference at all." He reached for his wife, eager to reconcile with her.

For an instant, one instant, he felt her body remaining firm against him. He cinched powerful arms around her middle, enjoying the familiarity and certainty of his wife, as he lifted her body up and against his. He felt her relent, felt her body ease into compliance, as she turned to him, wrapping her arms around him.

Jim kissed her hard, full on the mouth, his hands roving to places he knew she liked to be touched. "M-m-mmm," she whispered against his face, sliding one of her knees between his to caress his groin. "This is more like it."

He made a muffled, growling sound in his throat and threaded his lengthy fingers through her hair. His tongue delved deeply into her mouth. He eased the satin gown off her collarbone, off her arms, her breasts, her tummy, until finally, finally, they both laughed as they took turns kicking it past her ankles with their feet.

He reached for her left breast and enjoyed it with his hand, feeling it ample and warm inside his grasp. He felt her hands guiding him, cupping his head on both sides and moving it downward.

Jim followed her leading, lowering his head to her nipples. As he took her into his mouth, he thought he felt her twisting, wresting with delight. Oh, but he loved seeing her face when she wanted him! He raised his eyes to watch her, but found her propped halfway up, stretching across the pillow away from him, trying her best to see the clock.

"What are you doing?" he asked.

"Seeing what time it is," she answered.

"What for?"

"Wanted to know if it's too late."

He stopped altogether, raised himself up on one elbow, and stared at her. "Too late for what?"

"You know." She looked at him as if he was an idiot. "Too late for this to mean anything." She gestured toward the temperature chart he'd noticed earlier. "My temperature was already up when I got back from Charlie's party."

He sat up, naked. "Do you want to make love with your husband, or not?"

"Oh yes," she said, glancing once again at the nightstand. "Of course I want to do this. I always do."

"No," he clarified grimly. "Do you want to do this if it's not the right *time*?"

She tilted her head at him like an exasperated bird. "What do you think?"

"I think I'm not in the mood anymore," he said.

"Come on," she said. "Jim. Lay back down."

"I'm going down to sleep on the sofa."

She flopped back in the bed, covering herself with blankets. "This is ridiculous."

"Yes," he said. "I think so, too." He stood up, went downstairs, and pitched cushions off the couch. He tried to make himself a reasonable place to sleep, with only two decorator pillows and one undersized afghan. He closed his eyes against the pain, not liking himself, feeling empty, untouched, unloved.

Sarah had no right to long for her son. Even so, as night grew deeper, her longing came, and with it grieving, regret too powerful for tears. By morning her entire body was spent from the immensity of these things, the significance of her adolescent decision, the vastness of her life in some other place. Just as before, when she'd borne the consequences of her choice, she bore them alone.

The produce she'd ordered would arrive this morning.

She'd scheduled the store's opening for 8 A.M.

Rita Persnick would arrive to show the property for the first time at midday.

She'd scheduled time to meet with Paul Arthur and Rita at the title insurance company that afternoon.

As Sarah climbed down the stairs, she tied on her apron. She unlocked the front door and reached for the CLOSED sign, flipping it around to OPEN for the first time since her father had gone to the hospital to die. Her hand on the sign, she heard the school bus hiss to a stop across the highway. Red lights flashed. Cars braked both ways.

In the embarking crowd of children, she found the

one she sought, lugging his frayed backpack over one arm, his polar-fleece cap shoved recklessly into one pocket. Watching him climb into the bus, she felt a hankering so vast she didn't think she could bear it.

Last night she'd accused Jim of being cruel. She knew very well he was nothing of the sort. It would've been easier if she'd come for her father's funeral and then whisked out on the next plane, never suspecting, never needing to care about this particular boy. Yet, along with the terrifying denial came another thought, an empowering one, steeped in simplicity. Charlie was someone she could, should, love, even as she'd loved him when she held him in her arms so long ago.

As the bus closed its doors, its windows shone, glazed and dripping from the children's sweaty, bundled bodies. Cars sped past. The bus began to pull away. Mittened hands wiped peepholes in the frost. As they did, Sarah saw the array of their faces, the children of this valley as she'd been a child once, wide-eyed, rosy-cheeked, silly with happiness.

She walked back inside the store.

In the days since Thanksgiving, Sarah'd polished the counters and Murphy-Oiled the pine plank floors. She hadn't gotten to trapping mice or dusting shelves yet, both chores sorely needed, in view of the cereal aisle mess she'd found last night.

Sarah grabbed a rag now and began to make do. When she dusted past the canoes and snow shoes to the highest shelves in the camping utensil area, she discovered a pile of pans pushed back into a corner, the cast-iron set, thick with cobwebs and dust. She went for the ladder, climbed it, and pulled the heavy pans out as best she could.

They'd never sold, not since the day Will Hayden had cleaned them and pushed them into the corner the night before she'd left Star Valley for good. Seeing them now, she recounted word-for-word her father's speech as he'd buffed these pans. *"A man never likes to think that what he's spent his whole life providing for his children won't be enough to satisfy them."*

"It isn't what you've provided, Dad. It's me. I feel isolated from everything real."

"It is easy to undervalue whatever is close to home."

Sarah carried the pans to a visible shelf, aiming to sell them. The produce truck arrived. So did the milk truck from Star Valley Creamery. The driver of the Eddy's Bread truck unloaded two shelves of bread, wheat and white, plus an appetizing stock of donuts and pastries. Still, she greeted no customers.

It was while she unloaded and stacked the third crate of cucumbers that Sarah heard the stomping and the strains of a harmonica refrain from the split-log bench on the store's front porch. Strange how the idea of someone using the porch again, of someone marching in to purchase something, set Sarah's heart to pounding. Strange how something that had seemed so routine and ordinary once seemed so incredibly noteworthy this morning.

The harmonica kept playing. No one entered. Somebody banged on the screen and hollered, "Sarah Hayden? You in there?"

Wiping her hands on her apron just as her mother had done a million times, she went to the door and opened it. "Hello? Can I—"

"Howdy, partner," bellowed Ben Mitchum. "Welcome to business in Star Valley, Wyoming."

"What?"

"Howdy, partner," sang out Mrs. Coral Weatherby, who was so old and deaf she didn't realize anybody else had said anything. "Welcome to Wyoming, honey."

Jake Haux sat on the long, low bench beside her and, thumping his foot in rhythm, set forth with his harmonica into a rousing rendition of "Home on the Range."

"Howdy, partner," said Richard Jenkins of Jenkins' Building Supply.

"Howdy, partner," said Mac Johnson, who'd already seen her once this morning to deliver from the creamery.

"Howdy, partner," said Kender Budge, the other part-time waitress from Dora's Caddisfly Inn.

"Howdy, partner," chorused Mr. and Mrs. Lester Burgess from the Pronghorn Motel.

Homer Egan, owner of Egan's Greenhouse and Nursery, presented Sarah with a potted geranium. "Best get it in out of the cold. Won't be much of this thing left if these blooms get frostbite."

"What is this?" Sarah asked, halfway holding the screen door open to them, but not understanding.

Etna Bressler from The Valley Mortuary stepped forward. "This is an official greeting from the Howdy Partner Committee of Star Valley."

"We're brand new," Prentiss Smith chimed in. "Like a chamber of commerce, only better. We all called around and decided to come this morning, seeing as this is the day you opened your door."

"We stop over like this and welcome new businesses to Star Valley," Jack Gwilliam explained.

"But I'm not a new business," Sarah said.

"Might as well be," Ben Mitchum said. "Place has been closed up tight over six weeks. We welcome old businesses under new ownership, too."

That gave Sarah pause. She hadn't stopped to think of herself as the official owner of Hayden's General Store. Perhaps it'd be best to invite everybody in. "If you'll give me a minute, I'll make coffee," she said.

"What?" yelled Mrs. Coral Weatherby.

"She said to come in, Coral," Prentiss yelled back at her. "Said she'd make us all a cup of coffee if we'd be willing to stay long enough."

"I'd *love* coffee," Mrs. Coral Weatherby hollered back across the porch.

Sarah lead the Howdy Partner Committee inside and

placed the geranium beside the cash register. She hurried upstairs to dig out the old aluminum percolator again. "It'll be just a minute," she called down, surprising herself at how pleased she was that they'd come. "We'll have donuts, too. Just got a fresh batch delivered this morning."

The townspeople roamed the aisles, inspecting things. "Place seems just like it did when old Will was here," Lester Burgess said.

"No, it doesn't," his wife disagreed. "It's cleaner. Hasn't been this clean since Blythe was around. And the milk's fresh, too. Go look at it, Lester. It doesn't expire until Tuesday next."

"Would you have a look at these pans?" Richard Jenkins held up one of the cast-iron skillets Sarah'd moved just this morning. "Haven't seen anybody use these since my own grandfather took us camping down near Bridger. He used to fry up a skillet of trout that'd make your stomach bust, they tasted so good."

"I'll make you a fine price on that pan." Sarah came downstairs with a trayload of mugs. "It's been around too long."

Jake Haux had moved inside with his harmonica. Once he finished "Home on the Range," he moved right into the opening bars of "Springtime in the Rockies."

"This reminds me of Thanksgiving at Harve and Maudie's place," Carol Mortimer announced. "It's a good thing didn't all of us make it. You wouldn't have had enough to feed us, even if you *are* a food store. A whole other carload of folks broke down over on Person Street and had to go home. Can you imagine naming a street 'Person Street?'"

"They named it that," Mrs. Coral Weatherby butted in, and everyone thought it rather odd that she'd heard enough to comment now, "because when folks first settled this place, that street was the only street for five miles had a person living on it."

Sarah ran upstairs again and came down with a heavy mitt and the coffee pot. She planned to pour out in the store and leave the pot on the wood stove to stay warm. She didn't realize until she began to serve how many people'd been stamping around her front porch. A strong, callused hand, a familiar hand, picked up one mug and held it forward for her to fill. She glanced up, right into Jim Roice's face. She felt as if somebody'd slugged her right in the lungs. She couldn't catch her breath.

"Jim—"

He didn't look as if he'd slept more than she had. He hadn't shaved. His chin was covered with dark awn, as newly grown and bristly as the head on barley oats.

"I saw Charlie this morning," she whispered. "Saw him gettin' on the bus."

Dora Tygum took a steaming mug and clapped Sarah on the back. "Glad you're in business," Dora said. "Now that your door's open and your milk is fresh, next thing you've gotta take care of is that waterwheel outside. If your dad was still around, he'd've tinkered with it by now and gotten it going."

Desperately, Sarah turned to the woman at her side and spoke up. "Don't know if there's any hope for it, Dora."

"No matter how hard the winter, Will's overshot flume coming into the pond always had enough water to keep that wheel turning. Never seen an inanimate object look so dejected as that wheel looks now. Folks ask who's gonna fix it every time they sit down for supper at the Caddisfly Inn."

"Wondered about that once." Jake Haux laid aside his harmonica long enough to get a rise out of Dora. "Knew it had to be something besides your stuffed pork chops that kept people coming back to that restaurant."

Dora ignored him and went on. "That wheel wants to be turning just as sure as that water wants to be running through it. Wasn't meant to be a magpie nest, which is exactly what it is now!"

Jim Roice stood watching Sarah, never saying a word. She felt the force of him standing there the way she'd feel the force of wind or flame.

"Good morning," he said finally, not smiling. "Howdy, partner."

"Why did you come?" she whispered.

Apparently, she didn't whisper the question quietly enough. All the Star Valley townsfolk started answering her at once.

"Jim Roice always comes to these things," Ben Mitchum explained loudly. "He's president of the Howdy Partner Committee."

"Put his name in the hat, we did," said Prentiss Smith. "All of us came to the meeting and wrote down the name of somebody we thought could do a good job of it. Jack Gwilliam passed his Stetson and we all decided the first name we drew out would be the winner."

"Pulled his name out first thing." Lester Burgess said.

"Went through every name later. His was the only name anybody'd put in, except for one vote for Mac Johnson which we figured Jim put in because he didn't wanna vote for himself."

"No," said Mac Johnson. "That was me. I voted for myself."

"I put Jim's name in the pot because I thought he'd be best at this, after everything he's done to keep Wyoming Troutfitters going," Jack Gwilliam said.

"About lost the place first year he had it," said Jake Haux.

Though Jim said not a word, Sarah knew his answers. He'd come because he always came to these things, because if he didn't this morning something would've been different. His words from the night before resounded in her head. *"Nothing will change, Sarah. It mustn't. We won't act as if anything is different."*

"Never seen such a high tax bill as that one." Carol Mortimer delved right in, figuring she worked in the tax office and that gave her the right to tell this story. "Like to have died when I sent that bill out to him after they reappraised the place."

"We gave out his brochures to folks," Emma Burgess announced. "He even paid us a small commission."

"Everybody was planning on going to an auction by the time he got that land paid up," Homer Egan interjected. "Everybody watched him break his back and nobody knew how he'd pull things out. Guess we didn't take enough stock in how much he loves that land. Jim Roice wouldn't've lost that place for nothing."

"Even that wife of his didn't think he could do it," Dora Tygum announced proudly. "She told me that one morning when she stopped in for breakfast."

At that, Sarah shot one fast glance at him, one fast glance that he met head on, bespeaking silently of his pride, his pain.

Victoria hadn't believed he could do it? Victoria hadn't believed he should hold on to the land at every cost?

These people weren't telling her anything about Jim Roice that she hadn't known since he'd been a youth. His roots sank deeper into that place than the lodgepole pines or the shivering aspens or even the willows by the water. The very soil beneath his feet brought forth Jim's strength. Caddisfly Creek coursed through his soul as surely as blood coursed through his veins.

She remembered Victoria saying how he'd surprised her.

"Jimmy," she said, knowing him full well, aching for him.

At that moment, Kender Budge, Aretha's niece, stepped up wanting more coffee. "Just a half, please," the teenager said quietly. "I mix it with lots of milk."

Sarah poured, unable to speak at the magnitude of what she'd just discovered.

"I'm just out of school," the girl said as if Sarah'd asked. "Graduated last spring."

"Oh." She forced herself to concentrate on the girl. "Didn't realize you'd already finished."

"Would you tell me one thing, Miss Hayden?" Kender asked. "Would you tell me what you think about leaving this place?"

Sarah turned and stared down at the shy, pretty girl, intrinsically aware of the man listening, the father of her son, the man who knew all the implications of her answer. "What do you mean?"

"You left this place when you were about my age, didn't you? Tell me. Do you think it was a good thing to do?"

Sarah took a deep breath. "I don't always know," she said.

Tears of earnestness glittered in Kender's eyes, eyes the same clear lavender as fleabane. "I wanted to get out of this valley so bad. Momma never would let me go. She's scared she'll never see me again. But Daddy said he'd help me a little if I'd earn enough to make it through my first semester on my own. That's why I'm waiting tables at the Caddisfly. I'm trying to save up for college, which isn't easy."

As Sarah took the girl's arm, she glanced up momentarily and looked right into the darkness of Jim Roice's eyes. "If you want something that badly, you won't forgive yourself for not trying."

"I tried for the DAR scholarship last year, but I didn't get it."

"The Daughters of the American Revolution." Sarah had to smile. "Are they still awarding that thing every year?"

"Yes." And Kender obviously didn't see anything to smile about. "If they'd've given it to me, it would've meant everything. I could've started college last September."

"Missing the outside world won't be made easier by the fact you don't know exactly what you're missing," Sarah told her wisely. "I know that much."

Tears like glinting stars began to slip down the girl's cheeks. "It's okay, then, to go?"

"I'm not saying it's okay." Here Sarah realized she spoke honestly to herself, more honestly than she'd spoken before. "You'll often find it hard. But if you don't satisfy the thing that's restless inside you, you won't know if you've hidden some part of yourself away."

Kender's expression changed, taking on the ethereal shine of peace and certainty. "I want to be like you," she said. "Everybody around here tells me about you. You've lived in New York City. You're colorful. You think colorful things and see possibilities, so different from the people I know around this place."

"No, Kender." She was saddened and intrigued by the girl's view of her, brutally aware of the man who'd listened to every word. She thought of Charlie this morning as she'd seen him, romping up the steps onto the bus, eager and happy as she'd once been. "You will find, perhaps, that people who are different aren't always better. In time you'll see much of the same life around you, no matter where you've sought it. And, no matter where you seek it, you'll find a lot of it is good."

Rita Persnick arrived to show the property precisely at eleven-fifteen. She marched through the front door of Hayden's General Store brandishing that same black leather valise, leading a brigade of three suited, dour-looking men.

Sarah'd just finished washing up the last of the coffee mugs. She couldn't remember a day in her lifetime when the store'd held so many Star Valley townspeople at one time. The place looked right for a store now, clean underneath but disarrayed, as if shoppers had spent hours poking through items on the shelves.

Thanks to the visit from the Howdy Partner Committee,

she'd actually made several sales. She gave Richard Jenkins a good price on the cast-iron skillets and he proudly toted them off. Prentiss Smith and Ben Mitchum each purchased a package of Eddy's donuts. Emma Burgess carted home two gallons of milk, still swearing that the only place she'd find any milk fresher would be if she milked the cow herself.

"I'm the one delivered that milk here this morning," Mac Johnson spoke up. "Delivered some of the same batch over at Tom Happersett's store, too."

"Happersett has never carried milk this fresh," Emma insisted as she plunked down five dollars and forty-three cents.

Sarah shut the cash drawer and smiled. "Thank you, Emma."

She didn't know why, but the arrival of Ms. Persnick's potential purchasers disconcerted her. "Interesting place," one of the men commented to her as he walked around the place, jingling things in his pockets as if he was already wanting to depart.

"Yes," Sarah said. "It is an interesting place."

"Perhaps we should examine the property outside first," the realtor suggested to them. "Let's have a walk around the pond."

"Is the snow deep?" one fellow asked. "I didn't bring my overshoes."

"I've got pac boots you can borrow," Sarah said, gesturing to the row of Sorels her father'd always kept out so people could try them on and find the correct size.

The three men eyed the huge, rubber-soled pacs as if they had absolutely no idea what purpose they might serve. "I believe we'll be all right without them," someone said.

"You probably will be," Sarah said, knowing she could offer them snowshoes, too, and that they'd have absolutely no idea what to do with them. "The moose that come around keep things well trampled. You shouldn't sink in too far."

Rita Persnick and her delegation spent over forty-five minutes inspecting things, the chinking between the logs, the old door framing, the pine flooring, the mitered corners on the shelves. Everywhere they scrutinized, Rita Persnick suggested possibilities. "The floors could possibly be refinished," she said. "Maybe the logs could be sandblasted, too."

"What about the waterwheel?" one of them asked. "Could it ever be made to turn again?"

"Possibly," the realtor answered.

In the main room, she pointed to the potbellied stove. Sarah'd always warmed her hands at the old stove, laying her mittens along the nickel-silver fittings to dry. "If you planned to make the place a fine-dining restaurant," Ms. Persnick suggested, "you could remove the stove and build a large rock fireplace. Lord knows, there's enough smooth river rock in the parking lot to get a good start on it."

Upstairs, she pointed to the old claw-footed bathtub Sarah's great-grandfather had brought in by supply wagon through Yellowstone Park from Cody. "You could remove that, too. The roof line lends itself to a wrap-around shower arrangement."

"If the bathtub went," Rita Persnick suggested, "you could glass in the area."

"Don't have to worry about a bathtub," one said fervently. "We wouldn't keep the living quarters. We don't see a way to salvage any of it. The upstairs area would be open to dining."

"I've got it," one of them proclaimed. "This is the best idea I've had all day." The others waited with baited breath for him to continue. "If we buy the place, we'll bring the bathtub downstairs. We'll use it as a salad bar."

*   *   *

If good news and gossip travels fast in any small town, it travels like dry-storm lightning in Star Valley, Wyoming. By noon that first day, half of Lincoln County knew that Hayden's General Store was open for business. The other half of the county was soon to find out.

Most people who stopped by to see Sarah didn't need to do any shopping. They all stopped in to say hello or to offer congratulations, then picked up some little something to make the trip worthwhile.

"Your dad would be mighty proud, seeing you behind the counter like that," said Frank Weatherby.

"Does me good seeing this place lit up first thing in the morning," said Dawson Hayes.

"Used to see you like this, apron tied on, scurrying around trying to help your momma," said Francis Beery. "Just seems right, having you back, Sarah Hayden. It ain't fittin' for a girl of your talent to disappear into a place like New York City."

During all these salutations, Sarah lost count of how many gum packs and Eskimo ice cream sandwiches and chocolate milk pints went out the door.

The bell on the door jangled again at half past three. Sarah pushed herself away from the desk, where she'd been working on the ledger, and hurried to meet her next customer. "Good afternoon. What can I—?"

She stopped short.

Victoria Roice stood at the counter, fingering the national park scarves. Victoria lifted her chin, meeting Sarah's entrance with boldness.

"So you're open for business," Victoria said with strained courtesy.

"Yes," Sarah answered.

Silence hung between them, silence as tangible and

fixed as a wall. Another customer came through the door and picked up a newspaper, the one that came out in three sections every Wednesday. He lay the quarter in Sarah's hand. The bell chimed again as he left.

Victoria let the scarves alone. She bent closer to Sarah. "I know he came here last night. He told me."

Sarah wouldn't lie either. "Yes. He did."

"I don't know how you did it."

Victoria, Sarah wanted to say, only she didn't dare. *There are things between Jim and me that you mustn't know*.

"Charlie couldn't find his father last night. Jim got a phone call from Prentiss Smith and neither of us knew where he'd gone."

"You knew," Sarah said. "You knew because I asked you to tell him first."

"You had no right after I denied you. It was Charlie's birthday. That little boy walked all the way over here in the dark, looking for his father."

"You could've come with him."

"That's ludicrous."

"It isn't such a long way. Children have walked that path before."

"And not just any children, were they? You're talking about yourself and my husband. God, but how sick I am of hearing those stories from everyone. Jimmy and Sarah. Jimmy and Sarah."

"We shared a childhood. He's a part of who I am, Victoria. He'll always be."

"He's a part you walked away from. Remember that."

"I do remember," Sarah said, glancing down briefly, as if she needed to get back to her work. "I think of it much more than I ought to."

"If I could, I'd buy this run-down excuse for a shop myself, just to give you good reason to go back to New York City."

"Victoria. We've done nothing wrong."

"Makes no difference. You know this town better than anyone," Victoria said. "Folks've been talking about you and Jim for a long time."

At that moment, school bus number four, the exact bus Sarah'd seen loading children at the curb that morning, pulled to a stop in front of the store. Children spilled out in every direction, looking even more disarrayed than they'd looked in the morning, backpacks flinging, mittens and hats being hastily tugged over fingers and ears. Two girls ran to the willows, where they'd hidden sleds and began loading backpacks and other paraphernalia onto them, making ready to pull their belongings home.

"Meet you at Greybull Pond, Charlie," hollered Joey Sikes.

"I've gotta go home and get my hockey stick," yelled Brad Dilger.

"I play goalie," Charlie Roice shouted.

"You always play goalie," Joey argued. "You played goalie all day yesterday."

"Yesterday was my party. That doesn't count."

"Everything counts, Charlie. You've got to let us have a turn," Brad argued.

"Okay. Eric's goalie then," Charlie said.

"Look," Joey bellowed even louder. "The store's open again."

"All right!" chorused the three others at once. "We can get Bubble Jugs."

Inside the store, Victoria and Sarah watched as the whole gang of them changed direction and headed for Hayden's General Store. "My mom's in here," Charlie called out. "That's her car."

"Hi, Mrs. Roice," they chorused as they banged in through the door.

The same huge, horrible loneliness clogged Sarah's throat as the boys came toward them. "Hi, Charlie Chickadee." Victoria stopped to smile at the boy, a true smile that sparkled momentarily in her eyes. She was glad to see him.

"You call him chickadee?" Sarah asked as she reached for him and touched his forehead. Despite the snowy day outside and the disappearance of his hat, he was hot and sticky.

"It's her favorite name," Charlie said matter-of-factly. "She's been calling me that ever since I was about five, so I put up with it."

"Wrong. I've called you that ever since I laid eyes on you," Victoria corrected. "Ever since the social worker laid you in my arms and you started climbing up my elbows. Because your hair reminded us both of feathers, you had so little of it."

"Chickadee," Sarah's mouth scarcely moved when she whispered the words. She felt the words, almost didn't say them. "Charlie. Charlie Chickadee."

The boys selected two Bubble Jugs apiece and Victoria paid for them. They ran out the door as quickly as they'd come, backpacks bouncing.

Victoria waited until they'd gone, then turned back to Sarah.

"You see how happy we are," Victoria announced, her voice strained again. "Please. Do what you have to do to sell this store, then get out of this valley. I want you to let my family alone."

15

Marshall Upser often walked past Rockefeller Center long past evening, the collar of his jacket pulled to attention below his ears, his chin low. As he strode, he shoved his hands into his pockets and constantly rummaged, as if he searched for something deep inside them.

Fog had come up over the harbor and filtered into the city, sending restless fingers of damp gauze stirring through alleys and around street lamps. Still, even despite the murk, the lights on the massive tree glittered with gaiety, casting a puddle of merry light upon the scarved, mittened skaters that cavorted below.

Marshall paused on the sidewalk, watching all the fun, missing Sarah.

He began, right there and then, to resolve himself to spending Christmas without her. Thanksgiving had been perhaps the most difficult holiday he'd ever experienced, particularly because he'd continued to expect Sarah.

"Oh, she's coming," he'd told everyone over and over again at Sandlin and Bonham. "Haven't you spoken with her? She plans to be in the office next Monday."

Two days before, he'd purchased a fresh tom turkey at Choice Meat Market around the corner, one so plump he'd readjusted two refrigerator shelves just to make the bird fit. He'd ordered a squash casserole and two salads from a deli downstairs from the office. He'd even toyed with the idea of inviting friends.

In the end, he'd decided against that, eager to have her to himself, alone. He'd waited all day endlessly, thinking she'd phone and tell him when she'd be in at La Guardia. He'd hidden a huge cluster of flowers in the cooler downstairs, flowers he'd hand her when she stepped off the plane. But, when she called at last, she called from the store. She kept chattering on about some sweet potato pie she'd cooked and a huge dinner she was attending with Maudie Perkins and some little boy who'd brought his cousins over to play in the cattails.

"You aren't flying into La Guardia today?"

"No, of course not, Marshall. The title on the place is being disputed and I can't leave just yet."

"But you said you'd be back for Thanksgiving."

"Did I?" She sounded as if she'd forgotten. "Oh, Marshall. I meant to let you know the day it all happened. It's such a mess. All the old homestead rules, and they had no way to measure acreage except to tie a bandanna on the wheel of a wagon."

Now, tonight, Marshall thrust his ungloved hands even deeper into his pockets and resumed his heavy gait. As he went his way toward the apartment, Christmas lights beckoned from window after window, not the old-fashioned bulbs that glowed in gentle colors to be seen for miles, but the new, frantic sort, the ones that played music and deployed in patterns and reminded him too much of the strip in Atlantic City.

Seven blocks from home, he began to jog. *This is good*, he thought. *Good*.

Five blocks from home, he broke into a run, taking pleasure from the burning exertion upon his lungs, his slamming heart, his tightened muscles. By the time he unlocked the front door to the brownstone, he was ready to talk to her. Even when he dialed her number, he was still gasping for breath.

"Sarah? Sarah? Is it you?" he asked, never giving her the chance to say hello.

"Marshall? What's wrong?"

"Nothing's wrong. I've been running."

"At the club?"

"No, on the streets."

He could hear the instant fear in her voice. "From what? What were you running from in the streets?"

"Christmas lights."

"Dear sweet heaven, Marshall. Christmas lights? Are there Christmas lights up in the city?"

"Of course there are."

"We don't have any here. Guess everybody's just so far out in the country, they don't see much use in lights."

"When are you coming back to New York, Sarah?"

She didn't answer him for the longest time. He got the particular feeling she didn't know what to say. She only waited on her end of the phone, remaining silent.

"Give me an estimate."

"I talked to Joe Bonham this week," she said instead. "He's given me a leave of absence, for as long as I need one. He's hired someone temporary."

"You had that much coming to you, at least. You haven't so much as taken a vacation in four years."

"Keep reminding me of that."

"Is the deed mess being straightened out? Is anyone taking interest in the place?"

"Rita Persnick's shown it a time or two. I've opened

the place for business and am minding the store. She said I needed to do that, given the importance of keeping paperwork and turning a profit. She says the deed matter is close enough to hand to entertain offers."

"She sounds like a logical person."

"She's like you. She's told me to do all the same things you've told me to do."

"That's reassuring."

"Yes."

As the conversation tapered off, Marshall had a thought, one that gladdened him a great deal. "Guess if I got desperate enough, I could always jump on a plane to Wyoming to see you."

She fell silent again, not encouraging him.

"What is it?" he asked, knowing Sarah all too well. "You don't want me to come?"

"It isn't that," she said carefully. Her words sounded as if she extricated them through layers and layers of uncertainty. "I've often missed you. But things are unsettled here and I—" Here she stopped, knowing she couldn't go on, that she couldn't yet voice the truth about Charlie. "It's just that I've *found* something—"

"Found something of yourself?" he asked almost bitterly, because he should've guessed it could happen.

"Yes, Marshall," she said and, in her voice, he heard a meager smile. "Yes. That exactly."

Five times Rita Persnick lugged her briefcase into Hayden's General Store. Five times she escorted a delegation of possible buyers down the shelf-lined aisles and up the ramshackle stairs, pointing out bathroom improvements, fireplace possibilities, imperative kitchen updates.

When the first offer came on December 10, the real-estate agent advised Sarah to take it. "It's a good offer," Rita said. "Not full price, but strong. Honestly, it could be a long time before we find anyone else who's this enthusiastic about the property."

"What about a counteroffer?" Sarah asked, surprised.

"It's up to you, Miss Hayden, but I'd take this without countering. These folks are certainly qualified buyers. You never know, though. They may be stretching to give you this amount. With all the refurbishing they'll have to undertake—"

"I'm going to think about it, Rita," Sarah said, interrupting the woman before she could start listing much-needed improvements for what seemed like the hundredth time. "Give me a few hours to decide."

That afternoon, Sarah closed up shop and walked in the meadow again, bundled in the ageless sheepskin coat with no owner. A new snow had fallen, one that had drifted so deep, she followed the buckrail fence to find her way. *I could be finished with this*, she thought. *I could be away, in the city, with Marshall, back to who I used to be.* But she'd never be the same she'd been before she'd discovered the truth about Charlie. Never.

The figure they were discussing seemed a monstrous amount of money. Sarah called the real estate agent at dusk, after she'd turned out the lights downstairs and sat eating alone, watching the expanse of snow in the meadow take on the same blue hue as a sheer watercolor. "I won't accept," she said.

"Miss Hayden? I don't understand. Why not?"

"I'm not ready."

"Aren't ready for what? Aren't ready to sell?"

Sarah answered as frankly as possible. "I know it's a lot of money. I'm just not certain. Circumstances don't permit me to—"

Rita Persnick began to panic. "Will you counter? Will you come down on the asking price at all?"

"No. Not this time."

"You're making a mistake," Rita Persnick informed

her. "These folks'll be disappointed. *I'm* certainly disappointed."

"That doesn't make a difference to me," Sarah said. "I've made mistakes before."

Margaret Cox stomped snow off her boots on the front stoop at Peart's Barber Shop and lay the newest Cabela's catalogue on George's counter. "They're advertising spring stuff already," she said, inclining her head at the row of fellows waiting for George to give them a trim. "Tents. Hiking shoes. Backpacks. It isn't even Christmas yet."

"Guess they figure on people plannin' ahead." George Peart pulled a long, black comb from the jar of blue Barbi-cide and began to flatten the hair on Jarvis Miller's head. "Now hold still, Jarvis," he said. He replaced the comb and bent over, reaching for the electric clippers that hung on the wall. "Wanna make sure I get your sideburns level."

Jarvis Miller lay the weekly newspaper open-face in his lap. "You ought not to have any trouble with sideburns, George. Not after the art job you did for that kid, Joey Sikes, over the weekend."

George Peart straightened considerably, his demeanor obviously affected by the compliment. "So people are talking about Joey, are they?"

"Of course people are talking about him," said Ben Mitchum, who'd been waiting patiently in line for George to trim the hair in his nostrils. "You should've heard the teachers at the faculty meeting this morning. Claire Hallorin almost canceled the Reading to Kindergarteners program when she saw what you'd done to Joey's head."

Peart deflated a bit at that story. "Don't see why a kid with the shape of a hockey stick shaved over his ear has to give up reading to kindergarteners."

"Claire thought it set a bad example to the little ones."

"They didn't cancel it, anyway," Judd Stanford piped up. "Joey stood right on the front row and read aloud three pages from 'Balto—The Dog Who Saved Nome.' Francis Beery told me all about it when she stopped in to pick up her phone directory."

"Heard the thing over Joey's ear looked more like a check mark than a hockey stick," remarked Vern Chappell offhandedly. "Heard he was walking around in the halls this morning with what looked like a giant stamp of approval on the right side of his head."

"I went to barber school, not art class," George said on his own behalf. "I try to work miracles, but I'm just working with hair."

"Don't pay them any mind," Jim Roice said, folding his paper and laying it neatly on the counter beside Margaret's satchel. "Before next weekend, every boy who plays hockey down at Greybull Pond is gonna come in here and beg for one just like it. I can name 'em right now. Eric Ankeny. Brad Dilger."

"What about Charlie Roice?" Margaret Cox mentioned auspiciously. "You gonna let Charlie walk in here and get a hockey stick shaved on *his* head?"

Jim looked from Margaret to George Peart. George hung the clippers back on the peg and left them to dangle. He picked up a razor and turned it on. As it hummed ominously, he finished up Jarvis Miller. As Jarvis stood from the chair, it became obvious to everyone that George had gotten carried away with talk about the Sikes boy. He had, indeed, lopped the right sideburn a good quarter-inch shorter than the left.

"If his mother doesn't mind," Jim said neatly and, for one absurd moment, Sarah's face appeared before him instead of Victoria's.

Vern Chappell chortled. George Peart turned away and began whisking Jarvis's collar with a natural brush.

Margaret Cox swung her satchel over one shoulder and clucked at him reproachfully.

"If Charlie wants a hockey stick carved along side of his head, he's welcome to have one, George."

Judd Stanford rose and took his turn in the barber's chair. "Can you do mine the way you cut that fellow's from Cheyenne this weekend?" Judd instructed him.

"What fellow?" Vern Chappell inquired.

"Peart sure did have a busy weekend," Ben Mitchum said.

"Fellow who brought his wife and came up poking around Hayden's General Store," Judd said.

Margaret Cox began to get interested. She lay her satchel back on the counter again and leaned forward. "I heard about those folks, too. They stayed around a long time. Were they interested in the old place?"

"I heard they were." George soaped up Judd's hair, rinsed it, reached for the comb again, and began to slick it down in a slight resemblance to a sea lion. "I heard they spent Saturday morning down in Afton, doing their darndest to get financing from Afton State Bank."

The bell on the door jangled and in marched W. D. Owen, pastor of the Morning Star Baptist Church. "Got time to give me a cut, Mr. Peart?"

George gestured toward the empty chair at the end of the row. "If you don't mind waiting."

"'They that wait upon the Lord shall renew their strength, they shall mount up with wings as eagles.' Isaiah 40:31," quoted the pastor. He didn't sit down. Instead, he walked right over to Jim Roice and clapped him on the back. "Say, I heard a nice offer came in on that land next door to yours."

"Sarah Hayden got an offer on the place?"

"Guess those folks *were* interested," Ben Mitchum said.

Jim gripped the pastor's shoulder. "Did Sarah take their bid? Did it go under contract?"

Try as he might, he couldn't remember seeing the sign when he'd driven past Hayden's General Store this morning. In his mind he felt both elation and fear. Would it end like this, then? Would Sarah go her own way, knowing everything she knew, and leave him to raise Charlie as he'd prayed? She had no right to ask for things to be any other way.

Still, he stood vulnerable among his friends in the barber shop, feeling as if something he'd greatly treasured was gone. He'd had a dream like this once, a quiet, ambiguous, haunting dream, in which he'd searched through darkness for something he couldn't find.

"You sure oughtta be glad to see Sarah Hayden leave Star Valley," George Peart said, pointing the long, black comb in Jim's direction. "She had her chance around here a long time ago. Jim Roice, I've never seen two folks stand so stiff and strong about gettin' their own way. A girl oughtta know what's important to a man. She oughtta know better than to think she can run off and take a fellow off his land. Crazy girl. Sooner she sells her own father's place and heads back to the big city, the better for all of us."

Jim started to say something. "George—"

But before Jim got the chance, W. D. Owen jumped in and stopped all of it. "She turned the offer down. She's not selling out. At least not today."

"What?" George Peart bellowed.

"You don't say!" Ben Mitchum hollered.

"Can't believe that!" Margaret Cox yelped.

Jim's face registered a spectrum of rich emotion—shock, satisfaction, fear. But nobody seemed to notice the broad play but the pastor himself. "You thought she'd get rid of it at first chance?" W. D. asked.

"Don't know what I thought," Jim said.

At that moment, the bell jangled again and in came Jarvis Miller. "George?" the man inquired as he poked his head in the door. "Do you have time to work on me a little more? Just went home and the missus is complainin' because she says my sideburns don't match."

"You willin' to wait your turn in line?" George asked.

"Yeah," Jarvis said. "I'm willing."

"That's fine," George told him, gesturing with the comb again as if he was directing the community band. "Have a seat there and I'll get right to you."

Much the same conversation was going on at the Spotted Horse Station down in Hoback Junction, where Victoria Roice always stopped to have afternoon refreshment on her way home from a day's paperwork at the ski mountain. The bartender leaned over the pine table where Victoria had her elbows propped and said, "I heard real estate is moving down in Star Valley."

Victoria looked up at him and narrowed her eyes. "Good grief, Ed. Why would you say such a thing as that? Nothing's worth much down there at all, except come tax time."

Ed Tribitt, owner of Spotted Horse Station, had been quite a sportsman hunter in his day. Lined along the bar were the heads of his favorite conquests—a buffalo, an elk, a wild boar, and a moose—all staring down at his customers on their stools with glassy, knowing eyes.

Nowadays, every time he served liquor to Victoria Roice, she reminded him of the prey on his wall. Didn't know why exactly, except she seemed to be hanging somewhere she didn't want to be. Though he thought her nice enough, she reminded him too much of the wild boar, the one with eyes that protruded from each side of his head, the way God made him so he could see what was going on behind him easier.

"You want another drink?" he asked.

"I always want another drink," she said. "You know that."

"Yeah. But you've gotta drive all the way down the canyon. I've gotta watch you close and kick you out the door before you get too much."

"You've done a good job at it before, Ed," she said, smiling amicably. "I trust you to do it again today."

He went behind the bar and, with a steel scoop, dumped a good amount of ice into her glass.

"Now, tell me what you meant by the real estate comment," she prodded him.

Behind the bar, he mixed 7-Up and Seagram's Seven into her ice. "Just what I said," he told her. "Had a whole group of city folks in here Saturday going on and on about wantin' to start business up in Star Valley. Heard 'em tell Rita Persnick over their drinks that they'd be willing to offer close to full price on the old Hayden place. Drew up the papers right here at this table."

Victoria's eyes went as wide and round as the unfortunate moose on the wall. "They did?"

"Yep."

"Sarah's sold the store," she surmised breathlessly, and, as she jumped around the table searching for her coat, he became worried she might upset her glass.

"I'm gettin' you some coffee," he said. "On the house. No need to hurry out of here like this."

"But Sarah's sold the store," she said.

"Now"—here, Ed Tribitt wondered if he'd made a mistake telling her the story at all —"I didn't say that, did I?"

She swung her coat over her shoulders and, exactly as he'd predicted it, sent the full glass flying. It fragmented on the floor. "Hells bells, Ed. I've been waiting to get her out of this valley ever since old man Hayden's funeral."

"Missus Roice," he announced. "You oughtn't to be talking this way."

"Can't help talking this way. You have any idea what it's been like living under her shadow these past years?

There's still something soft about Jim's face whenever her name gets mentioned. But after this deal goes through, she'll be gone."

"That's what I'm trying to tell you," he said, crunching glass with his boots and hastily wiping the table, doing everything he could to keep himself from having to meet her eyes. "She isn't selling it. She won't be gone."

"What?"

"They offered her almost full price for that ramshackle property and she turned it down."

"Dear sweet heaven."

"Whole group of 'em had a meeting back in here last night. Rita Persnick told 'em there wasn't anything she could do. Said she'd pushed as hard as she could but to no avail. She's either holding on for top dollar or she's having second thoughts about getting rid of the place at all."

To Ed's surprise, this information didn't slow Victoria down one whit. Now that she'd gotten into her coat and shattered one of his best highball glasses, she was hell bent to get on her way. He shoved a cup in front of her and tried to fill it with coffee, but she shoved it right back at him.

"Don't see why you're in such an all-fired hurry," he said, half annoyed. "You've got a good hour before anybody in Star Valley expects you home." She'd told him as much many a night as she'd sat listening to the snow plows go past on the highway, watching the sun disappear behind Beaver Mountain.

"I'm not going home just yet," she said. "Clinic's open late on Monday nights in Jackson. I'm driving back in to see Dr. Barkley."

Ed Tribitt was intrigued, and certain she'd had one drink too many. He was suddenly glad she'd broken the glass on the floor. "My daughter-in-law had to wait two months for an appointment with Barkley last summer. You just waltz in there and see him like that, no questions asked?"

"If I make a big enough stink I can. I'm one of his best customers."

He stared at Victoria. Dr. Barkley was an OB-GYN specialist. If what he'd heard around his bar was right, Victoria'd never borne a baby.

She seemed to read the bartender's mind. "Infertility," she stated casually. "I'm one of his infertility patients."

"Oh," Ed Tribitt said.

She dropped her purse and straddled the chair neatly to retrieve it. She reached as far to the left as she could before losing her balance and landing flat-seated right where she'd started. As if her renewed placement gave her license to tell all, she announced to everyone in the general vicinity, "We've got a beautiful boy, Jim and me. But we adopted him right off the bat without trying for our own first. God's got his own joke going, I suppose."

Ed tried to stop her. "Missus Roice. You don't have to—"

She held up a hand and kept going. "Makes it easier to talk about, you know. Jim's always thought I was obsessed with the idea of a baby. Guess every woman is, at one time or another. How else would the species be propagated?"

Several people on stools along the bar stared down at her. Ed tried to make light of it, tried to protect this woman from saying something she'd regret tomorrow. "You giving us the biology lesson of the day, Missus Roice?"

Victoria seemed not to hear him. "For me, it's more than being obsessed," she said. "A baby would tie us together. A baby would mean he'd look at me and go all soft. A baby'd make him forget he settled for his second choice when he settled for me."

16

Jim was waiting up for her when she pulled across the front cattleguard late that night. "Where have you been?" he demanded. "Charlie and I were scared to death you'd skidded off the road and landed in the Snake River or something."

Victoria climbed out of the Wagoneer and swept past him into the house. "Clinic was open late tonight. I stopped by to see Dr. Barkley. Had to wait a long time."

"Mom." Charlie ran up and grabbed her middle. "Where were you? We were scared."

"Let go of my legs," Victoria said evenly. "You know I don't like it when you cling."

Jim wouldn't let her get away with her excuse. "Your appointment with Dr. Barkley was last month. I just got the bill a week ago. You didn't need to go again."

"Don't tell me what I need," she said. "And don't talk about this in front of Charlie."

"What?" Charlie asked. "What can't you talk about in front of me?"

"Charlie." Jim stooped down to his eye level. "You'd best go to bed."

"I'm sick of going to bed," Charlie bellowed indignantly. "Every time you and Mom talk about this weird stuff, you make me go to bed."

Jim smelled the whiskey on Vic's breath. Out of sheer desperation, he couldn't relent to his son. "Don't use that tone of voice with me, young man."

"It's the only tone I've got," Charlie said defiantly. "I wanna be with *Mom*. I was scared about her."

"Upstairs." Jim pointed toward the hallway. "Now."

Victoria waited until Charlie thumped slowly all the way down the corridor and up the stairway. She shrugged out of her coat and left it on the oak rack beside the door. "I don't want to talk about this now, Jim. I've other things on my mind."

"You don't want to talk? After you're three hours late getting home and you've been to Dr. Barkley's for no reason?"

"For no reason?" she asked artlessly. "How can you know about my reasons?"

They stood at opposite ends of the family room. For the first time, Jim realized the house had grown cold. He'd built a fire in the wood stove long ago, but he'd been so worried about her late arrival, he hadn't taken time to stoke the logs in hours.

He took one step toward his wife. He saw her shiver.

"It's difficult," she said, as if to humor him. "It's difficult being a woman and wanting something you cannot have."

"Victoria," he said, not understanding what she meant. "Are you talking about the baby?"

As she moved toward her husband at last, Vic's expression became decidedly seductive. "I'm talking about a great many things, Jim. There now," she said quietly, reaching him and starting on his top shirt button. "It's time we went to the bedroom ourselves, isn't it?"

Her disappearance was an odd thing. "You scared us to death, Vic. You act as if nothing's wrong." Perhaps it was the blend of his son's innocent alarm, of his wife's canny orchestrations, that caused Jim to go on and take her to task now. He recalled the chart he'd found propped on her bedside table. "And why would you want to take me to the bedroom? You've already ovulated this month."

She took his hand to lead him. "I have. Does that make such a difference?"

"I would think it made a difference to you," he said.

"I don't know what you're talking about."

"I'm talking about loving each other," Jim told her.

"I'm talking about the same thing."

His shirt fell open. With cool hands, she slipped inside the cambric and wrapped her fingers around his ribcage.

"You don't want me," he said, finally admitting it, his eyes probing hers as if he could see everything no one else could see. "You want something *from* me. That's a significant difference."

Victoria stopped, her fingers no longer working his skin. "What?"

"You heard me."

"Yes." She stared up at her husband as if he were someone she didn't know. "I heard you. But I don't know what you're saying."

"I'm saying I don't want to do it like this anymore, Victoria."

She pressed closer, her finger tracing a tantalizing line from his shoulder to his navel.

"You've been drinking." She had that lingering rankness about her, that long-spent acrid stench of good Seagram's gone bad. He grasped her shoulders, practically shaking her to reality. "Why don't you come out and tell me what you want from me? Why not play it straight?"

She dropped her hands, indignant at being denied. "You think you know everything about me."

Jim tried to recall what she'd last told him about the doctor's instructions. "Do I need to put on different underwear again? Do I need to watch my temperature, too? Does he want us to try it upside down? Right-side up? Standing on our heads?"

Anger blazed in her eyes. "You sorry—" She brought up a fist in one wide, wild swing.

Jim instinctively raised his left arm to knock her blow aside. When she aimed for his exposed chin this time, he grabbed her arm and squeezed it blood-stop tight against him. "Get a hold of yourself, Victoria. I'd like a baby, too. But we've already got a child upstairs."

She screamed, doing her best to wrench away from him. "You care more about him than you care about me. You think my needs have no significance."

"That isn't true," Jim said. "I know your needs and the importance of them, Victoria. Just once I'd like to see you holding on to those who love you, holding on with no strings attached."

She stepped back from him; he set her arm free. "How can you say that, Jim? After all the good times we've had making love—"

"No," Jim said. "We haven't had good times making love. Not since you decided having your own baby was more important than anything. We do commit the act, but there's nothing warm and loving about it. What we do is calculated to your specifications."

"I don't have specifications tonight."

"I don't believe you."

He waited for her without saying anything else, knowing she was wrong, knowing she'd never admit to it.

"Forget it, Jim. Just forget it."

"I'm not going to forget it. I want to know what Doc Barkley told you tonight at the clinic."

She started to tell him, then stopped, obviously realizing he'd caught her. "Damn you."

"Tell me."

She took one deep breath and started in again. "He won't sign me up for surgery until you're willing to have those tests."

"Tests?"

"I went in tonight to schedule surgery, Jim. He hasn't been able to find anything wrong with me any other way. But he won't do surgery unless it's a last resort. Says he won't do anything invasive unless he has to."

"We talked about tests before," Jim stated, trying to get his bearings in this conversation.

"Yes. For you. We talked about tests for you." They had and he'd nixed the idea, because of the money, because he knew he didn't need them. "They're simple tests to see if you're able to get anyone pregnant."

"I don't need tests," he said quietly.

"Jim, you don't know that," she pressed. "Doc Barkley will check for motility, to see if your sperm are sluggish or fast."

"I have fast sperm," he said. "I know I have fast sperm."

"That's not all of it. They check for appearance, color, and coagulation. They check for volume, how many sperm you emit in one milliliter of liquid. They check their shape to make sure the sperm have healthy, oval heads."

"I'm not going to go through that," he said, his frustration mounting. "Victoria. My sperm are healthy. There's no reason to—"

"They might be abnormal or large or immature. And your pH balance might be too acidic." She kept talking merrily along, never noticing the storm building in Jim's dark eyes. "There are things that could be wrong with you, things that could prevent my pregnancy." Too late, she realized what he'd said. She stopped suddenly and turned toward him. "What do you mean, there's no *reason*?"

An icy shard of warning pierced him as he realized that, in his outrage, he'd taken the conversation much too far to back down from his words or redeem them. He'd ruined it now, ruined everything for Victoria. Although he would devastate her, he had no choice but to stand strong for the truth, and for Charlie.

"I mean exactly what I said," he said guardedly. "There's no reason to put either of us through that part."

"But you don't know that." She said it slowly, sounding out each word, sampling it, as if she suddenly realized that, indeed, he might. He might.

"Yes," he told her strangely as the seconds ticked by between them in slow motion. "I do know, Victoria."

"How?" she asked, her face gone ashen. "How do you know?"

"I know I'm capable of fathering a child," he said, "because I did it once."

"Dear sweet heaven. Jim." She backed away, looking nauseated and lost, as if someone'd thrown a punch to her vitals and knocked her lungs clean empty. "With who?" He waited, never answering his wife, knowing the havoc would be complete when she realized the answer. The monstrosity of it was she knew already. She knew the name, knew the face. And, as reality slowly began to dawn for Victoria, she gripped on to him from sheer pain. "No, dear sweet heaven, no."

He reached for her, wanting to support her, wanting to spare her the anguish, but it couldn't be done.

"Tell me it isn't Sarah. Tell me you didn't father a child with Sarah Hayden."

He peered down at her sadly, knowing he could tell her no such thing.

"Jim."

He said nothing.

"Say it out loud," she pleaded. "Say you didn't have a baby with Sarah Hayden."

"I can't say it," he whispered steadily, his eyes bleak, "because it would be a lie."

She jerked away from him, wailing hideously with the deep-rending cry of some primitive, wild mourner. "Let me alone. Get out of here."

"Victoria." He proceeded toward her, trying to stop her from doing some damage to herself. Instead, she picked up a pottery bowl from the sideboard and hefted it clumsily at him.

He ducked. The bowl smashed into jagged pieces against the log wall behind his head. "She doesn't have a baby. She went off to college. She ran off to New York City like everybody says."

"That's right." Fear began to ice his heart, fear so intense, so debilitating, that he didn't dare give credence to its source. What if she guessed he was Charlie? "Of course Sarah doesn't have a baby now."

"What did she do with it?" Vic yelled. "Did she get rid of it? Did she have an abortion?"

Jim shook his head, answering as calmly as he could to sidetrack her. "Neither of us wanted that."

"The Star Valley townfolks know nothing of it. If they did, they'd've talked." She picked up another breakable thing, something of Charlie's that had been sent for Christmas, a glass ball filled with water and snowflakes and a teddy bear reading in a rocking chair.

"Sarah went away. She gave birth in Laramie before she put him up for—"

Victoria froze, her neck rigid like an animal caught in a searchlight. "Him?"

"—for adoption." He realized his mistake after it was too late. He should never have mentioned the baby's gender. Never.

Victoria scrutinized the Christmas ornament in her hand. She gaped at it as if it might be a crystal ball, as if it might reveal secrets to her. He saw her mouth moving, saw her numbering back the years. "A little boy?" she asked weakly, raising the glass sphere over her shoulder as if to aim it at him. Suddenly, suddenly, all Jim's quiet satisfaction began to make sense.

"Don't throw it, Victoria," he managed. "That's—" He couldn't bring himself to say it.

"This is Charlie's." She looked at it, then back at him. Her voice wavered. "It belongs to the little boy we adopted ten years ago."

"Don't do this."

"Dear heaven, Jim. Is it Charlie?"

"Victoria. You don't want to—"

She didn't fling the thing at him. Instead, as reality struck her, she clutched the glass so firmly that it broke magnificently in her own hand, slicing the width of her fingers, sending droplets of blood and water oozing down her skin.

She seemed not to notice. "Jim?" Her voice was child-like, as if she knew she had to coax, as if she knew she'd never pry it from him any other way. "Have you adopted your own boy?"

"Victoria. Let me do something for your hand."

"Tell me." She had the look of a crazed animal in her eyes. If Ed Tribitt could've seen her, she'd have reminded him more of his trophy animals than ever. "Tell me what you've done."

"Put that thing down."

"Am I raising Sarah Hayden's son?"

"Good God, Vic. Don't make me say it."

Sarah Hayden and Charlie Roice resembled one another. Now that Victoria thought of it, she could see every similarity. "Charlie belongs to Sarah."

"No. No," Jim tried desperately. "He doesn't belong to

Sarah. You've raised him since he was an infant. You're the only mother he knows."

She sat on the sofa and stood the jagged remains of the water globe on the coffee table, cradling the bleeding hand with her uninjured one. "That's why you married me then," she stated stoically. "Of course, you needed a wife so you could take legal custody of that baby."

"No. Yes. I mean—I had custody of him, anyway. This just made it . . . better."

She didn't help him along now. She sat there, holding her hand, blood dripping onto the knees of her pants.

"I didn't adopt him, Vic. I didn't have to."

"But all the papers you brought home to sign, all the times we went to court . . ."

"That was for you. If we'd've done it differently, everyone would've known. It would've been talked about."

She would accuse him. She would accuse him of everything. "You did it this way to protect Sarah. Everything you've done has been to protect Sarah."

"No. Perhaps I did it to protect us from Sarah."

"I can't sit here and listen to this."

He went to the kitchen, retrieved a large square of cheesecloth she kept in the pantry, and brought it back to wrap her hand. "Do you have glass beneath your skin?"

"I don't know. I don't care."

"Let me look at it, Victoria."

She held her fingers out for him while he inspected the wound.

"Looks bad," he said. "I'll get disinfectant." And, as he did, he saw that, in his way, he'd pursued his own heart as recklessly as had Sarah. Because he'd loved old Will and that boy, because he'd been true to himself, he'd caused hurtful things.

Victoria touched him on the sleeve when he came back. "Jim?" she asked. "Remember when I told you I tried out for the Olympic team? Remember when I told you I didn't make it?"

"I remember," he said.

"I lied to you then," she told him now. "Didn't try out for the team, Jim. Didn't have any reason. I knew I didn't have the endurance for it."

He swabbed her hand, not wanting to meet her eyes. He'd known that about her before. He'd figured it ever since they'd almost lost the land and she hadn't fought beside him.

"I want a baby," she said. "I want a baby more than anything in the world."

"I gave you one. One more precious to me than my own life," he said, still dabbing with disinfectant and cheesecloth, knowing he'd just killed her, knowing there had been no way to stop it. Oh, but he was tired of keeping this from people. "I did the best I could for you a long time ago."

"Need to ask you something, Jim."

"What? What do you need to ask?"

"I need to know if you've ever loved me."

He looked up at her, holding her hand, hesitating only slightly. "Yes," he said finally. "I loved you. I'd never have done this any another way."

"But now?" she questioned. "What about now?"

"Now," Jim echoed. He met his wife's eyes, thinking of how so much was changing. "Sometimes I don't know."

Her fingers were still bleeding. For this moment, he knew she found it easier to stay sane dealing with common matters. She focused on her hand. "I'll need stitches, won't I?"

"We'd best drive over and wake Doc Bressler."

"I'll get my coat," she said.

"I'll check on Charlie Chickadee," he said. "We oughtta wake him and take him with us to Afton. A drive down that far'll take awhile."

"He could stay asleep," Victoria said. "He's been alone at home before."

"If he wakes up, he won't know where we've gone." Jim climbed upstairs, pushed open his son's bedroom door, and stepped inside. He expected to see his spindle-legged boy sprawled across the bunk, asleep in the thin silver glow spilling over from the window.

Charlie's bed was empty.

"Charlie?" he called. "Son? Where are you?"

No answer.

"Charlie?"

Except for Victoria rummaging through a bathroom drawer downstairs, the house was itself, squeaking or silent in its rightful places.

"Son."

Again he waited for an answer. None came.

Jim commanded in his best father voice, "Charlie! Can you hear me?" Inside, his fear multiplied. He felt peculiar, as if some great force had taken the night in hand, away from him. "Charlie?" Jim went to the top of the stairs. "Victoria? Have you seen Charlie?"

"He's in his bed," she answered, as if he'd asked her an idiotic question.

"No, he's not."

She had her coat on, buttoned and ready to go. She'd wrapped makeshift bandages completely around her hand. "Where could he be?"

"Don't know. Unless—"

A thought struck him. Jim ran back to his son's bedroom and crossed to the window. The sash stood open an inch, when it hadn't been ajar before.

Outside, the moon gilded the snow into a giant patchwork of shadowed frets and burnished reflection. He could see most of his property, from the dark skeleton of the dilapidated barn to the snugly bound hulls of the Mackenzie boats kept for next summer. To the east he saw Caddisfly Creek, its unfrozen waters weaving back and forth against jutting rocks and snowdrifts, reflecting a filigree stretch of moon.

Directly below Charlie's window stood the winter-naked crab apple tree. It held no snow on its branches and had the look of being recently jostled. Long ago, when this room had been Jim's, he'd spent many a late summer's night gallivanting through the stubbled meadow, snipe hunting with friends or sneaking to the store, all after he'd departed from this window at bedtime and clambered down from the topmost limbs that had grown across the high ledge even then.

Victoria came to his side. They stood together looking out the window, the pain between them a tangible entity. "Charlie's climbed out the window and gone," Jim said.

"Look there." Jim pointed to small indentations in the newly fallen snow, foottracks that began beneath the latticelike branches and led to the edge of the trees, on the path across to the store.

"Damn you and Sarah Hayden," Victoria said. "Damn you both."

17

Every night, Sarah stood at the old oak counter to balance her cash and shut down the store. She did it the exact way she'd seen Blythe do it for years, totaling each tray, turning bills right side up, top to the left, using a paperclip to hold them singly in place. She noted the sums on an appropriate column of the deposit slip before moving to coins, dutifully separating pennies, nickels, dimes, and quarters into lockable bags. As she began with quarters tonight, she heard someone tromp up onto the front porch.

She'd turned off the porch light and flipped around the CLOSED sign at least an hour ago. She stuck the money bags beneath the table and poked the tray inside the register. "Sarah?" she heard a little voice call. "Sarah, are you home? I wanna come inside."

"Charlie." She immediately flipped on the light, unlocked the door, and welcomed him. "What's going on?"

"Don't be mad at me, will you? Don't wanna hear anybody else bein' mad." He stood outside the screen, his eyes shining with tears, wearing nothing but plaid bedroom slippers and a San Jose Sharks nightshirt. He'd wrapped his arms around his belly to keep himself warm.

She swung open the screen, reaching for him. "Charlie. Little guy." It was the first time she'd held him and known he belonged to her and, if she hadn't been so worried, it would've been enchantment. "You'll catch your death of cold running over here like this. Your lips are almost blue."

"Can't help it," he said, sniffing and backhanding his nose. She could tell he was trying to keep himself from those tears, to be tough, as newly turned ten-year-olds should be.

She gathered him close against her, burying her face in his cottony hair, hair the same color as autumn-cured grass, the same color as hers once had been. "If you need to cry, it's okay," she said. "I won't tell anybody."

Her words brought the invitation he needed. He clung to her for everything he was worth and began sobbing. "Momma didn't come home for the longest time and Dad was stomping around the house and she got there and she didn't even wanna *hug* me."

"Oh, Charlie." And, inside, Sarah's heart was breaking, breaking for all of them, for the boy who had been pushed away, for herself, who could finally hold him, for Jim, who knew the truth. "You mustn't take it to heart. I'm sure she was upset about something."

"She's *always* upset about something."

His snow-wet slippers had fallen onto the floor. Sarah tossed them away and felt his soggy toes. "I'll get you a pair of Will's old wool socks," she whispered.

"No," he whispered back. "Not yet. Don't let go yet." He was seventy-five pounds of boy, all miracle, scrunching right on her knees and, without his consent, she couldn't go anywhere. He kept both arms circled around her and hung on.

"You scared?" she asked, touching his hair.

"Yeah," he said, sniffing again. "I know it's dumb, but I can't help it."

"No. It isn't dumb. Not particularly."

"It was harder coming through the trees tonight because nobody knew where I was," he told her. "Until I could see the light from the store, kept thinkin' about mountain lions and coyotes and stuff."

"You've gotta be careful," she said, agreeing with him. "Once when your dad was a little boy, he was out one night wearing a sheepskin cap and an owl dove right down at his head and took it in his talons right off him."

Charlie backhanded his nose again and sat up straighter. "An owl got my dad?"

"Yeah," she said, nodding. "Scared him to death, even made him cry. He thought something'd jumped out of the sky and was trying to take his head off."

Despite himself, Charlie giggled. "I like it when you tell stories about Dad."

"Well"— she bit her lip for a moment, aching, just taking in every feature of his face —"I could tell you a lot of those stories."

"Grandpa tells me stories, too. Sometimes he tells me stories about you."

"He does?"

"Told me once how you and my dad were best friends."

"He did?"

"Yeah." A pause. "Were you?"

She shook her head. "Sometimes. Not always."

"I thought you were all the time."

"I was a girl, remember. Your dad used to pick on me a lot and make me run away."

"Like I pick on Heather Hess?" he asked, wide-eyed.

"I put a garter snake in her lunch sack because she chases me at recess."

"Yes," Sarah said, laughing, and glad to distract him. "Exactly."

He plopped into the chair beside the stove and immediately caught his heels on the rounds. "I'll get you those socks." She hurried up then came back down again, stooping before the fire to tug the thick woolen socks onto his feet. "You're looking warmer."

"Don't wanna go back home," he said. "Wanna spend the night here with you."

She glanced at the old black phone. "I'm going to call your dad, Charlie. He'll be worried when he doesn't know where you are. Your mom will be, too."

"They won't be worried. Won't find me missing until morning. I climbed out the window and down the trunk of the crab apple tree."

"In your slippers?" Sarah went back to her task at the register, thinking it best not to pass judgment or give advice, only to let Charlie tell her.

"I lost 'em. They fell off and I had to pick them up when I got to the bottom."

"You might've fallen out of the tree, too."

"Mom and Dad wouldn't't've cared. They were too busy hollerin' at each other."

Sarah felt the sudden discomfort of knowing things she shouldn't know. She started on the quarters again, counting them out. Four makes one dollar. Two dollars. And three.

"They were hollering about Dr. Barkley and the bills and Mom's temperature. Then Dad was saying she was drinking something bad and tonight he said she doesn't want him except for sexing."

"Sexing?"

"Do you know what that is? I learned it when I watched *Wayne's World* on cable. Sexing. That's when they get in bed together and jump around on top of each other and make babies."

"Charlie!"

"They always have to do sex some certain way because Doc Barkley said to. I'm just an adopted baby and Mom wants a real one that's her own. Dad wants her to just love us instead of worrying about somebody she doesn't have or know."

Sarah's heart lodged in her throat. She lost her place on the rolls of quarters and had to start all over. *That's what I did*, she thought. *I left everyone I loved once because I wanted something I didn't have, something I didn't even know.*

She said the only thing she could think of to say. "Guess that makes you kind of sad, huh?"

Charlie spoke with renewed bravado and delicious honesty. "Of course, she should be happy just having me. That's what Dad tells her, too. But she says he doesn't understand. She got real mad and threw something at him and broke it on the wall."

Sarah didn't know what to say to that. "You want to help me wrap these pennies?" she asked suddenly. "I've still got a long way to go."

He stood from the chair and came over, his nightshirt flopping, the huge socks wrinkled like elephant knees at his ankles. She pulled out a stool so he could stand tall at the cash register.

All of a sudden, the hated tears were beginning to roll down Charlie's face once more. He scrubbed them away. "Now that she doesn't want me, maybe nobody does."

Sarah gave up tallying quarters altogether. She touched Charlie's chin and said with gentle solemnity, "You mustn't think that."

"But what if she gets so mad at Dad, she makes him give me away or something?"

"Oh, Charlie. Your father would never give you up. He

loves you a great deal." She said it with total conviction. And she thought, *So do I! I love you that way, too!*

"But I'm just adopted. If they could have their own baby, they wouldn't want me."

"They'll always want you, Charlie. I know that better than I know anything in the world. I know what your father went through to get you."

"But he's not my real father. My real father didn't want me. My real mom signed papers and gave me away. And my real father did the same thing."

No, he didn't, Sarah wanted to say. *At risk of everything, he brought you back to himself and this place. It was only me who gave you away, Charlie, only me.*

"Think of your dad. Think of your evenings searching for rocks and bugs and fishing on Caddisfly Creek." She gripped his shoulders and told him the only simple thing she was free to say. "You're loved, Charlie. Probably more than you'll ever know."

"You really think so?"

"I do. Sometimes adults get confused about important things. It often takes children to make them realize it."

He finished the penny rolls and lay them in a pile. Next she let him do the nickels and dimes, showing him his own space on the deposit slip to jot down the total.

"There now." She held out the last bag for him to drop in the coins. "Tomorrow I'll take them down to Afton to the bank." Just as she locked the last bag, Sarah noticed him stifling a yawn. "You sleepy?"

"Uh-huh," he said, nodding.

"Come over here to the chair," she said, just this once unable to resist. "I'll show you what my mother and I used to do when I got sleepy."

"Don't wanna go home," he said. "Wanna stay with you."

"I'm calling your house in a while so they won't worry. But just sit with me for a while," she said. She propped her own feet at the base of the stove, where they'd stay toast warm. "Now. I'm going to tell you a story, but you're going to make it up, too. I'll say a little piece and then I'll stop and you fill in, using something you see in the store. Got it?"

"Yeah," he said, situating himself in the chair with her and taking all of her lap and then some. "Sounds like fun."

"Okay," she began. "You ready to start?"

"Yeah."

"Once upon a time, far, far away, there was a prince who didn't have—"

"—a canoe—" Charlie piped up, grinning, pointing to the massive Coleman hung directly over their heads.

"He set off in search of a canoe," Sarah continued, "taking only his—"

"—snowshoes—"

"—and—"

"—a can of green beans!"

"Very good," Sarah told him proudly. "You're very good at this game."

They made it all the way to the ancient land of coffee cans where the prince fell in love with an obstinate princess who built her castle from Woolrich sweaters and wouldn't, for the life of her, eat pickled beets. And each time Charlie selected an item, his voice grew slower, softer.

Soon, very soon, Sarah felt his head sink heavily against her shoulder.

Jim stood on the porch at Hayden's General Store and peered inside the window. There they sat, Charlie and Sarah, their backs to him, their heads together, and so alike.

He didn't know what caused the constriction in his throat as he watched them, other than the realization that it had been forever since he'd seen Victoria holding the boy that way.

He rapped on the window so he wouldn't frighten her. She turned halfway, saw him, and motioned him in.

"Has Charlie been here long?" Jim whispered.

"A while. Long enough to close out the cash register and tell stories."

"Thank you, Sarah."

"I was about to phone you," she said. "I was afraid you'd be worried. He was pretty upset."

"I can imagine."

Neither knew what to say for a moment. She sat before the fire, a huge tumble of boy in her arms, her eyes speaking every emotion she couldn't dare say. He stood beside the doorway, his eyes grim.

He snapped his fingers twice at his side out of sheer nervousness. "Can he stay here a while?" he asked finally. "Victoria's out in the car but she won't come in. She's cut her hand. I've got to get her to a doctor."

"He can stay here," Sarah whispered, "tonight, or whenever he'd like."

As he stood in the doorway and she watched him, for some reason she remembered a day together, a day when they'd fished by hand in the stream, and made love in the willows, and Jim's dog, Barley, had discovered them, bounding through the scrub timber with no advance warning at all. The big, breathy pup greeted them in his slobbery fashion, his whole body wagging with joy as they laughed and rolled and tugged on various damp articles of clothing before Barley stepped on them. "Good dog, Barley!" She'd giggled as he stood over her, his tongue flailing.

"Bad dog, Barley!" Jim'd said instead. "You about scared us to death."

She thought, *Just suppose. Just suppose that was the day we conceived our son.*

"I'll be back to pick Charlie up in a little while." Jim turned and took the screen in hand.

"Jim?" she asked before he could open it. "What happened over there tonight?"

He didn't look at Sarah when he answered. He stuck his chin toward the ceiling, following the whorled patterns in the pine above him the way a child would lazily watch a cloud. "Not much happened I'm willing to talk about," he said simply. "I've told her about Charlie, Sarah. So now she knows."

18

Christmas in a small, alpine town is different than Christmas spent anywhere else. As the holiday came on that year, even the breeze stayed still. When snow came each evening, it fell in unhurried flakes as big around as demitasse saucers. Down in Jackson Hole, someone strung red and green lights among the antler arches that marked the four corners of the town square. Across the main road, down by the Star Valley post office, the Howdy Partner Committee hung a painted banner that read: Seasons Greetings! Happy Holidays!

Sarah decorated the store. One afternoon, she donned a pair of snowshoes and walked deep into the forest to cut boughs. She toted back a pile of limbs, dropping them onto the porch with satisfaction as the resinous fragrance of fir, balsam, and spruce carried into the frosted air. She tied them together into three sconces of evergreen, adding dry rosehips and cedar berries for color, then hung each one onto the three posts that lined the porch. On the door, she hung an old willow wreath she'd found upstairs in the attic, one she and Blythe had woven ages ago.

As she decorated the wreath with tiny pinecones and festive red ribbons, oh, how she missed her mother! For so long Sarah'd kept herself removed from the memories of this place. For so long she'd convinced herself that the quiet days of her childhood here added no merit to her life. But the holidays brought forth in her the same thing they bring forth in all of us, the blessed portion that expects miracles, the portion that always waits for magic.

Try as she might, Sarah couldn't stop seeing things through Charlie's eyes. When Prentiss Smith invited everyone over for a sleigh ride on the back of his haywagon, she couldn't help thinking, *Charlie will ride on the highest bale, giggling mercilessly and poking hay in Brad Dilger's ear.*

When Aretha Budge down at the Wyoming Driver's License Bureau gave out candy canes to everyone who came in to renew, she thought, *If Charlie comes in here, he'll wait until she's turned her back and take two more.*

After the gathering of carolers came from Morning Star Baptist Church and circled around the front stoop to sing "Joy to the World," she thought, *Charlie will stand right in the middle of them and sing, too.*

As she pictured Charlie, she pictured herself when she'd been ten, serving hot chocolate to the carolers who stopped by, helping herself to delectable candy canes from the tree in the lobby of Afton State Bank. She even thought of the year when one of the cowboys from down the Hoback had stopped by for soda and had roped an elk. The poor animal happened to be wandering aimlessly past the place on his way to feeding grounds at the refuge and Will had tied him to the front porch for two hours.

Everybody in Star Valley stopped by to feed him carrots. Blythe tied a red bow on his antlers. Sarah could hear

Will's voice now: *"He's Santa's reindeer, all right. Santa has a hard time getting out this far, what with his busy schedule this time of year and all. This here's Blitzen. Sarah's asked for a new bike and Blitzen's come all this way to make sure she's minding her manners."*

This year, two days before Christmas Eve, Rita Persnick showed the property again. She strode into the door fifteen minutes before the scheduled appointment and dangled the exclusive listing agreement from two fingers. "Miss Sarah Hayden," the realtor announced, "as far as your store is concerned, I do not bring anyone out this many miles without believing that the buyers may be hot prospects."

"I understand that," Sarah said.

"I do not want to feel as if I'm wasting my time, or yours."

"Yes."

Rita flipped open the agreement to page three. "You did not see fit to add any contingencies when we both signed this contract, Sarah. You realize that, if one buyer offers you full price for your property, you must abide by this contractual agreement and sell."

"Yes. I realize that."

"This document is legal and binding for its entire length, a length of six months, which you specified yourself in writing."

"I'm aware of that, too."

"This contract does not expire until May 15."

"I'm perfectly aware of the date," Sarah said calmly, not rising to Rita's obvious indignation. "If someone makes a full-price offer, I'll honor it accordingly."

The agent from Teton Valley Real Estate tucked the listing agreement back inside her imposing black attaché. "I wanted to make certain you understood the details. There are those in my office who have expressed concern about you, Sarah. They are concerned you might think you have a right to back out on us."

"I knew the rules when I signed the contract," Sarah said. "I wouldn't back out."

"Good." Rita smiled for the first time during the exchange. "I'm glad that's settled."

Fifteen minutes later, the realtor met another set of prospective buyers down the highway, at Spotted Horse Station. When she brought them inside, they were no different from the others. "What an unusual place," the woman exclaimed delightedly. "It would be perfect for an antique shop. I could put the old bathtub on the front porch and use it as a planter for geraniums."

"Why doesn't this waterwheel turn anymore?" asked the man. "Why wasn't it better maintained?"

"They love the place," Rita Persnick whispered to Sarah on their way out. "Expect to hear from me soon."

On Christmas morning, Sarah had only one gift to open, a ponderous silver package Marshall had sent from New York City, with a sticker beside the ribbon that said simply: Macy's.

The evergreen boughs across the facade of the store and the old wreath on the door were her only concessions to the season. Sarah'd seen no cause to trim a tree. She sat alone in the kitchen with Marshall's box now, just staring at it for a time, feeling close to the man she'd left behind in New York City, feeling far away at the same time.

Purposefully, she made the opening take an entire ten minutes. She sliced each length of tape with her fingernail, one at a time. She folded the paper nicely and tucked it beneath her chair before she went to the next step and raised the lid off the box.

From inside the billows of metallic-flecked tissue, she lifted a black felt hat, a Breton roller with a turned-up brim and one black velvet bow on one side. "Oh, Marshall," she whispered to no one. "It's—"

She stopped, not knowing exactly how to classify such a hat. It was perfect to wear to dinner at 21 or to an opening on Broadway. And she had just the suit to wear with it—the Donna Karan she'd brought for her father's funeral.

Sarah stepped to the mirror in old Will's room and adjusted the brim low over her eyes. She turned to the right, then to the left, examining it.

From below, she heard a knock on the door. Seemed odd to have someone come to the store on Christmas morning. She hurried downstairs, forgetting about the haute couture on her head, and poked her nose against the front window. Outside stood a family, three strangers—a father, a mother, and a little girl.

"Can you help us?" the man asked through the glass. "Name's Dave Burnham. Our car broke down on the highway and we need a phone. Stopped at the Caddisfly Inn across the street first, but that place is locked up tighter than a drum. You don't suppose there's anyone around who'd fix a carburetor and get us back on the road this afternoon, do you?"

Sarah invited them in and showed them the phone on the counter. "Don't know of anyone offhand. Star Valley Sinclair does mechanic work, but I'll bet Carl Kohler is home with his family."

"That inn across the way won't be open for lunch, will it? We've been on the road since Omaha, trying to make it into Jackson this afternoon so we can use our time-share. Don't have food with us or anything."

"Nope. Dora'll be closed all day, too," Sarah said, trying her best to think of something that might help them. "I've got food here. Why don't you pick out what you need?" And, as they walked up and down the aisles, an idea came to her. "You know, my neighbor next door knows how to work on cars. I know he's home because I saw their lights on last night." In fact, she'd sat on her bed for the longest time, watching the lights from the Roices' tree. "If he can't fix it altogether, I'll bet he could jerry-rig something to hold it until you made it up the canyon."

"You think so?"

"His name is Jim Roice," Sarah told them. "Here. I'll dial the number."

While Dave Burnham talked on the phone, Sarah brought down a fresh pot of coffee and a tray of hot cinnamon rolls she'd baked just that morning. "Oh, yum!" the little girl squealed. "Look, Momma. It does seem like Christmas, after all."

Dave Burnham hung up the phone and gladly took one of the rolls. "Well, I'll be darned. Fellow said he'd be happy to walk over and take a look at it. Says that if it's what he thinks it is, he knows he can get it up and running good enough for it to make it to a dealer tomorrow in Jackson. Can you imagine? Somebody being that helpful during a holiday like this?"

"Oh, Dave," Mrs. Burnham admonished. "Surely he expects you to pay him."

"And I will, if he'll let me."

"Guess people around here get all caught up in the season," the woman said skeptically. "Can't imagine anybody being so willing to go out of his way."

"Doesn't have as much to do with the season as you might think," Sarah said. "People around here are just good people."

"Country people." Mr. Burnham smiled with solicitude.

"Doesn't have as much to do with the country as you might think, either," she corrected him, and, as she did, the realization came to her, too, as new and precious as any gift. "Just has to do with the way people *are*. Everywhere you look, you'll find good people. Problem is, we've learned to close ourselves off from them. We've made it too easy to forget or to stop believing or to stop being one."

Burnham and his family stared at her. Dave finally said, "Never had anybody put it that way before. Guess you're right at that."

By the time Jim Roice's truck pulled up in front of Hayden's General Store, Sarah had supplied her guests with a grocery sack filled with bread, cheese, meat, and a dozen Hostess Twinkies. "Just so you don't get stranded without something more to eat," she said, winking at their daughter.

"At least let us pay you something," Mrs. Burnham said, rummaging around in her purse for her wallet.

Sarah shook her head, feeling honestly content, and not nearly so alone. "Couldn't take money from you if I had to. Cash register's all closed out and empty. I want to know you folks have had a meaningful Christmas."

"Oh, we have!"

"We will!" Mr. Burnham called.

"Thank you!" they said, waving as they hurried down the steps to jump in the truck with Jim.

It wasn't until they'd left the porch that Sarah heard the little girl say in a clear-bell voice, "That lady was so nice, Mommy, but why was she wearing that funny hat?"

An hour later, after Sarah'd tucked the hat back in its Macy's box and slipped it under the bed, Jim Roice came to the store. He came right on in without knocking, just the way he'd done so many times before, and gazed up at her while she came down the stairs to greet him.

"Thanks for helping those folks," he called up to her. "Isn't often we get somebody stranded here. But, when we do, they're really stranded."

"Thank you, too," she said. "I fed 'em well, but I never could've gotten them on their way like you did."

He couldn't resist teasing her a little bit. "I remember when your mother used to solve every problem in the world by giving away boxes of Hostess Twinkies. She solved a lot of your problems that way."

"For a while," Sarah said quietly. "Until I grew up and my problems got too big for anyone to handle except me."

He was still holding his army-green bag of tools in one hand. Slowly, he set the bag onto the floor. "You got a rag or something I could borrow? I've still got grease all over me."

"Yeah." He just kept looking at her. She felt disoriented suddenly, just having him in the store, as if someone had come in unexpectedly and moved things. "They're around here somewhere." She finally found them in a box by the storeroom door. "Here." She brought him two or three. "These oughtta do you some good."

He rolled up the sleeves of his flannel workshirt and began to wipe down his powerful arms, arms that had held her once, arms that now held his wife.

"Thank you, Sarah." He wiped down his face, too, but his efforts didn't do much good. "You should've seen me when I was workin' down at the Sinclair. I looked bad like this every day."

"You don't look bad to me, Jim. Not at all."

The terrycloth rag stilled against his tanned skin, light against dark, and he raised his eyes to hers. "What're we doing, Sarah girl?"

At Jim's use of his favored name for her, Sarah's very breath ceased to come. She stood as proudly before him as an antelope stands in a Wyoming sageflat, her head high, her eyes dauntless. "Don't know," she whispered. "Never expected to come here and find the many things I've found. Never expected I'd come back home and wish to stay."

He jammed his fingers through his hair. "Charlie loves you," he said. "No matter if he never knows who you are, he loves you."

"I didn't aim to make him feel that way."

"Some things just happen," Jim said. "Trying to stop them would be like trying to stop something of nature."

Sarah stood watching Jim, knowing her ties to this man, this place, had become as unstoppable as nature's forces, too, as unstoppable as wind or snow or fire.

Jim paused, waiting for her, thinking that, if she kept standing that way, her eyes distant, her chin raised, he might have to take one step forward and kiss her, kiss her like he'd never kissed her before, kiss her like a man he was now, instead of the boy he'd once been, a boy in the throes of discovery.

"How is Victoria?" she asked him.

So she'd known what he'd been thinking. He shook his head, knowing they'd both been wrong once when they'd been young, and they were both wrong to be needing each other the way they did now. "She isn't happy, Sarah. All she thinks about is having a baby."

She watched him, sad for him, sad for Victoria, too.

"Would you let me take a look at the waterwheel?" he asked, obviously wanting to change the subject. "I've got my tools with me and my work clothes on. It's a good time for me to take the thing apart and see what's keeping that wheel from turning, it being Christmas and all."

"Ice is frozen around it. Don't know if you can do much good."

"I'd like to try."

She stepped into her snow boots and looped her coat over her shoulders. "I'll go with you," she said.

"You got some sort of a shovel or something? That'll help me break through if need be."

"I'll get Dad's old spade."

He hefted his bag and donned his gloves. She followed him, tromping across the snow-tufted meadow to the water. The cattails had long since folded in every which direction, forming a forest of frost-bent triangles at the north end of the pond. Sarah waited until he'd unbolted the huge box and was examining the ironworks before she dared ask the next question. "What was she like with Charlie?" Sarah asked. "What was it like when you first brought him home?"

His big hands paused on the machinery for a moment. "It was the most incredible day of my life, of both our lives." Jim stopped, unscrewed a rotor from what looked like a primitive turbine, and pitched it aside. "That woman from the Wyoming Parenting Society handed him to me and I thought he seemed so wise it was odd, like a little wise man who'd just come from somewhere I'd never been. I kept looking at his face, thinking I'd see you. But all I could make out was him, just Charlie, with those big blue eyes that have turned green since, and all that funny bunch of hair."

"And Victoria?"

Jim stopped all pretense of working on the wheel. He didn't turn to Sarah. He only declined his head and spoke to the ice laying in fragments below him. "I wanted to shout it to the world. 'He's mine! He's mine!'" And, as Jim spoke, it was everything Sarah could do to keep from reaching for that vulnerable hollow at the base of his neck, to keep from touching him with gentle reassurance.

"Victoria loves him, too, Sarah. We hadn't been married for long and I convinced her it would be such an adventure to have him. She set up a nursery that could've been featured in a magazine it was so pretty, with teddy bears and a rocking chair and a lace blanket her grandmother'd crocheted in record time. She sat up at night holding him, saying, 'Oh, Jim. Just look at his beautiful face. If we pushed it a little, we could tell folks he looks just like you.'" He stared at nothing for a while, then set to work again, rolling his sleeves and poking both arms into the innards of the waterwheel. He pulled out fists of debris, leaves, grass, stones. "Don't know when it started to change between us. Don't know when what she didn't have started being more important than what she did."

"Are all those rocks what stopped the waterwheel from turning?"

"No. Shouldn't be." He left them piled beside his knee. "This here's an old, rugged contraption. Crazy thing's just seized up for no reason I can see."

"Can't imagine," she said. "Can't imagine why the thing would just up and quit."

Jim still hadn't looked at her. He bolted the frame piece back onto the wheel, taking care to give the wrench his full weight as he fastened each nut.

"Thanks for what you did for Charlie last week, Sarah. I'm obliged to you over that. He didn't hear much, but it scared him to death, just listening to the fighting. He needed a friend. Don't think anybody else would've sufficed that night. He needed you."

It wasn't thirty minutes after Jim had gone before Sarah heard another knock at the front door. "Goodness," she said aloud. "Haven't had so much company since the Howdy Partner Committee decided to welcome me to town." This time, when she went to answer, she saw two green eyes peering in through the glass, a nose pressed up against the screen, and a cowlick sticking straight up.

"Aren't you afraid your nose will freeze to the screen?" she asked grinning, happy, oh, so happy to see this particular boy on this of all days. "Merry Christmas, Charlie."

"Came to visit you," he said, keeping something hidden behind his back. "Wanted to find out if you're having a good day."

"Yes," she said. "I am."

"What'd you get for Christmas?"

"A new hat."

"Can I see it?"

"Sure. It's under the bed. Come upstairs and I'll show it to you."

"I got pajamas and underwear from my grandma. Grandmas always think you need pajamas and underwear."

"Yep," Sarah said. "Mine did, too."

"This morning Santa brought me a new hockey stick with a curved blade. Makes it much easier to control the puck if you've got a stick with a curved blade. I've already gotten my stick tape and wrapped it up. We're gonna have a game down on Greybull Pond after everybody gets done visiting their relatives and stuff." The whole time he followed her up and chattered, he kept his hands anchored behind the small of his back.

Sarah pulled the box out from beneath the bed and put it on again. "Ta-da!" she said, tilting the brim at him. "What do you think about this hat?"

Charlie frowned. He walked all the way around her. Then he shook his head. "I think that is a dumb hat," he said.

"You do?" she asked, but, for some reason, she wasn't surprised.

"Never seen anything quite like it," Charlie said matter-of-factly.

"It's fancy," she explained. "In New York City, people wear hats like this to all the fancy places."

"Don't have many fancy places in Wyoming," he said.

"You're right about that."

"Won't keep your ears warm, either. In Wyoming, what good's a hat if it won't keep your ears warm?"

"I don't rightly know, Charlie," she said. She turned to examine herself in the mirror again, deciding she looked ridiculous. She pointed to her own fancy reflection in the mirror and, together, they began giggling.

After Charlie's mirth died down, he revealed what

he'd been hiding. "Brought you a Christmas present that's a lot better than that," he said, bringing a dilapidated box out from behind his back. He'd wrapped it in the latest issue of *The Thrifty Nickel* and tied it with one strand of green yarn.

"Oh, Charlie."

"Hope you like it." He dropped down on the bed, waiting for her to open the paper.

She began to open it exactly as she'd opened the hat, making the unwrapping last a long time, tearing off each strip of tape individually with her fingers.

"That isn't the way you do it," he told her. "You rip it open in a hurry. I've been working on this two weeks. Can't wait any longer."

"You help me then."

"Okay."

Together, they tore the paper to immediate shreds. Newsprint and wood chips went flying everywhere.

"There," he squealed. "Take it out of the box, Sarah."

"It's something made out of wood. There's wood all over everything."

"Quit trying to guess! Take it out! Take it out!"

The box was crisscrossed shut with electrical tape. She couldn't get the lid off. She had to tear the thing practically in half to get at it. When she did, she found another wrinkled, taped lump of *Thrifty Nickel*. Carefully, she unsealed the object.

"Oh, Charlie," she whispered in awe. "Oh, Charlie." She flung the hat to the bed and knelt. "This is the most wonderful present anybody's ever given me."

"Made it myself," he said proudly. "Copied it out of Momma's bird catalog. See? It's a wood box with this wire mesh on it. You open up the wire mesh with this little hook, and this stuff inside's called suet. It's beef fat from Happersett's and sunflower seeds and cut peanuts and cracked corn and millet all together."

"You nailed the box together by yourself?"

"Not *all* by myself," he said. "Dad had to help me a little. One corner kept coming apart."

She held it carefully, carefully, in the palm of her hand. She'd never treasured anything quite that much.

"Sorry I had to buy the beef fat from Happersett's. Won't ever buy anything over there again. But I had to do this or else you'd've known I was up to something."

"Did you mix all the ingredients together, too?" She planted one kiss, their first kiss, on his nose. "This is wonderful."

"I've written down the recipe in there so you can make more when you need to. Forgot to change clothes when we got home from church and I got fat all over my Sunday school tie," he said proudly. "Look at the *s* hook. Dad helped me bend it. So now it's ready to hang in the low branches of any tree. It's a bird feeder."

"It's a beautiful feeder."

"Momma's catalog says that the chickadees love it. They have a hard time finding anything to eat under the snow. The fat gives 'em extra energy when the wind gets high and winter gets cold. In that book, says it guarantees chickadees to come to your window every morning."

"Thank you," Sarah said, tears coming to her eyes, thinking what a perfect Christmas it had turned out to be, how simple and how real.

"Why are you crying?" he asked her.

"Because I love you," she said.

"Can we put it in a tree now? I wanna see if it works."

"Come with me." She took his hand and, together, they trudged out into the heaps of snow beside the house. "We'll find the perfect place."

"That one," he suggested, pointing to a blue spruce sheltered slightly by the corner of the store. "It's right beside the window. You'll be able to see them all even when you're helping people at the cash register."

Sarah placed the suet feeder on one low, lacy, snow-covered limb. "That looks just right, doesn't it?"

"Yes," he said. "Just right." Then they went inside and drank hot chocolate, looking out the glass as the birds began to come.

19

In late January, Victoria packed a bag of toiletries, drove to St. John's Hospital in Jackson, and admitted herself for surgery.

"You're one of Dr. Barkley's?" the admittance clerk asked her.

"Yes."

"You undergoing this surgery on an outpatient basis?"

"Yes, I am."

"I'll need to give instructions to somebody. Who will be driving you home?"

"You'll have to give the instructions to me," Victoria said. "No one is driving me home." In fact, no one knew she'd come at all. Only Dr. Barkley had eased a bit, finally giving sanction to the surgery after she'd explained Jim's abilities to father children. It had been one of the most ridiculous conversations she'd undertaken in her life.

"You see, Jim isn't just being stubborn. He knows he

doesn't need tests. He's fathered a healthy baby. How do I know? Because I've raised him, that's how I know."

"I don't advise this," the nurse said as she read Victoria's records. "Who's ever heard of driving all that way after surgery? You're going to be woozy."

"I make the drive to Star Valley every day," Victoria insisted. "I can do it this time as well."

In the end, Dr. Barkley wouldn't release her until she agreed to call a taxi. "That's what outpatient surgery is, Victoria," he told her almost angrily. "What your body has undergone is invasive and traumatic. You're still under the effects of anesthesia. Part of your agreement with me and with the hospital is that someone will administer your pain pills and care for you once you get home. If you don't hold to your part of the bargain, I will not release you until tomorrow."

"You can't do that. No one even knows I'm here." Although, she thought grimly, Jim wouldn't notice her missing until the hour grew very late. Since she'd found out the truth about Charlie, she'd spent too many late evenings at the Spotted Horse Station.

"I'm phoning Buckboard Cab."

"It'll cost a fortune to pay them to drive me down the canyon."

"I'll put the charges on your next bill," Dr. Barkley told her. "I want to see you alive next week when you come into my office and I report my findings. We've got a liability question here, Mrs. Roice. One way or another, I think it best to cover my losses."

If Star Valley's December weather had been peaceful, Mother Nature—as was often the case—made up for her benevolence during the first brutal week of February. For days, the sky stayed gun-barrel gray, the wind lashing those who dared poke their noses out with quick-sting shards of ice. What snow didn't come from the sky came from the ground, cavorting in great blizzardy drifts and piles, twirling into corners, hindering visibility, etching each log of Hayden's General Store with ice.

At least five black-capped chickadees hopped about each morning in the protection of the old blue spruce, feeding on Charlie's suet. They did so now, in spite of the storm. These days, Sarah constantly kept a coffee pot warming on the wood stove for customers. The wind had taken down two power lines close to Lake Palisades. Neither the Mac Johnsons nor the Farrell family had any electricity for almost seven hours.

In these parts, folks were used to getting by without lights and conveniences. Dinner could be cooked and the house could be warmed with the wood stove. The table could be lit with beeswax candles or kerosene lanterns. If the refrigerator quit working, things to stay frozen could be set on the back stoop.

Only one kink remained, or had started, in this pioneer country life that still marked so much of Wyoming. Anyone who used water in Star Valley relied on the quiet, constant service of an electric water pump. You could get by for an hour or two without power doing normal, run-the-faucet things. But let somebody forget and flush, and the whole household suddenly found itself out of luck and out of water.

"Sarah?" Becky Farrell asked as she stuck her head in the front door and shook off the snow. "Matt flushed the toilet three hours ago and we're totally out of water over at the house. Do you still let people pay for baths the way your dad used to?"

"Of course," she said. "How many?"

"Three of us."

"Do you need towels, too?"

"Nope. We brought our own."

"Three dollars apiece then. Nine dollars total. No tax."

"I'm walking over to Greybull Pond," Matt Farrell announced. "Gonna go over and watch that hockey game. Those little boys have really gotten good at it."

"Called off school today because of the wind and the roads being bad and what do those crazy kids do?" Mac Johnson asked, smugly laying a run of eight spades, from four to jack, across the table. "They put on their skates and go outside to play ice hockey."

Down past Greybull Pond, where the boys were playing, Jim and Victoria Roice stood outside beside the Wagoneer, debating the sensibility of her driving these roads.

"Can't we go inside to discuss this?" Jim asked. "Snow's blowing so hard, I can't see you across the hood."

"No," she said. "I'm on my way to Jackson. You're the one who followed me out here. This trip isn't up for discussion."

"Victoria. There's no reason to drive to Teton Village today. Nobody can go up the mountain. The tram won't be running. You know for yourself it's too windy."

"Damn it, Jim," she said. "Why does everybody treat me like I'm fifteen years old and just learning to drive? I'm on my way and nothing's going to stop me."

"Okay. I'll pick up Charlie at Greybull Pond and we'll go with you."

Her voice rose. It rang as keen and sharp as the wind around them. "I don't want you and Charlie to go with me."

"We'll drive to the village. We'll find out that the lifts and the ski tram are closed. We'll find that the offices are closed. We'll drive back home."

She shrieked at him. "I've already called Teton Village. I know the tram is closed. I'm not going out there today."

"What else could be so important that you're willing to risk traveling on these roads?"

"I'm seeing Dr. Barkley this afternoon."

For one long moment, he remained speechless. Of course. Why hadn't he realized it? Dr. Barkley. The only motivating force in Victoria's life these days. "How stupid of me for not figuring it out on my own." His words were dry, hard.

"But it's more than just an appointment," she told him through the biting wind. "He's giving me the results of all the tests."

"What tests?" he asked. "I thought there weren't going to be any tests."

"No," she told him. "Not tests on you. Tests on me. The results of the surgery are back. He's giving me his final report this afternoon."

"Surgery? You had the surgery?"

"Yes."

"When? Why didn't you tell me?" He realized, somewhat chagrined, that her telling him would've been the only way to know such a thing. He would not have noticed changes in her body. They hadn't touched each other in weeks.

"This is my own project, Jim. I don't want you involved. I don't want any support. I will do this by myself."

"Do this by yourself? Victoria, have you gone crazy?"

"Stop leaning on the car, Jim. I want to get going."

"I would've gone to the hospital with you. I would've sat with you while you were under anesthesia. I would've driven you home. Victoria, how did you get home?"

"Dr. Barkley called me a taxi."

"Great. Just great."

"I told you the car had broken down in Jackson and then I went to bed by myself."

"Just great, Victoria. I'd like our baby, too. But, you're seeing this all wrong. A baby is a blessing, a life, not just a seed planted between a lucky, healthy egg and a shapely, athletic sperm."

"You're just satisfied. You're just satisfied because of Charlie."

"What's wrong with being satisfied, damn it?!" he roared. "I told you why I didn't need to go in for testing. Sweet heaven, at such a cost to you, I told the truth. Accept it, Victoria. Accept that such a thing could happen, and that I'd still want to be a good husband to you."

"I'm going to Jackson," she said stoically as she opened the door and climbed inside. "I'll let you know what the doctor says."

The nurse didn't direct Victoria to one of the regular poster-lined examining rooms. Instead, Victoria was led to Dr. Barkley's private office, a wood-paneled library with framed photos of his own kids lining one wall. She sat in a deep leather chair across from a placard that read: Dr. Lars Barkley, M.D., and waited.

"Hello, Victoria," he said when he walked in and dropped her folder onto the desktop. "How was your taxi ride home last week?"

"I'd rather not discuss it."

"Thought you might call and cancel this appointment," he said. "Are the roads bad down your way? I've had several patients who couldn't come."

"Not me," she said. "I didn't want to miss this meeting."

He seated himself in a chair that was exactly like hers. He leaned back and crossed his arms. He didn't have to look at her charts before he spoke to her. She thought wryly, *He always has his speeches planned.*

"Well. I don't know if the information I'm going to give you is going to sound like good news or bad news, Victoria."

"Try me," she said. "I'll let you know."

He took a deep breath and watched her for a moment before he spoke. "I couldn't find anything wrong with you."

"What?"

"It's odd, considering the Clomid I prescribed you hasn't worked at all."

"What? What's odd?"

"There's not a thing I can find that should keep you from having children. I found no signs of endometriosis. Your fallopian tubes are fine. Your ovaries are fine. Your uterus is fine. Egg production is right on, considering your age, of course."

"But certainly there's something—"

"No. Nothing I could find at all. That's why I introduced my speech to you the way I did. If I'd found anything, we'd know what we're up against. We'd know if we needed to change anything or treat anything. On the other hand, everything about your reproductive system is functional."

"What does this mean?" she asked, halfway standing from the chair and leaning over him. "What does this mean?!"

"It means I don't need to see you anymore," he said kindly. "There isn't anything more I can do for you at this point, Victoria. I'd advise you go home to your husband, break open a bottle of champagne, put on soft music, and keep trying."

Electrical power over at the Johnson and Farrell places went on during the late afternoon. The gale, which buffed the hockey ice on Greybull Pond to a faultless polish, kept blustering well past the evening news. Still, wonder of wonders, the snow clouds began to drift apart as the sun set, leaving ragamuffin tendrils to catch the color.

Sarah's best-loved time of evening came just as the store closed, when the moon hung like a new-minted coin over countryside still backlit by the sun. She went to the porch, flipped the sign to CLOSED, untied her apron, and enjoyed the watercolors, the pure twilight green, blue, lavender, of the winter range rising to her west.

"Dadblast this thing," she heard a voice say. She turned toward the pond and saw Jim Roice working on the wheel again, grunting with exertion, nearly losing his footing in the snow when the rusty nut suddenly broke free and turned. "Didn't have a problem with these workings the first time. Bet the first time, that crazy thing hadn't been unscrewed since the 1930s. Today I've tightened it down myself and it takes all this pushing just to break it free."

"What are you doing working?" She dried her hands on her apron. It was getting to be a nervous habit, something she did every time she didn't know what else to do.

"Looking to fix this wheel."

"Seems to me there'd be plenty to do over at your place, without having to fix up mine. You've already tried once."

"Charlie's spending the night with Eric Ankeny. Victoria's gone down the canyon to Jackson. I expect she'll be late returning."

"This pond is a good place to watch the road."

"It is."

She dried her hands again, even though they were already dry. She liked the looks of him around the place, liked him tinkering with equipment that had been in the Hayden family for almost a century. "Best close up the register," she called to him. "Don't get too cold out there waiting for her, Jim. I've got the coffee on."

A while later, he came to the door, his breath chuffing in billows of frost, and rubbed his gloved hands together for warmth. "Looks like a family of muskrats has been living in your wheel, Sarah. I'm guessing five or six generations of 'em."

"If we clear them out, can we get the thing going again?"

"Don't know. I'd like to move the whole bunch of 'em down the river. It may take some time before we figure out what's shutting the whole thing down."

"Kimmy Jo from over at Caddisfly Inn has been telling me it's muskrats ever since I came back for Dad's funeral. She told me she'd seen them swimming in the pond."

"Couple of the blades on the runner are rotted through. I'd best see about replacing those."

"You start spending much more time worrying about that waterwheel, and I'll have to start thinking about paying you for it. Right now, you'd best see about coming in and warming up," she told him. "Your nose turns red just like Charlie's."

"I'm not coming in," he said. "Get your coat and mittens on. Come out for a walk with me, Sarah."

He didn't have to ask her twice. She ran for the dusty sheepskin coat, buttoned it tightly beneath her neck, tugged on cap and mittens, and joined him.

"Gotta ask you one thing," he whispered. "Long time ago, you remember talking to Kender Budge?"

"I remember," Sarah said. "She reminded me a lot of myself."

"You were saying that people who are different aren't always better. You were saying a lot of good people can be found in a lot of different places."

"Yes," she told him. "I was saying that. Going away, coming back, I've learned a great deal about people, about what is important." She stared off into the stars.

They walked together through the trees, on a course that had once stayed open, and now drifted closed with crust upon crust of ice and currents of snow.

It was a night of thin starlight, of bitter wind, of bleakness as cold and sharp as the frozen ground beneath their boots. Not for weeks, not since the night he'd told her about Charlie, had they spent time alone without some-one else knowing where they were. They dared not. And now, in these few sterling moments together, the years seemed to retreat between them.

"Sarah," he said quietly after they'd tramped through the deep snow for a while. "I wonder if you know what my life is like now."

She didn't stop or answer him.

"We have to talk about this, you know."

"We don't. No good can come from talking about such things."

"You don't know it. You're judging by what you think you know."

"Damn it, Jim," she said, finally coming toward him, clenching mittened fists at her side. "You've got a family, Jim, a little boy who I love more than I love myself. After everything, I won't jeopardize everything he holds secure."

He gripped her shoulders, made her turn toward him. "And what about me? What about loving me?"

"Don't ask it of me," she said. "Don't ask me to stand before you and tell you about everything I regret."

"You regret your freedom, don't you? You regret you ever left."

She reached up with one hand, meaning to cuff him across the jaw despite the ragg-wool mittens she wore. He gripped her wrist and wrested her close to him. "Oh, no, Sarah girl," he said with a slight tinge of amusement in his voice. And then, he couldn't help himself. He laughed with true mirth at the remembrance, his breath making a puff of vapor in the cold. "I hope the days of you decking me are over."

And so it became childhood laughter that closed the breach between them. Jim Roice gathered Sarah at once into his arms, held her tight against broadness she recog-nized, and lowered his mouth to encompass hers.

Before she knew what she was doing, she had committed herself to his kiss, a kiss that was at once a commemoration and a burgeoning hope, a kiss as immediate as it was tender, so like him and so unlike anyone else in the world. Not until it was over did she realize what it meant.

The kiss was a complete, fervent giving of selves, neither Jim nor Sarah holding back or hiding from the other. The years passed away between them. And even as time faded, the lesson of life itself—the frustration, the hope, the acute joy and gritty pain—stood in its stead.

The remembrance should have frightened her, reminded her that while she released herself now to discover these old, good things, he could not. Until this moment, she hadn't realized her fate. She hadn't realized that, since she left the valley so many years ago, she'd unconsciously compared every kiss, every man, to this kiss and this man and, in the comparison, found others lacking.

"I'd best go in, Jim," she told him. "Victoria will be coming home."

"Think back," he said, poking his hands in his pockets and marveling at the stars. "Think back to all the times we've stood out here together."

He walked her back to the porch and waited, watching her from the frozen meadow while she stood half in darkness, half illuminated from the plate-glass windows of the store. She took the screen door in hand but didn't open it, didn't want any sound to disturb the stillness.

"Jimmy Mill Roice."

She said his name once, just once, to remind herself that he stood beside her in the darkness, that he'd always be some place, not quite far away.

"See above you, Sarah," he said softly. "Turn around and just take a look at this broad Wyoming sky."

"I know it," she answered. "I know it. No matter where I go, I'll never see anything quite so fine and new as this."

20

As Victoria drove home from Jackson Hole, the heater in the Wagoneer blasted full speed. Still, no matter how high she turned the defrost, she couldn't get warm. She couldn't stop shivering. Seemed as if the cold didn't come from outside tonight. It came from somewhere deep within herself.

She drove slowly, aware of the thin gloss of ice that often coated this stretch of road after a windstorm. As she rounded a curve, her headlights played on a young cowboy walking along the highway shoulder, his hat bent into the wind, a guitar looped over one shoulder. As the lights caught his face, he poked his thumb in the direction Victoria was going.

During the summer months, it wasn't unusual to see hitchhikers along the way, often sitting on their guitars and accompanied by dogs, holding up cardboard signs to mark their destinations: Pinedale or Denver or Salt Lake City. This time of year, though, the weather made it almost impossible for moneyless travelers. Victoria pulled onto the shoulder and opened the door.

"What're you doing out here? Do you need help?"

"Hitchhiked over from Boise," the cowboy said. "Thought I'd play a little guitar and earn my keep at some restaurant or something. Only problem is, my dog's disappeared. Jumped outta the back of the truck I was riding in up by the intersection. Fellow I'd hitched with wasn't willing to come this way. Thought I'd just walk along and call her. She'll hear me soon."

"What's her name?"

"Bob. She's a bloodhound. Brought her all the way with me from Idaho."

"Idaho isn't too far. You expect she's trying to go home?"

"Don't know what I expect. It's awful dark out here, but she can smell herself through just about anything."

"What makes you think she came this way?"

"She's always out running. She's always thinking she's gotta find something better than what she's already got. For that, she spends a lot of days going hungry."

"Well, get in," Victoria said. "Don't wanna read in the paper in the morning that somebody froze to death walking by the roadside. I'm going as far as Star Valley. That's back west, toward the Idaho state line. Maybe we'll see Bob."

"Thank you, ma'am," he said, tipping his hat to her and revealing a pile of sandy brown curls. "Much obliged."

Victoria didn't expect to find his dog. It sounded like an unlikely story to her. "So where are you headed tonight?"

"Don't have a plan. Just out to find my dog."

Victoria glanced across the front seat at him, thinking him young but handsome. "You really a cowboy, or do you just wear the clothes?"

"I'm a vet student at Boise State. Do a little rodeoing on the side. Steer roping with my brother. Won $1,000 in the Jackson Hole Rodeo last summer."

"You must be pretty good."

She felt his eyes on her as he answered strangely, "I'm pretty good at a lot of things."

"Oh, really?"

Victoria turned her attention back to the highway. She wondered if he could see her hands trembling on the steering wheel. She kept thinking, *There's nothing wrong with me at all. No reason I can't get pregnant.*

"So what about you?" he asked, leaning a little ways toward her. "Where have you been? And where are you going?"

"I've been to a doctor's appointment," she said, stiff beside him, suddenly afraid of herself, afraid of all the possibilities. "Then I've been to a bar. And before I get home to Star Valley, I might go to another bar."

"Are you driving drunk?" he asked, sounding honestly worried.

"No. These roads are bad but I'm a good driver."

"No reason to get mad about it."

"I can't help it. Nobody thinks I'm a good driver."

"Lady? Are you okay?"

"Sometimes I don't know."

"You sick or something? Is that why you were at the doctor's?"

"No. I was at the doctor's because my husband and I can't have a baby. Dr. Lars Barkley, M.D., was trying to find out what was wrong with me."

Suddenly the headlights illuminated something brown running along the edge of the road. At first Victoria thought it a calf that had slipped through barbed wire and gotten out of somebody's pasture. But the cowboy at her side started hollering: "It's Bob. Stop now. There's my dog."

She braked. "I don't believe it."

"See? I told you so."

Victoria parked the car again and the fellow jumped

out to retrieve his animal. "Come on, Bob. You crazy fool dog, I thought you were gone for good this time." He peered back in at her. "You mind if Bob rides along, too? I can put her in the back seat."

"By all means," Victoria said, shaking her head. "I'm not gonna drive off and leave the two of you out here." The huge dog had a jowly brown head with massive black lop ears. Bob hung her head from the back seat to the front and drooled in Victoria's lap.

When the familiar Spotted Horse Station sign appeared on the left-hand side of the road, Victoria breathed a sigh of relief. "You wanna go in here for a while?" she asked. "I'll buy you a drink. We'll celebrate that you found Bob. Ed Tribitt's a good man. He might give you a place to sleep tonight if you play your guitar for his customers."

The cowboy touched her on the leg, then moved his hand up to her thigh. "Is that what you want? We could stay out here in the car."

For a moment, she considered it. She thought, *It's a possibility, trying it with someone else. I ought not to be afraid. No one would know but Bob the dog.*

He saw her hesitation and took advantage of it, bending across the seat to kiss her.

She kissed him back, wrapping her arms around him. He tasted like tobacco and leather. Perhaps a baby he fathered would look like him. Perhaps it would have those tousled sandy curls and that cocky grin. *Or perhaps,* she thought, *perhaps the baby would look like me.*

He lifted her buttocks and pulled her toward him, then started to unzip her jeans. "Gotta get these off . . . there. Oh, look at you. You look real good. I like your panties."

She reached for his hands to stop him, but he wouldn't quit.

"Come on, lady. Just let me feel you. Your panties are all wet."

Lady. He'd called her lady.

With shocking clarity, Victoria realized she was about to do this with someone who didn't even know her name. Furthermore, she didn't know his name, either. He had to be at least ten years her junior. And all she'd been able to think about was conceiving a baby, a baby she didn't know, a stranger . . . a stranger . . . when she had Jim and Charlie waiting back home.

Dear, sweet heaven. What had she done to them all?

"I don't want this," she said. "Don't touch me."

"Of course you want this," he said. "I can tell an eager woman when I see one."

It occurred to her that this was exactly what she'd done to her husband. She'd calculated, planned, manipulated, using Jim and their marriage bed with the same reckless self-absorption that had brought her to this place.

Suddenly, she understood why Jim had pushed her away.

"Oh, lady—"

She sat up, her pants wrinkled down around her ankles, and said to him, "Get out of my car."

He tilted the brim of his Stetson at her. Strange, it was one of the few things he hadn't already begun to remove. "But you've got me all hot, woman. Hot and ready."

"Please. Just get out of my car."

Bob whimpered at the window, as if the dog had been trained to depart at the words "Get out of my car."

He ran his hands up the inside of her thighs and left them there, parting her, his fingers almost inside her. He waited a long minute, waited to decide.

She closed her legs against him. "Get out and take your drooling dog with you and don't come back."

She saw the remoteness come into his eyes. Thankfully, he took his hands off her and started buttoning his jeans. A real gentleman, Victoria thought wryly. "Just because you're mad at yourself doesn't mean you've gotta be mad at me," he said, his voice shaking. "Thought you wanted it, lady."

"Don't call me lady."

"Guess this means you aren't gonna buy me and Bob a drink."

She got herself dressed without answering. "I'm going to walk into that bar by myself, do you understand? I'm going to have one drink to calm my nerves, and, when I come out, I want you to be gone. I don't care where you go. I don't care who you catch a ride with. I just don't want you sitting here in my front seat when I get back."

"No wonder you and your husband can't have a baby," he said as he climbed out. He whistled for Bob, then finished it. "You probably never do it with him, either."

Victoria didn't look back. She walked in through the front door of Spotted Horse Station. She glanced around for Ed Tribitt, or anybody familiar. She was both disappointed and relieved not to see anyone she recognized. She sat at her favorite stool, right beneath the stuffed moose head, and ordered her favorite drink.

Ed wasn't here to keep count the way he usually did. She ordered three drinks and drank them fast. After that, she ordered another one. She still didn't know if she could face going home.

"Hey, lady." She jerked to attention when she heard the word, but it was only the bartender who didn't know her. "We're closing in five minutes. Can I get you anything else before I clean up back here?"

"No thanks," she said. "I've had enough." She lay too much money on the counter, but she couldn't figure out how much everything cost. She needed to get back. Only, she couldn't remember where she needed to get back to.

She walked outside, welcoming the cutting wind against her face. The wind made it easier to think. She opened the front door to the Wagoneer and looked in. Nobody was there. Good. The only trace of her hitchhiker she could find was a wealth of stubby brown dog hair sticking all over the back seat.

When she turned out onto the highway, she turned the wrong way. It took her a while to realize she needed to go to Star Valley tonight instead of back to Jackson. She hung a U-turn right in the middle of the road and drove past Spotted Horse Station again. Victoria followed the road very slowly. She negotiated each curve very carefully. Twice she turned on her blinker for no reason. Nobody was behind her. Above her, the stars seemed far away and pale.

She didn't want to have a wreck. She didn't want to end up in the Snake River, or else Jim would never let her drive again. Twice she passed road signs and jumped, afraid she was passing someone walking on the side of the highway. Once she thought she saw Bob.

In Star Valley, she couldn't figure out how to find her driveway. She saw the sign for Jenkins' Building Supply and Charlie Egan's greenhouse. She'd gone all the way down past the Pronghorn Motel before she realized she'd missed the turn. The turn into their driveway had no sign, only darkness and a cattle guard.

She made another U-turn, looking for her own driveway. In her headlights, the horrible thing loomed, the hand-painted brown sign she'd driven past every morning since the day she'd married Jim.

Hayden's General Store. She aimed her front fender directly for the sign, floored the gas pedal on the Wagoneer, and ran into it.

The wood cracking sobered Victoria a bit. She tried to back up and take another run on the sign, to do more damage. She put the four-wheel drive into reverse and floored it. Nothing happened. She threw it into neutral, then back into reverse, and tried again. Still nothing.

She rested her forehead on the steering wheel, exhausted. It had been a long day. And, from somewhere in her stupor, she never did realize that the sound she heard in the distance was that of her own horn honking.

Sarah stepped into her snow boots, threw on a flannel robe, and ran downstairs. Someone'd run into her sign and was stuck in the middle of the parking lot, honking. She threw open the screen and ran toward the vehicle, yanking the door open to make sure no one was hurt.

There sat Victoria, snoozing away, her forehead on the horn.

"Victoria," she hollered. "Stop. You're gonna wake up everybody in Star Valley."

"What?"

"Victoria. Pick your head up. You're honking your horn."

"What?" But this time, Victoria picked her head up to ask the question, and the horn stopped its incessant blare.

"Are you hurt?"

"Hell no. Sarah Hayden, what are you doing here?"

"You're in my yard. You ran into my sign."

"That was fun. The best fun I've had all day."

"You're drunk. You could've gotten killed driving up the canyon like this."

"I don't need you to tell me that."

"Move over. I'll drive you home."

"You can't drive me home. The Wagoneer's stuck on your sign. We'll have to call a tow truck from Star Valley Sinclair tomorrow."

"You'll have to walk then. Can you walk far enough for me to help you home?" Sarah backed up and Victoria unfolded from the driver's seat. She stood up, swayed, and grabbed on to the hood for support.

"Damn it."

"Loop your arm over my shoulder," Sarah instructed her. "I'm strong enough. I'll help you get home."

"Don't need any help from you." Vic turned toward Sarah and let fly one wild punch. Sarah ducked out of the way.

"Nobody will ever let me forget," Victoria said as she grabbed the hood again. "No one ever let me forget that he'd loved you."

"Vic," Sarah said. "Don't do this to yourself."

"Don't wanna go home," Victoria said. "Don't want Charlie to see me drunk. Mustn't let Charlie see me like this."

"He won't see you. He isn't there. He's gone over to Eric Ankeny's to spend the night, then tomorrow morning they're playing hockey. You've got time to recuperate."

Victoria stared, her eyes seeming to focus on something for the first time since she climbed out of the car. "How do you know? How long have you been keeping up with my family like this?"

"Since I found out it was my family, too."

She made as if she might swing again. Sarah put up one hand to deflect the blow, but it never came. Victoria said, "I knew what I was getting into back then. I've played second-fiddle to you since the day I first saw Jim Roice's face."

"Come on, Vic." Sarah reached for the woman with both arms and bore her weight as they both moved toward the road. "Let's get you home."

"Sorry about your sign," Victoria said. "I was driving along. All of a sudden, it just jumped out in front of me, like it was in the middle of the highway or something."

"That's okay. I'll get a new one. I wish you'd run over Rita Persnick's realty signs, too."

"Maybe I did."

"Maybe so. Guess we'll find out in the morning."

They'd walked halfway up the Roices's driveway when Victoria began to sob. "Don't know what to do anymore," she said, weeping loudly. "Just don't know what to do."

Sarah turned and took the woman by the shoulders. Their eyes met. "Accept what's been given you," she said to Victoria and to the darkness and the ancient trees. "Love your family. And let your family love you."

On Saturday morning, the Chinook winds began.

Dry breezes whistled down the slopes of the mountains, warming as they blew. Old-timers talked about Chinook days, days that often came during the worst of winter, warm temperatures that churned packed ice into deep, wet piles of slush.

The warm winds set snow everywhere to melting, sending water dripping from every eave, as icicles formed or took on new, monstrous proportions. You could go with no hat and not freeze your ears. You could sit on a protected porch and grin into the sun.

Chinook days carried with them an odd sense of decadence, of freedom. They seemed a slight reminder of seasons gone by. Everywhere, ice melted. To the frozen Wyoming upland, Chinook winds brought the first tantalizing, timid illusion of spring.

"Going out to check the Mackenzie boats," Jim informed Victoria as he tugged on his boots. "It's been almost three months since I looked 'em over good. Gotta make sure those tarps are holding, with all the water that's coming off the roof."

The whole time he talked, he never looked at her. He just kept yanking his bootlace tighter and tighter.

"You tie that boot any tighter, you won't have a right foot by nightfall," she said.

"When hard weather comes back, we could have damage if water gets caught against those hulls and freezes."

Victoria sat across from him, sipping a steaming mug of coffee. "Jim, you got time to talk?"

"Feels like spring out there today. The aspens are

gonna be leafing out before you know it. You'd half think it was May out there this morning instead of just February."

"You got time to talk?" she asked again. "Won't be satisfied if I sent you off this morning without saying something."

He finally stopped and looked at her. "Send me off? You're not going down to Jackson this morning?"

"No. Someone's covering for me today. I needed time to"— she hesitated, not knowing exactly how to say it — "be."

He touched her arm. "You want to tell me what the doctor told you?"

"I'll tell you sometime," she said. "Not right now."

He took his coat off the peg and shrugged into it. "Gotta see about those boats."

"Jimmy." She stood up. "I've gotta tell you one thing before you go down to the barn."

He zipped his coat. "What?"

"I've gotta tell you I'm sorry."

"Sorry for what? The fender? Carl Kohler said he'd have the new one by next Monday. We'll fix it then."

"No, not for that. For other things. For things that can't be fixed."

He stood in the doorway, his back toward her. "I don't know what you mean, Vic."

"Yes, you do," she said quietly. "I'm talking about us."

At last, he turned toward her. "I've been so damned consumed with the idea of hanging on to things, haven't I?"

"We've both been consumed," she said, tears coming to her eyes for the first time in years. "Sometimes a person's greatest strength is also a great weakness. We've caused each other pain."

"Yes," he said. "We have."

"I think about our wedding sometimes. I think about how I felt standing out by Lake Palisades with a bouquet of mums and the breeze blowing just right. Remember? Remember how far you could see across the water? All that blue, like seeing into forever. And saying our vows—"

"Victoria." He didn't move across the room toward her. She hadn't expected it of him. He said somberly, "Vows are best kept. We made ours before both God and Pastor W. D. Owen."

"Even so, I often don't know the best way of loving you," she told him. "Perhaps I should love you as I've seen you love Sarah. Perhaps I should release you as you once released her. I know how it all ends, don't you see? After all, Sarah's come back."

He clutched the doorknob and said nothing, jutting his chin toward the ceiling, looking at nothing, the sinew at his neck a drawn, taut line.

"Go see to your boats, Jim," she said quietly.

Milt Hoover of the Lincoln County Highway Department always stopped by the barber shop of a morning to help himself to a cup of coffee and talk about the weather.

"What do you think, George?" he asked the barber as he gave Lowell Anderson a shave. "You think it'll be warm like this through the whole week?"

"Don't want it to be. We need to keep the snowpack up above timberline where it belongs. We lose much more snow this winter and we'll be looking at a forest-fire summer for sure."

"Guess that's planning ahead for you. I don't ever worry about summers around here when it's so cold, air crackles through your nose."

"Air ain't crackling today."

"Chinooks always make me think about summer," said Lowell Anderson. "I'll bet it's over forty-five degrees out there. Warmer than that down in Afton.

Harvey Perkins and Jack Gwilliam've been out in their snowplows since six this morning, trying to scrape slush off the highway."

"Now don't start talking, Lowell," George Peart said. "You know what happened last time I shaved you and you got talkative in this chair."

"Yeah, I know," the postmaster said. "You about cut my nose off."

"That's an exaggeration." George reached for a larger razor. "Only took off about half an inch of skin."

"Well." Milt plopped the *Rural Electric Tidbit* back on the shelf and stretched. "Now that I'm caught up with the local news, best get on my way. I've got some DANGER, THIN ICE signs the department wants me to spread around this afternoon. Wanted me to drive the truck out on Greybull Pond, too, and see how the ice is holding."

George Peart stopped his shaving. Even so, Lowell Anderson didn't make any comment at all. "Folks at the highway department think it's warm enough to make that ice give way?"

"Could be. I can tell you one thing, though," Milt said, chuckling. "I'm not gonna chance ruining another good vehicle. Remember last year when Joe Markman got a whole backhoe stuck in the mud down by Caddisfly? Crazy thing, driving a rig out in the ice like that. Figure I'll just stick those signs around the edges and go home. That oughtta scare everybody away until it's miserable cold again."

Brad Dilger and Joey Sikes were already waiting at Greybull Pond when Eric and Charlie dumped their gear on the bench, snapped on their helmets, and began to lace their skates.

"This is a great day," Eric said.

"Yeah," Charlie answered. "The best."

"Hurry, you guys! My dad's making me come home in an hour!" Brad called. "It took you two all day to get here."

"Charlie slept over at my house," Eric answered. "Took us a while to get all his stuff packed up."

The two boys ran pirouettes upon the ice, raising their sticks high, making slapshots, lauding the sun. They joyously rehearsed, wrapping runs around the outside of the goalie net, shaving to a stop when they chanced upon opposite moves to their liking. Eric Ankeny poked his neon-orange blade guards into the snow and Charlie followed his friend, taking to the ice with bent legstrokes and scissoring skates.

"How are we playing it?" Joey asked. "The usual?"

"Yeah," Eric said. "Two on two."

"I play with Charlie," said Brad.

"No, I play with Charlie," said Eric.

"I'll pick," Charlie said. "Joey's on my team."

"Good," Joey said. "Brad versus Charlie on the face-off."

"I'll pitch it in." Eric lobbed the puck toward the middle of the pond. Charlie gained control immediately, weaving the puck away from Brad, then passing it to Joey.

Joey skated fast, trying for a breakaway. When Brad zipped in front of him and waggled his stick, Joey passed back to Charlie.

"Shoot!" Joey hollered. "Shoot!"

Charlie shot. Brad jumped, diving to a slide, and stopped the puck.

"Good defense," Charlie yelled, huffing with exertion.

Brad passed the puck to Eric. Eric shot. The puck zoomed perfectly into the net.

"One-nothing!" Eric bellowed. "Get ready for the face-off."

As Charlie and Brad stood, sticks ready, they felt

something jostle at their feet. A sound, like the rending of cloth, echoed against the trees.

"What was that?" Charlie asked.

"Don't know," Joey said. "It was weird, wasn't it? Like an earthquake."

"They've had earthquakes here before."

"I know that, silly."

"Here comes the face-off. You guys stop fooling around." Eric lobbed the puck into the air.

Charlie took control again, but Brad tipped it away. Joey came up and checked Brad, poking his stick beneath his friend, falling against him to knock him away from the puck.

"No fair! Checking. There's nobody here to call penalties."

"If you check right, you don't draw a penalty," Charlie hollered as he took it into a breakaway and lifted the puck into the air, scoring in the upper left-hand corner of the goal. "This new stick is great. I've never been able to get it airborne like that before."

"Next goal wins it," Brad said. "I've gotta go in a minute. My dad's gonna be mad if I'm not home by one."

"Come on. Hurry."

Charlie took the face-off again. He got a breakaway and shot immediately. The puck hit the goalpost and bounced out. "Ah!" he shouted as he hit the rebound. "Score!"

"You think you could've given the rest of us a chance?" Brad asked, disgruntled.

"You told me to hurry so I did."

"Show-off."

"I've gotta go too," Joey said. "My mom wants me home for lunch."

"Me too," Eric said. "We've gotta go shopping this afternoon. You want to come, Charlie?"

"No." He pivoted once around the goalie net, his

skates flashing, as silver blades caught the sun. "I'm gonna practice my crossovers."

"You sure?" Joey called.

"Yeah." He waved them off with one red glove. "You guys go ahead. I'll skate a while."

21

Milt Hoover whistled as he parked his truck alongside the highway. Couldn't remember what song he was whistling, just something he'd heard on the radio, a tune that made him feel good. He stepped up on the back bumper of his truck to dig out the THIN ICE signs.

He'd been putting them around since he'd left Peart's Barber Shop two hours ago; he'd saved Greybull Pond for last because it was his biggest job. Crazy thing, anyway. Ice wouldn't give way on Greybull in this weather. Once the trucks had been out on it in November, kids always skated on it until past Easter.

Now, where were those signs? He'd kept at least five just for this purpose. But everything in the back of the truck had jostled on top of everything else during the drive. Darn slush. Might as well have been driving all day over potholes. He'd spent all day steering through stuff the same consistency as snow cones.

Milt climbed clear into the bed and shoved his

strongbox aside, scooting shovels, chains, and spools across the metal with a resounding grate.

Ah. There they were.

He gathered the signs into a bunch and propped them against one shoulder, carrying them the same way he'd carry a fishing pole. Milt hopped out of the truckbed and made his way through the snow toward Greybull Pond, still whistling the same song.

It had been years since Victoria had walked in the snow, years since she'd enjoyed the sun-gilded colors at her feet, the squeaking of lodgepole pines as they swayed, the flight song of birds as they flickered through the trees. She did so now, letting the sun warm her face. Perhaps pain was good, she thought. Perhaps with pain came this first, full sense of being alive. Perhaps she'd needed to let herself feel those things a long time ago.

As she walked through the forest, sunlight shone through spruce needles and glimmered like patches of debris on the snow. As she broke through the trees and came to the shore of Greybull Pond, the place was strangely quiet, almost hauntingly so. She heard no children's voices, only the sound of one pair of skates carving ice, making turns.

Victoria expected to see them playing hockey. She'd decided, when she set out on this walk, to find Charlie and watch him use his new Christmas stick. He'd been bragging about it for weeks. She found him skating alone at the far end of the rink, circling round and round the net so fast as to make himself dizzy, his skates crossing, paring the ice into thin shavings as he made each revolution.

"Hi, Mom!" he called when he saw her.

Oh, but she was glad to see him this morning, glad to see the particular boy she'd known and loved for so long. "What are you doing?" she called. "Where's everybody?"

"They all had to go home. I made two goals in the game. Eric only made one."

"Good for you."

Charlie skated toward her, sun glancing off his skates. As he came close, he asked, "How was your doctor appointment? Did you find out why you can't have a baby?" He sliced to a stop.

"No. Doctor didn't find anything wrong," she said, surprised at his awareness, and pleased because he'd asked. "But that can be good news, too."

"All right," Charlie said, raising his stick. "I'm glad he told you something nice."

"Hey." She took one step forward through the snow, knowing she wouldn't reach him on the ice, but wanting to draw closer to him. "Charlie."

"What?"

"I love you. I always have, you know."

"Sure," he said, cocking his helmet at her. "But sometimes you thought so much about that baby, you forgot is all." He balanced his stick low across the ice and started to skate away. "Love you, too, Mom. I'm practicing crossovers. You wanna see?"

"Sure. Show me," she said even though she'd already been watching.

He skimmed across the rink, then came barreling away from the edge of the pond toward her, crossing his skates at top speed as he rounded the corner.

"Great," Victoria yelled from the snow. "Charlie, that's amazing. You're really getting better."

"I'll do it again. Watch." But, as he circled the corner a second time, he felt something odd give way beneath him. He caught the toe of one skate upon the heel of the other. He lost his balance and began to fall. He saw a jagged crack moving toward him across the surface.

"Charlie!" he heard his mother scream. "Charlie. Get off the ice."

He pitched forward, trying to catch himself with his hands.

"Hang on!" she screamed. "Charlie, hang on!"

Hang on to what? He set his hands in front of his face, expecting the jar that would stop him. But Charlie never felt himself hit anything. The ice he grasped crumbled beneath his gloved hands. He plummeted straight through into water, clear blue and eerie, fiery cold.

He exhaled halfway, the bubbles tickling his face inside his helmet. His skates filled up with water. His hockey breezers did the same. For seconds, a minute maybe, he fought to unsnap his helmet.

Charlie tried to swim, but the water in his clothes held him down. He couldn't undo his helmet without yanking off his gloves. He pulled the right glove off and tried again at the helmet. He couldn't get the snap without both hands. He yanked the left glove off and, for one weird, disembodied moment, watched the glove float away. With hands as clumsy as something dead, he fought to find the snaps on his helmet. He found one again. He tugged hard on it, then on the chin strap. The snap wouldn't budge.

Charlie couldn't get his helmet off. He couldn't even find his helmet. He couldn't hold his breath anymore. What he'd give, oh, what he'd give, for one full, sweet breath of air.

As the water began to go dark around him, he wasn't afraid.

He realized he wasn't alone.

Charlie'd barely felt the jolt as another person slammed into the water. At first, he thought the thing that swam beside him and with him might've been an angel. Now he felt her arms go around him, felt her holding, lifting him. He knew as a boy, as he'd known as a baby, to rest in Victoria's arms.

He couldn't see her. He only knew the feel of her, the safe sense of her.

His mother.

When his head reached the surface, he had on his helmet. His stick lay on the ice where he'd dropped it. His lungs burned. And though his head stayed above water, he couldn't climb out.

"Kid! Hang on!" he heard a man shout, as the guy dropped an armload of signs on the snow and began to untie a yellow rope looped to his waist. "I'll be there. Don't let yourself go back in. Under all this ice, we might never find you."

"I'm—"

"Sh-h-hhh. Don't try to say anything. Just save your strength. You're gonna have to hang on to this rope."

As Milt Hoover approached the spot where Charlie had gone in, he knelt to his hands and knees, distributing his weight so not to stress the ice further.

Charlie couldn't talk. He didn't have the strength or the ability to hang on. But, for some reason, he didn't have to clutch the jagged, broken edges to stable himself. Something stayed beneath him, lifting him, lifting him, keeping his head above water.

Milt worked fast, knowing the ice around them could go at any minute, too. He knotted the rope around Charlie's bread basket. "Now. As I pull you out, lay flat on the ice," Milt instructed. "Don't try to stand up or even get on all fours to crawl. I'll take you all the way to the edge, where it's safe."

"My—"

"We've gotta go fast. You ready?"

Charlie nodded. "But, my mother—"

"We've gotta get you out of there." Slowly, ever so carefully, Milt Hoover began to draw Charlie Roice out of the water, toward safety. Charlie lay prone on the ice, too exhausted to help. When they got to the edge of the ice, Milt Hoover knelt beside him and easily unfastened his hockey helmet. He pulled it off and dumped the icy water. "There you go, son," Milt said. "Any other time of year and we'd've been dumping fish right out of that helmet with you."

"You going in that hole?" Charlie asked, his eyes dazed. The boy was obviously in shock and probably suffering from hypothermia, too. "You gonna get her out, too?"

Milt Hoover felt his heart constrict. "Who? Get who out? You're the only one I saw."

"No. You've gotta go back," Charlie said, beginning to wail. "You've gotta go down there. My momma's still there. She held me up so I could get breath."

Milt reached for his radio. He broadcast to anyone who could hear him. "Somebody call 911. Get a rescue team out to Greybull Pond. We've got a woman under the ice."

The Lincoln County Search and Rescue Team sent divers down for two hours before they found Victoria's body. An ambulance came to take Charlie to St. John's Hospital in Jackson, but he wouldn't go. "No," he screamed. "I'm staying with my dad. I'm staying with my dad!"

The paramedics wrapped him in blankets and let him stay.

Another ambulance stood waiting nearby, but, as the minutes dragged on, everyone understood there wouldn't be a use for it.

At Hayden's General Store, Sarah heard the sirens. "Anybody know what's going on?" she asked the first group of shoppers as they came in. "I keep hearing trucks and sirens pass by."

One of them selected a box of instant hot chocolate and set it on the counter. "Didn't you hear? A big accident. Some little boy fell through the ice over at Greybull Pond. I think it was bad. They're saying somebody died."

Comes a time when you meet something dangerous in life, when the mixture of adrenaline and fear so overpowers your body that it prickles like sharp nettle on your skin. Sarah knew the full sensation of it now as she stood, the hot chocolate purchase halfway punched into the cash register.

"Here you go," she said, shoving the item into a sack. "Just take this."

The woman had change in her hand. "But I can pay—"

"No. Just take it. I must go."

Sarah left the store open. She left customers standing in the foyer. She left the phone ringing and the register set halfway through the purchase. She pulled on her pac boots and coat and ran. As she neared Greybull Pond, she heard voices, saw red lights flashing in macabre circuits through the pines. And the whole way, as she sloughed through the heavy slush, she prayed, "Please, God. Please don't let it be Charlie."

Sarah broke through into the clearing and for long, agonizing moments, couldn't see anyone she knew, couldn't fathom what was happening. "Charlie?" she screamed. "Where's Charlie Roice?"

"He's over there, Sarah." Harvey Perkins took her by the shoulders and physically turned her to see them. "Charlie's over there and Jim, too."

Across the broken ice, she saw Jim standing, his shoulders squared, his head bowed, holding on to a child wrapped in blankets. She had to get to them. The slush made it slow going as she skirted the pond and the huge Lincoln County rescue trucks. She ran as best she could until, breathlessly, she came to them. "Charlie, oh, Charlie," she cried, reaching for the little boy to gather him into her arms. "You're safe. You're safe."

But Charlie didn't move toward her. And, when she raised her face to Jim's, she saw torment in his eyes, as if he'd been the one to die.

She took one step back into the deep snow. Chunks of ice spilled over into her boots and soaked her ankles. "Jim? Jim? What is it?"

"Victoria's gone," he said. He didn't look at her. He couldn't. "They're searching for her body under the ice."

"Jimmy," Sarah whispered, finally realizing that, for the past few minutes, she'd been crying. She reached to take his hand. "How?"

Jim held his hand away and wouldn't let Sarah touch him. "She saved Charlie's life under there. He says she pushed him up—"

From across the way came a shout. A wet-suited diver rose from a break in the ice and pushed his mask off his face. "We've found the body," the diver told everyone.

Sarah reached for Charlie, but still, he wouldn't come to her. "Let me take Charlie back to the store, Jim," she whispered frantically. "Let me spare him this."

"I'm staying with my dad," Charlie hollered, putting his fists out as if to push her away. "I won't go. I won't go."

Jim stared down at her, agony in his eyes. "Dear God, Victoria," he said again.

"Come with me, Charlie Chickadee," Sarah whispered as she reached for his hand and cried.

"Take him." Jim shoved the boy toward Sarah. "He shouldn't see this. Get him out of here."

Victoria Tayloe Roice's funeral seemed much, much different from the last one in the valley. Last funeral had been old Will Hayden's and, for Will, no one had cried. Folks knew he'd been satisfied and, if not for his daughter leaving, he'd have been all-the-way happy.

With Victoria, things were different. Star Valley townspeople filled Morning Star Baptist Church to standing-room-only. Flowers and greenery arrangements covered the front altar. Before the service began, four extra rolls of toilet paper in the downstairs bathroom had completely disappeared. Mrs. Coral Weatherby blew her nose right on the spot, from the third pew on the left side, and made such a racket over the sound system that the choir had to stop during the third verse of "How Great Thou Art" and wait until the pianist could find her place in the music again.

W. D. Owen talked on and on about Victoria. He told of the sunny day he'd married Jim and Victoria Roice on the shores of Lake Palisades. He told of the good mother she'd been, and of the good wife.

As the pastor talked, Jim Roice kept one arm around the little boy beside him on the front pew, their heads bowed together, their shirt collars perfectly white above their suit collars, their new haircuts from George Peart perfectly aligned along each of their napes.

"Such a shame," someone from the ski corp commented.

"Ought not happen to a young family like that," someone else said.

"She was a good lady," Ed Tribitt, who'd sent one of the largest arrangements of greenery, said. "Wasn't always cheerful when she was drinking, but she was good."

"Seems a waste," Maudie Perkins muttered. "Little boy losing his mother like that, and a man losing his wife."

Sarah sat on the back row right beside Maudie, scarcely able to see through all the heads and hats, scarcely able to hear through all the sniffing. Once, she saw Jim pull a hanky out of his pocket and hand it to Charlie so he could blow. Once, she saw Charlie reach to touch Jim's face with his small hand.

How she longed to take the front pew with them. How she longed to grieve Victoria with them and, in that tender grief, claim them as her family, too.

At the cemetery where they buried her, Jack Gwilliam

brought in a backhoe to break through the frozen ground. Cold weather had set in again; folks came bundled in everything they owned. The wind howled. Red rose petals blew haphazardly across the snow. No one talked about the president's foibles or the fact that landfill rates had gone up down at the county dump. Star Valley folks somberly paid homage to the woman they'd known only a decade or so, the woman who'd married and cared for one of their own.

Everybody from thirty miles around waited in line to pay their respects to Jim Roice and the boy. "Don't know what to say," some said. "We're so sorry," others commented. "She done a good thing, saving her boy's life like that," said George Peart. "God's will is often impossible to understand," announced Beulah Hardaway.

And when Jim Roice and Sarah Hayden met face-to-face in the midst of that line, words failed to come.

His back went rigid. She stooped low to hug Charlie. "I'm glad you're my friend," she said, taking his hand while huge tears flooded the little boy's eyes for the umpteenth time.

"My momma died," he told her.

"I know, sweetie," she said back, her heart breaking because she couldn't stay beside them. But, when she spoke, she didn't say, "Victoria died knowing what I felt for you, Jimmy. I'm scared she knew my regrets, that I wished you both belonged to me again."

"Thank you for being here, Sarah," Jim said. He didn't say, "I'm guilty and she knew it. I'm guilty because I loved you even while I loved her."

"I'd best move on," she said, touching Charlie's wheat-ripe hair for the last time. "I don't want to keep you."

Mr. and Mrs. Miller Roice came home right after the burial. They parked their huge motor home with the Arizona license plates directly outside Jim and Charlie's front door. Sarah watched from her window as a cavalcade of visitors drove into the Roices' driveway. For days, Sarah expected Charlie to appear at the screen door of Hayden's General Store with just enough change shoved in his pockets for a grape Bubble Jug. For days, he didn't come.

A week after the funeral, Sarah got up enough bravery to bake a lasagna and carry it to them. Jim's mother met her at the porch. "Why, little Sarah Hayden," she said, clucking her tongue. "What are you doing here?"

"I brought you dinner tonight, Mrs. Roice," Sarah, said quietly.

"Oh, how nice of you." She took the casserole from Sarah, but held it away from her slightly, as if she wasn't certain she wanted to eat it. "We've got a lot of food. I'll probably just put this one in the deep freeze."

Charlie's grandmother turned to go inside. "Mrs. Roice," Sarah said, stopping her. "I'd like to see Jim, if you don't mind."

"He isn't up to seeing anyone." She bent lower over the casserole and stared full into Sarah's face. "He especially isn't up to seeing you. Folks've been talking since we got back. Folks've been saying Victoria was having a hard time these past few months, that she might've thought something was going on between her husband and you."

"The person to blame for that isn't me," Sarah said. "The person to blame for that is whoever's doing the talking. Her husband is your son. You know we've always loved each other."

"Don't call it love," she said. "Don't call it love when a girl up and leaves everything she should be holding dear to her heart. You deserted him, Sarah, the same way you deserted your daddy."

"A person's got a right to be sorry," Sarah whispered. "A person's got a right to change."

"You made your choice about my boy a long time ago. About put him through hell and back, you did. It was awful being his mother and watching him hurt that way. Now he's lost his wife, too, and you come nosing around again. Don't you think my boy's been hurt enough, Sarah? Don't you think it's time you left him alone?"

As the Chinook winds promised, spring did eventually come to Star Valley. It began with dripping eaves and mud puddles and tiny alpine crocuses poking up through the snow. By early April, the ducks came in pairs, feeding on sproutlings in the meadows.

The snow-melt left in its wake an array of looking-glass pools scattered across the lowland. Mallards, merganzers, and teals waddled from place to place, quacking merrily and taking to the shallow, standing water for a swim. Ice on the waterwheel pond began to turn blue and then to dissipate. Trout season began.

Jim often walked along Caddisfly Creek alone, line arcing from his fishing rod as he silently plied the waters. He went out at dusk, anxious to escape the chaos in his home and his heart, eager for the music of the river.

His parents had stayed longer than he could tolerate them. His father had painted each Mackenzie boat brown for the upcoming season. His mother had insisted he sort through Victoria's things while she could drive to Browse 'n Buy in Jackson and discard them. Charlie often cried for Victoria and, more times than not, after the tears he plain got angry.

"Why did Momma have to die?" Charlie asked over and over again. "How come God lets stuff like this happen?"

"Be mad, Charlie," Jim said as he held his son and stroked his hair. "God would much rather you be mad with Him than to think He hasn't a hand in your life at all."

Came the day when Jim willfully asked his parents to leave the house. "You've protected us long enough. It's time we got back to our lives again," he said.

And so the senior Roices departed.

During the days Jim recorded reservations over the phone for what would be a banner fishing season. At dusk, he took Charlie onto the river. They fished until dark, then went home hungry, scrounging in the kitchen at bedtime to find something worthy of eating.

"Why don't we go to Sarah's store?" Charlie asked innocently one night while they were driving home. "We could get stuff to make sandwiches."

Jim stared straight out the front windshield and kept driving. "No. We aren't going to the store."

"Why not? We haven't gone there in forever. Please? We could get Twinkies, too. And a Bubble Jug."

"Don't work on me, Charlie. I said no."

"Are you mad at her?" Charlie asked point blank. "She didn't have anything to do with Momma dying. Are you mad at her the same way I get mad at God sometimes?"

Every night, as his son fell off to sleep, Jim kept vigil at the boy's bedside. Each night, he waited until Charlie's breath came even and slow before he stepped out onto his porch, shoved his hands inside his coat pockets, and searched high above in the night sky, scanning for some oracle in the spinning stars.

He often lingered long enough to watch the lights go out, one by one, at Hayden's General Store. Other times, he watched through the trees and knew her kerosene lantern burned past midnight upstairs in the window. Sometimes he saw Sarah walking, illuminated by moonlight so pale she might've been nothing more than a haunting. He thought, *We won't let her take us with her. We're alive, Sarah. Even though Vic's gone, we're alive.*

One night, he walked the path to meet her. He waited until she'd almost passed him before he stepped from the trees and reached to catch her arm. "Sarah," he said. "Don't be afraid."

"Jimmy," she whispered.

"Don't want us to go on avoiding each other."

"We must, and for good reason. You know what folks're saying."

"No," he said quietly. "I don't."

"They're saying she died unhappy because of us. They're saying we—" She stopped, unable to go on.

Jim said, "They're fools."

"Even your mother," Sarah told him. "Even your mother thinks it."

"Damn them, Sarah." He took her shoulders in his hands, holding her away so he could read her face. "Don't listen to what they say. Do you have any idea what it's been like grieving for her and wanting you, too? Do you?"

"I know what it's like to want two things."

"Victoria didn't die because she was unhappy," he said. "She might've, but she didn't. She died because she loved Charlie."

"Yes," Sarah reminded him, "but does that make it worse, because she knew he was my son?"

"I don't want to lose you twice," Jim said.

"Makes no difference what we want," Sarah answered. "She stands between us."

At John F. Kennedy Airport in New York City, Marshall Upser boarded an American Airlines 757 that would connect with the West in Chicago.

He'd started Sue Bell, his secretary at Sandlin and Bonham, searching for a flight into Jackson Hole three days before. He hadn't counted on the sparse selection of planes available to take him into Wyoming. Two days and two travel agents later, his secretary had finally found one seat going into the valley, by way of an overnight in Chicago and Idaho Falls and a little puddle jumper airplane that Marshall wasn't even sure could fly high enough for a pilot to bring in over the mountains.

"You're on a jet all the way into Salt Lake City," Sue Bell told him apologetically when she lay the itinerary on his desk. "If you'd be willing to wait two weeks, I could get you on something the rest of the way that has more than fifteen seats."

"Hell no. I've waited too long already," he yelled loud enough to send his secretary scampering out of the office. "Something's wrong with Sarah."

Funny thing was, during the months he hadn't heard from her, he'd known she'd be okay. Each time they'd talked long distance and she'd sounded haunted—as if something beckoned her away—he'd known she drew nearer and nearer to that elusive assurance she sought as she'd stood by his fire, telling him of a baby she'd cast aside.

Now, suddenly, she called New York every evening. She told him of Victoria Roice's funeral. She even began to speak of selling the store again.

"Sarah," he'd demanded over the phone. "Tell me what's wrong."

"I think it best I return to New York soon," she recounted slowly, as if she persuaded herself even as she persuaded him.

"Why, Sarah?" he asked. "Frankly, I don't understand this sudden conviction after you've hesitated for so long."

"I've got to get out of Star Valley, Marshall," she said. But she wouldn't tell him why. She told him instead of the prospects Rita Persnick had brought to the store, of each different idea to utilize the bathtub. She finally announced that she even liked the fancy Breton roller he'd sent her for Christmas. Marshall didn't like it. He didn't like it at all. Something in Sarah's voice was gone, some lilt of hopeful lyric, as if she'd given up something provident that had sustained her. He intended to get to that godforsaken place in Wyoming, no matter what size of peashooter aircraft they placed him on. Marshall

Upser had every intention of invading the mountains and finding out what—or who—had taken the spunk out of her.

Marshall crawled into a plane at Salt Lake City International Airport that made even his closet look big. He experienced relief, as each propeller started spinning and the thing bounced up the runway, to see that the plane actually had a bathroom. He'd long since stopped looking for the stewardess. Someone had stuffed each oxygen mask into a seat pocket with the assortment of flight magazines and the air-sickness bags.

The plane landed in Jackson Hole at 4 P.M. The airport had three gates—Gate A1, Gate A2, and Gate B. He hailed a taxi, a huge red van called Buckboard Cab.

"What's a buckboard?" he asked the taxi driver after he gave him the address of Hayden's General Store in Star Valley. "Why do you call it that?"

"You don't know what a buckboard is?" The driver poked a wad of tobacco into his cheek and adjusted his hat. "It's a supply wagon with a fancy seat. Got springs underneath it, so, even if you go over ruts, your bottom won't get bumped around. You didn't know that? You must be from New York or something."

"I am," Marshall said defensively. "I am from New York City."

The cab driver had a hard time finding their destination because the store had no sign. After they'd driven back and forth through Star Valley three times, Marshall finally found the place with a long, low porch set back into the trees. He saw Sarah's silhouette through the wide front window.

"This is it," he said. "Let me out right here."

When he walked inside, she didn't look up to see him. He stood in the doorway and watched her, scarcely recognizing the woman who stood behind the register. She wore an apron that looked like it might once have belonged to her mother. She'd pulled her hair back into a simple ponytail with one small, pearl barrette.

She finally glanced up from her paperwork. "Can I help—?" She stopped, staring at him.

"Yes, Sarah. You can help me. Or maybe I can help you."

"Marshall." She could scarcely say his name. And when she looked up at him, he saw the same death in her eyes that he'd heard in her voice. "Oh, Marshall."

"Maybe I've overstepped my bounds," he said. "Maybe I've done a foolish thing."

"Maybe you have," she whispered, "but I'm grateful for it."

"What can I do?" he asked. "How can I help you find the part of yourself that you've lost? How can I help you find the part of yourself you want to sell away?"

Tears began to stream down her face. She shook her head and held out her arms to him. "There isn't anything. Please hold me, Marshall," she said. "Just hold me."

22

Marshall Upser allotted himself one week, one week, to accomplish his task in Star Valley. He slept on a cot in the corner of the storeroom, wedged between two huge burlap sacks of fresh-milled flour and a peg rack lined with Nordic skis. Sarah'd asked him when he arrived to hold her, and he did so with generous arms and frequency, every time he glanced up to catch that little-girl-lost expression in her eyes.

"You're grieving your father," Marshall said.

"I'm grieving a good many things," she answered.

"Why now?" he asked. "Why not in November, when you first came?"

Seemed like every time Marshall wanted to relax, Rita Persnick came to show the property again. "Excuse me," Rita said, brushing past him and leading another group of businessmen. "I'd like to show these clients the fireplace area."

"Can't you show it to them with me sitting here?" he asked.

"I cannot. They're considering purchasing the place for a restaurant. They need to be able to view the entire panorama."

"Oh, excuse me," he said, plopping his feet onto the floor and gathering together his many sections of the *New York Times*. "I'll go to another area."

"I'm leaving soon," Sarah told him as soon as Rita Persnick had left. "Next offer that comes in, I'm going to take it. It's time to sell the store."

"What is it, Sarah?" he asked, begging her. "Confide in me. It's the reason I flew all the way out here, so you'd tell me. We must discuss this."

"I've let myself want something that can't be mine," she said, defeated. "I've caused something terrible, almost as if I'd killed someone."

"You think leaving for New York will make anything easier?"

"I'm not looking for ease," Sarah told him. "I'm looking to lay my past to rest."

"You're doing penance? Is that it?"

Three days after Marshall arrived, a small, tow-headed boy pushed in through the screen door of Sarah's store. He walked in unannounced and headed straight for the Bubble Jugs. The child helped himself to two of them, one grape and one cherry. Sarah glanced up from the cash register as he began to dig coins from his pockets and, when she recognized the child, the complete joy on her face threatened to overwhelm him.

"Hey, Charlie," she whispered, her voice wobbling. "How're you two doing over there?"

"Sometimes bad without her," he said. "Sometimes good. Dad's usually too tired to help me with my homework. Momma never was."

"I figured it was that way."

The little boy looked past her out the window. "You still gettin' chickadees? I've got some extra suet over at the house, if you need it. Maybe I'll bring some tomorrow."

"Will you?" Sarah asked, almost desperately. "Will you come tomorrow?"

"Yeah." Then he whispered to her, "Dad's been afraid to come shopping at the store, but I sneaked out."

"Charlie," she said. "You mustn't disobey your father."

"This is my favorite place besides Caddisfly Creek. Don't see how come I have to quit coming to my favorite place because Aretha Budge and Beulah Hardaway like to gossip so much."

"Charlie!"

"Well they do, you know. Though I don't know what they think's so bad about everything. Heard 'em the other day at the post office, right before Maudie Perkins shushed 'em up because I walked in the door. They talk like it's the end of the world or something, just because you're here and you love us."

Rita Persnick brought another potential buyer to see the place that afternoon. She kindly asked Marshall to move away from the wood stove again, but this time she said, "If you're going to be around for a while, why don't you go out and see if you can make the waterwheel work? That would be a useful thing for you to do."

The more he thought about her suggestion, the angrier he got. Who was this lady to tell him to go out and work on machinery? Finally, after she'd been in the house a good hour talking about changes that could be made in the bathroom, he gave up. He scrounged through a collection of old Will's tools and came up with a hammer and a wrench. He didn't know exactly what problems he'd encounter at the wheel, but maybe these would do some good.

When Marshall arrived at the pond, he found a man already bending beneath it. "Figure if Sarah won't let me fix anything else, I'm gonna fix this waterwheel for her," the fellow muttered to himself. "Crazy muskrats. There's no accounting for where some living things think they have to make a home. Almost as much a damn fool notion to live in a place like this as it is to live someplace like New York City."

"I beg your pardon?" Marshall said.

Jim pulled out of the waterwheel so fast he hit his head on one of the runners. "Ouch."

"This is private property," Marshall announced. "What are you doing?"

"Been doing things all wrong, is what. I've been letting Sarah judge things through the eyes of grown-ups," Jim said. "She's been listening to a bunch of old biddies when we both should've been listening to one little boy."

"This the same little boy who's been talking to Sarah about loving him?" Marshall asked.

"The very same." Jim leaned against the wrench with his full weight, levering his legs against the turn. "You see any reason why I shouldn't be thinking that little guy is smarter than we are?"

"No," Marshall answered. "Don't see any reason at all."

Jim set a willow laundry basket beside Marshall.

"What's this for?"

"I'm hoping you'll give me a hand with these muskrats. I've got a whole family's worth I'm planning to move upstream."

"I'll help you move muskrats," Marshall said. "Just take care of Sarah. I've known her a long time now, long enough to know she needs this mountain place."

"Yes," Jim said quietly, "and Charlie and I need her."

While Marshall had gone toting the third pair of muskrats up Caddisfly Creek, Rita Persnick led Sarah and the prospective buyers out toward the pond. "Look at this place," Rita announced. "It lends itself to many purposes. You may decide to incorporate a child's fishing pool. Or you might decide to build a deck beside it for alfresco dining. You might even try to repair the antique waterwheel and get it turning again."

"So it's an antique now, is it?" Jim climbed out from under the thing and wiped his grimy hands on his jeans. Then, with no further ado, he reached for Sarah and pulled her solidly against him while he announced to the realtor, "You'd best take these folks down to Jackson Hole where they belong. Hayden's General Store is no longer on the market."

"Of course it's still on the market," Rita insisted. "I have a signed listing agreement in my briefcase. Someone offers Sarah full price, she has to accept it."

"Someone offers Sarah full price, and there's a rich man from New York City up the river with muskrats who's told me he's willing to buy them out and pay more."

"Marshall?" Sarah asked. "Up the river with muskrats?"

"You're off the job, Rita," Jim said. "Go home."

Rita marched to the parking lot, jerked up the realty sign, and threw it, along with her briefcase, into the Suburban. Her three bewildered clients climbed into their car, staring after her as she drove away.

"Sarah girl. Listen to me." Jim Roice turned to her in front of God and the traffic on the highway and everybody. He took both of her hands into his. "I'm not willing to turn you loose because of what folks're saying. I'm only willing to see what's real through Charlie's eyes. I see my son. I hear his words. I know my own heart. I've always loved you, Sarah Hayden, ever since I was ten years old."

Sarah said, "Perhaps it isn't proper to love each other after all this."

"No," he told her. "Perhaps not. Perhaps it isn't proper or easy but, for us now, it will be right."

She turned to this man she'd known for as long as she remembered, secure in him, and secure in whom she'd become. "Yes," she said, laying her head against his chest, hearing the constant thrum of his heart. "I believe it is so."

"No matter what else happened, Victoria gave us a gift, Sarah. She gave us Charlie's life to share." He pulled her full against him, knowing he'd never let her go. "I honor her most by accepting that. In time, others will come to accept it, too."

"Hey!" Marshall Upser appeared over a knoll from the direction of the creek, swinging a willow basket in one hand. Charlie walked at his side. "Found this kid out by the shore. Anybody know who he belongs to?"

"Wanted to see those muskrats but they all swam away," Charlie bellowed. "Guess they were looking to make a new home."

"Hope so, son," Jim said, tousling his son's hair, never letting go of Sarah. "They'd best be getting settled in up there. This waterwheel won't be livable any longer. It's ready to go."

"Really?" Charlie hollered.

"You think it'll turn?" Marshall asked.

"Never know about things until you try them, do you?" Jim tightened the last old nut, stepped back, and opened the water flow in through the blades.

The wooden wheel jerked once, then seemed to pause as they each waited to breathe. Finally, the thing began to revolve, jolting once, then falling into rhythm, spilling long, silvery streaks of water into the pond.

"Yeah!" Charlie hollered. "It's going. It's going!"

"How about that?" Marshall Upser dropped the basket on the ground and dusted his hands off as if he'd just completed the greatest feat of his life. "The old wheel still has life in it, after all."

"Haven't seen it run this smooth since I was a boy myself," Jim announced.

Cheeks weather-stained red, the four stood beside the wheel, satisfied beyond words with their efforts, gratified with all the day had wrought. Where the spring thaw had already taken most of the ice to task, Jim could see light riffles extending across the pool, extending as they had when old Will had been here, when he and Sarah had been playmates.

Jim rubbed his chin and looked thoughtful. "When are you going back to the big city, Mr. Upser?"

"Tomorrow," Marshall said. "As soon as I can get a flight out of Jackson Hole."

"Gonna miss having you here, Marshall." Sarah picked up a rock and pitched it toward the pond. It landed, plunk, setting off a circle on the surface. "Thank you."

"Water won't be still anymore," Jim said. "This water was never meant to be still."

"Anybody hungry?" Sarah asked, looking from one to the other. "I could come up with a whole hot supper in there."

"Yeah," Charlie hollered. "I'm starving to death."

"Okay. I'll fix us something. We'll have a party."

Charlie ran toward the store. "Wish Momma was—" Then he realized, stopped, stared up at Sarah as if he didn't know what to say.

She stooped low, holding her hands out to her own son. "It's okay," she told him gently. "You miss her, don't you?"

He nodded. "Yeah. Sometimes I just forget she's not here."

Sarah buried her face in the boy's sun-fragrant hair, her heart overcome with thankfulness. "We'll remember her together. We'll remember how much she loved you, okay?"

Charlie stepped back and eyed her. "I love both of you, you know. I love you and I loved Momma, too."

"I know it, Charlie," Sarah whispered. "Oh, how I know it."

Above them, a slim, ash-colored crane soared across the sky with neck, legs, wings outstretched. *Krooo kroooo*, it called. They watched momentarily, hoping to see the bird alight, disappointed when he wavered northward along the creekbed and flew out of sight.

"Can I help with the cooking?" Charlie asked. "I'm best at macaroni and cheese."

"Sure you can help," Sarah answered. She stood, took the child's hand, and led them all inside for supper. And outside, on the pond that had stood mirror-still since old Will had died that autumn, the waterwheel kept at its slow, undeniable pace . . . turning . . . turning.

$1,000.00

FOR YOUR THOUGHTS

Let us know what you think. Just answer these seven questions and you could win $1,000! For completing and returning this survey, you'll be entered into a drawing to win a $1,000 prize.

101 Days of Romance
BUY 3 BOOKS, GET 1 FREE!

CHOOSE A FREE BOOK FROM THIS OUTSTANDING
LIST OF AUTHORS AND TITLES:

HarperMonogram

____LORD OF THE NIGHT Susan Wiggs 0-06-108052-7
____ORCHIDS IN MOONLIGHT Patricia Hagan 0-06-108038-1
____TEARS OF JADE Leigh Riker 0-06-108047-0
____DIAMOND IN THE ROUGH Millie Criswell 0-06-108093-4
____HIGHLAND LOVE SONG Constance O'Banyon 0-06-108121-3
____CHEYENNE AMBER Catherine Anderson 0-06-108061-6
____OUTRAGEOUS Christina Dodd 0-06-108151-5
____THE COURT OF THREE SISTERS Marianne Willman 0-06-108053-5
____DIAMOND Sharon Sala 0-06-108196-5
____MOMENTS Georgia Bockoven 0-06-108164-7

HarperPaperbacks

____THE SECRET SISTERS Ann Maxwell 0-06-104236-6
____EVERYWHERE THAT MARY WENT Lisa Scottoline 0-06-104293-5
____NOTHING PERSONAL Eileen Dreyer 0-06-104275-7
____OTHER LOVERS Erin Pizzey 0-06-109032-8
____MAGIC HOUR Susan Isaacs 0-06-109948-1
____A WOMAN BETRAYED Barbara Delinsky 0-06-104034-7
____OUTER BANKS Anne Rivers Siddons 0-06-109973-2
____KEEPER OF THE LIGHT Diane Chamberlain 0-06-109040-9
____ALMONDS AND RAISINS Maisie Mosco 0-06-100142-2
____HERE I STAY Barbara Michaels 0-06-100726-9

To receive your free book, simply send in this coupon **and** your store
receipt with the purchase prices circled. You may take part in this exclusive
offer as many times as you wish, but all qualifying purchases must be made
by September 4, 1995, and all requests must be postmarked by October 4,
1995. Please allow 6-8 weeks for delivery.

MAIL TO: HarperPaperbacks, Dept. FC-101
        10 East 53rd Street, New York, N.Y. 10022-5299

Name_____

Address_____

City_____State_____Zip_____

Offer is subject to availability. HarperPaperbacks may make substitutions for
requested titles.   H09511